───────── ★ ─────────

What I saw in the rearview mirror seemed to be a big old beater, but the street was so dark I couldn't make out the color, model, or driver's face. I pulled away from the curb, whereupon the beater rammed us again. Once more came a jingle of fractured glass, and Keith and I were whiplashed in our seats. On our left a chain-link fence ran all the way down to the Hill Street curve. On our right rose a stone retaining wall. In essence, we were trapped, skidding down a short chute to the channel. Our only chance to avoid the cold black water was a sharp curve to the right. But the heavy old beater had slammed us with ample force, and my car was running, in gear, and pointed down a steep incline, so it offered no resistance. We were halfway to the channel, flying so fast, that if we tried to turn right, we'd run smack into the brick building.

In a split second, I weighed my choices: channel or brick building?

───────── ★ ─────────

Big
Black
Hole

Wilma Kahn

W♦RLDWIDE®

TORONTO • NEW YORK • LONDON
AMSTERDAM • PARIS • SYDNEY • HAMBURG
STOCKHOLM • ATHENS • TOKYO • MILAN
MADRID • WARSAW • BUDAPEST • AUCKLAND

For my parents and especially my sister…
I think of you each day.

BIG BLACK HOLE

A Worldwide Mystery/March 2008

First published by Oak Tree Press.

ISBN-13: 978-0-373-26630-2
ISBN-10:   0-373-26630-8

Printed in U.S.A.

Acknowledgments

Yes, there really is a Kalamazoo.

I would like to thank the following entities and individuals for providing helpful information: Citizens Seminar on Criminal Justice, offered by Kalamazoo County Sheriff's Department, Kalamazoo, MI, and City of Portage Police Department, Portage, MI; Daniel R. Gustin, Director, Irving S. Gilmore International Keyboard Festival, Kalamazoo, MI; Kathy Hoekstra, Program/Operations Manager, Alzheimer's Association, Michigan Great Lakes Chapter, Southwest Region, Kalamazoo, MI; Staff at Yingling & Mauzy Agency, Inc., Kalamazoo, MI.

In addition, I'd like to thank my friends at Triad of Kalamazoo County; Survivors of Suicide, Gryphon Place, Kalamazoo, MI.

Finally, I thank the following women for their insights and encouragement: Luanne Castle, Esperanza Malavé Cintrón, Kathy Griffin, Jennifer Hranilovich, Sonya Keller, Barbara Markowitz, and Eloise Metheney.

ONE

IT WAS SEPTEMBER, month of mellow days and crisp nights, with everyone in Collingwood as happy as crows at harvest time. And since everyone was happy, no one needed a private eye. At least that's what I'd been telling myself. See, I'm a P.I. and no one seemed to need me. I waited in my office with the door wide open, welcoming business yet gathering nothing but flies. House and horse. Frustrated, I gave the buzzing creatures a swat, then I began to spruce up my minuscule office. I ran a feather duster over the old oak desk, the venerable swivel chair, the two decrepit client chairs, the ancient file cabinet, the temperamental electric typewriter, the Mac Quadra 660AV, the black phone/answering machine, and the tiny white fridge. This took all of five minutes, whereupon I fell back into my chair, batting at flies.

At 2:30 the phone squealed. I seized the receiver, fervently hoping that the job I desperately needed was on the other end of the line. When I say *needed,* I mean as in needed to pay my bills—phone, electric, car insurance, health insurance, credit card. I was up to date on nothing but office rent, and that was only due to the insistence of my landlord, Mr. DeKats. It's not that I'm a deadbeat. Quite the opposite. But August had been slow and…. Well, you know that old soft shoe.

My caller turned out to be Marty Klein, who at seventy-five is the oldest divorce lawyer (and the only undivorced divorce lawyer) in Collingwood County. "Just thought you'd like to know," he said. "You're about to be subpoenaed in a divorce case, Naylor vs. Naylor."

"Oh, no," I groaned. I'd done some snooping for the husband and found that the wife had cheated all right, but her lover was dead. I liked the wife—Therese was her name. It was clear to everyone that the husband, Alex, was eager to shake those last few coins out of his wife's deep pockets before she got shed of him for good. I preferred not to expose the identity of Therese's lover: Lynne Jeffers, a radio talk-show host whose murder I had solved the previous spring.

My dad had testified in many a divorce case, providing the pivotal information, so to speak. A P.I. before me, he had specialized in photographing cheating spouses in *flagrante delicto*. As for me, I'd confined most of my sleuthing to unmasking catnappers, foiling fortune hunters, and serving those beloved subpoenas. Yet the idea of receiving one, then blabbing my mouth in open court, made me cringe.

"Look," said Marty in his kindly grandfatherly way, "you did the investigation and, yeah, Naylor's a bloodsucking leech, but you're a professional, so finish the job."

Rah rah. Regret does not begin to describe what I felt for having told Marty the identity of Therese's lover. However, I was tied to the lawyer by strings of gratitude, not to mention ropes of ethical behavior. So I said, "Okay, Marty," and hung up.

I was appalled at the prospect of having to embarrass Therese in court. And what about Lynne's family? They had been shattered by her murder and would be crushed to dust when details of the love affair rolled out of my mouth under oath.

At that moment, a man in a dark blue suit entered the DeKats Arms, Collingwood's only flophouse and the location of my office. No indigent transient, he was young and clean and walked with a purpose. I surmised that he aimed to hand me a subpoena. As you may recall, my office door stood agape. *Gayle Fisher* is painted on the door, but the name looks like *rehsiF elyaG* when the door's open. Hoping that the man couldn't read backwards, I grabbed my purse, slunk out of the Arms, and scuttled across the street to the nearest bar.

The proprietor, Georgie, was relaxing in a booth, tapping her toe to an old Chet Baker tune. I joined her. She was draped in a loose dress of cobalt blue, sipping a wine cooler. Before long, she was holding forth on Chet's album, *My Funny Valentine*. It seems that it was remastered from vinyl onto a CD. Her first love is vinyl, but she's been playing more CD's of late. "Those old disks, Gayle? They just wear out."

"That's what my granny tells me," I replied, thinking of Gramma McKenzie's lumbago. Clearly, I was too preoccupied to engage meaningfully in such an esoteric conversation. Yet, as though unaware of my wavering attention, Georgie nattered on. Chet, it so happens, was just a pup when he made the album—all love songs. Georgie is not the type to decry Chet for being white or playing white. But she hated that he wound up a toothless junky. Georgie's the guru of jazz in Collingwood, a woman with warm brown skin *and,* as everyone in the know knows, a warm heart.

Chet's voice was so calm and sweet, the image of the courtroom nearly melted from my mind. Therefore, I was sorry to see Blue Suit enter the bar, in no way resembling a guy idling in for a drink and jazz, given his purposeful stride. "God dammit," I said, "here comes a subpoena."

He stopped at our table. "Gayle Fisher?" he said.

"Yes?" I replied through clamped jaws.

Georgie rose to her magnificent five feet eleven inches. She said, "See you in court," and made for the bar.

"So what's this all about," I growled, giving him the grim eye.

"I'd like to hire you."

I glowed with relief. Literally. I blushed. "Oh, gee. Please. Have a seat."

Blue Suit slid into the booth. He was angular and thin, about five-ten, black eyed, black haired, thirty-ish. The blue serge looked new, a tad formal, but fit him well and favored his pale skin. He had a sharp chin, full lips, thin nose, and large eyes with heavy lids above, dark circles below. The eyes, face, and body were charged with electricity. I knew the look: he'd had a nasty shock and gone on alert.

"Sorry," I said. "I thought you were someone else. Someone I wanted to avoid. So how'd you find me?"

"An older gentleman at the DeKats Arms. He saw me waiting outside your office and said you'd come over here for a break."

The hotel burgeoned with old men, but the "older" so-called "gentleman" was most likely Vaughn DeKats, owner of the Arms. Mr. DeKats hates to see any fish escape my hook.

I said, "Yes, well, what can I do for you?"

"My sister passed away last week. I think she was murdered—"

"Wait a minute," I interrupted. "Murder's not really my line."

"What about the Jeffers case? The *Free Press* ran a full-page article, how you solved the murder when the police couldn't."

Ah, yes. The *Detroit Free Press* had picked up the story—mistakes and all—from the *Collingwood Evening News*. His newspaper reference made me wonder where he was from. Since the *Free Press* enjoys statewide distribution, his home could be anywhere from Ishpeming to Detroit, though his citified ways suggested the latter. "Yes, I solved the case, I said, "but maybe it was a fluke." That's what Lieutenant Steven Leversee of Collingwood Public Safety liked to imply, and I was inclined to agree if only to keep peace in the bedroom. And to tell the truth, murder investigation is tricky; I keenly desired never to be shot at or stabbed by a crazy person again. Besides, my knowledge of the Motor City was sketchy at best. I knew that the Lodge Freeway dead-ended in Cobo Arena, but that was about it. How could I conduct a murder investigation over there?

"Maybe it wasn't a fluke," the man said evenly. "My sister's death was declared a suicide, and yes, it looked like one, but it couldn't have been. My sister would no more have killed herself than murdered another human being."

"Did you talk to the police about your misgivings?"

"Of course. But Chief Glenn said he had found nothing to suggest that the death was anything but suicide."

"Chief Glenn? You mean over in Shore Haven?"

"Yes, that's where it happened."

I knew Shore Haven. Sort of. It's a tourist town on Lake Michigan, fifty miles west of Collingwood. When I had tracked a con man there in May, Chief Glenn had let me prowl the town without interference of any kind. Either he was completely *laissez faire* or he simply didn't give a damn.

"How did your sister die?"

He struggled to get the words out: "They said she, she—she hanged herself."

I thought about this a moment. "Were there signs of a scuffle?"

"No. But here's the worst part. The room where she died was locked from the inside. Bolted."

"Oh." I was beginning to side with Chief Glenn. "What would you like me to do?" I asked.

"I'd like you to check it out, talk to people, see what the police missed. I'm sure she was murdered—cleverly murdered—and I'd like you to find out how and by whom."

"I don't know…."

He took a black-and-white photo from an inside pocket of his jacket. "This was Eleanor," he said, offering me the picture.

From her upswept hair to her lacy blouse to her long black skirt, the young brunette might have come from the year 1901. She was seated near a window, a silver flute resting in her hands, her face dreamy. She looked so calm, so sweet, that it was hard to believe she could have committed violence toward anyone, including herself. But sweetness can come at a terrible price. In high school, I'd had a friend, Mary Pfeiffer. She was sweet, everyone's pal, always there for someone in need. She was so sweet that the night before graduation, she blew her brains out with her father's .45.

"I see the family resemblance," I remarked. "The eyes."

When I tried to return the picture, he said, "No, keep it. I have another copy."

I placed it on the table, for to claim the photo was to claim the case. Then I thought that getting out of town for awhile might be a good idea, what with the subpoena hanging over my head like the proverbial ten-ton weight. I could sniff around Shore Haven a couple of days, make sure the police investigation had been, if not thorough, at least on the up and up, then report back to—

"Say, what's your name?" I asked.

"Bill. Bill Feinstein. My sister's name was Eleanor Montague. She was married."

"I'll take the case. I can't say that I'll prove you right, but I'll check into it, see if anything's irregular. Okay?"

He nodded. "What do you need to get started?"

I said with a straight face, "An advance of five hundred'll do it."

He took out a black calfskin wallet and withdrew five one-hundred dollar bills.

"Make it six," I quickly amended, remembering my car insurance.

He placed a sixth bill on top of the rest, and I slid them all into my purse. He gave me his card, said, "Need more money, just call."

I peered at the card: just *William Feinstein* and a phone number with a Detroit area code. I gave him my card: just Gayle

Fisher and a phone number with a Southwest-Michigan area code.

"What about a receipt?" he muttered, as though ashamed to be practical, what with his sister newly dead.

I dreaded returning to my office, for fear of encountering the subpoena. But Bill did deserve a receipt, just as I deserved a contract to protect my interests. So I said, "Sure. Let's take a hike." I dropped the photo of Eleanor Montague into my jacket pocket and we left.

Back at the Arms I scanned the lobby for any process-server types but saw no one except Mr. DeKats and three of his cronies from the track. Bill eyed the matted carpet, the flaking paint, the stained couches, the butt-filled standing ashtrays, and the low-rolling denizens. "Quite a place," he said.

"It's private," I replied, euphemistically.

I showed him into my office and motioned for him to sit in a client chair. I sat opposite in the squeaky swivel chair, which, like everything else in the office (except the Mac), I had inherited from my dad. He had died eight years before of a killer coronary, induced by hundreds of hours staked out in a car, munching Spud-Nuts while awaiting a great photo op. I was twenty-one at the time, working for him fifteen hours a week while I studied library science at West Michigan U.

When my dad died, I dropped out of school. I took a non-professional job at the library for five dollars an hour, married my suave but over-controlling supervisor, and divorced him—all in the space of a year. How's that for efficient? Then I had to admit to myself that although I love libraries, I hated working in the same place as my ex.

That's when I applied for and got my P.I. license. Several people helped in this process: Mom, who loaned me the fifty-one hundred dollars for bonding and license; Marty Klein and Captain Carry Veen, who vouched for me; and even my dear, dead dad, who had trained me and given me part-time employ as an operative for the required three years.

As I dug out a sheet of twenty-pound bond, Bill Feinstein surreptitiously glanced about the office, which like the lobby of the Arms is, well…private. At least the flies had gone into hiding. I typed up an agreement and a receipt, we signed our names, and my new client told me more about his sister.

"She was younger than I, twenty-three years old, a highly talented musician. Classical. She played the flute. Eleanor married a couple of years back," he said in a restrained voice. "Sean's a pianist, egotistical, put his career first."

"And she went along with it?"

"Unfortunately, yes. They lived in Chicago. He was preparing himself for one competition after another the whole time they were married. He never held a job. Meanwhile, she had a few students and played with the Manning Chamber Orchestra."

"Never heard of it."

"It's a prestigious group…but not wealthy. She received a stipend of twelve thousand a year."

"How'd they get by on that?" I asked.

"She had a small inheritance from our dad. And I gave her money if she needed it."

"What do you do?"

"Me? I work for G.M. I design concept cars."

An artist, more or less. I glanced at his hands. A little hairy for my taste, but long fingers and well defined knuckles made them attractive. "So what brought your sister and her husband to Shore Haven?" I inquired.

"He's got family there. A father with Alzheimer's disease—he's had it a number of years—and a sister who takes care of him. Eleanor and Sean weren't making ends meet, so they moved in with the old man and the sister in June. They have a house on the lake. Eleanor was helping out with Sean's father—he's too much for one person to handle—and they all lived, modestly, on his money. I didn't like the situation, but my finances were just as bad when I was Eleanor's age, so who was I to butt in? Besides, she and Sean were musicians, and I'm not, so we weren't even in the same sphere." His dark eyes were filled with loneliness and longing, the expression of a kid spying on a delightful party to which he had not been invited. I knew exactly how he felt.

I asked him to tell me more about Sean.

"Ever see a lamprey?"

"Not in person," I said.

"It's sort of a yellow eel with a sharp ring of teeth and a big sucking funnel of a mouth. It latches on to its prey and drains it dry."

"Oh."

"Why was everything about Sean?" he demanded. "Eleanor was very talented. She was principal flute with the Manning. The flute is the most expressive instrument in the orchestra."

"Perhaps. But it lacks the glamour of a piano."

"Glamour? What about James Galway?"

Galway was the only famous flute player I could think of while I could name pianists galore. I shrugged. "So you have this *feeling* your sister was murdered. Any idea by whom?"

He said, "No," but as if he didn't mean it. "Her husband's an ass, all right, but she was crazy about him. The sister-in-law's an odd duck, very wrapped up in her father and his needs. And the old man, well, he's senile."

"What about someone from outside the family? Someone from Shore Haven or Chicago?"

"All I can tell you is that Eleanor called me two weeks ago, very agitated. She said she hated Shore Haven, then asked for a loan so she and Sean could move back to Chicago."

"Did she say why she hated it?"

He shook his head.

"Are you sure she wasn't under some kind of emotional strain, something that might have driven her—"

"No! My sister did *not* commit suicide."

"Did you send her the money?"

"No."

"Mind telling me why?"

"I was tired of supporting that leach, her husband. So I didn't send the money!" He covered his face with his hands. "*I didn't.* But I wish to hell I had."

We remained silent for a few ticks of the clock. Then I remembered the process server and shifted nervously in my chair. "Bill?"

He made no reply.

"Bill, I'm expecting someone in a little while."

"I'm sorry," he said, dropping his hands. His face was flushed, moist with tears.

I felt like a rat or maybe a psychiatrist who had hit the fifty-minute mark. "Please, there's no need to apologize."

He pulled a handkerchief from his pocket, pressed it briefly to his eyes, then tucked it away. We stood and shook hands, and I have to say that I do, to a certain extent, judge a man by his grip. Bill's was good. A bit tense, a bit damp, but firm and not too tight.

We said our goodbyes and he left. I counted to sixty, then got the hell out of there.

TWO

I ESCAPED TO THE STREET and took off for home in my ten-year-old silver LeMans—neither the fastest nor the coziest car in the hemisphere, but it was cheap. My last car had been a dented gray Pontiac 6000 that I'd sold for a pittance due to the huge blood-stain on the front seat. Yes, I had collected estimates for having the upholstery replaced. But each estimate had exceeded the Blue-Book value of the car. Meanwhile, the blood had turned black, as blood is wont to do. The bottom line? Some spots not even K-14 will remove, and I'd be damned if I'd drive around town sitting on the black evidence of my having shot and killed a man—even if it was in self-defense. So I sold the car.

It took me five minutes to get to Laurel Street. I live in the "Historical Section" of Collingwood, two blocks of old Victorian homes newly rescued from squalor by a grant from the Malden Foundation. Most of the houses remain cut up into apartments, but all have been painted, the sidewalks replaced, and new "old-fashioned" streetlights installed. The dentist who owns the blowzy house where I live has splashed it yellow but failed to go the extra mile of keeping the lawn weed free or even mowed most of the time.

I cruised the old house, vigilant for strangers. I saw none yet took the precaution of parking a block away then sneaking back home. I unlocked the front door, fished my mail from its box, and scaled the stairs to the third floor. Except for wrestling with my beau, Lieutenant Leversee, and taking the occasional swim, climbing those stairs was the most exercise I'd gotten since June. Up in my apartment, I tossed clothes into a big black shoulder bag for my getaway to Shore Haven. The main tourist season had ended, so finding a place to stay would be a breeze, and the price of rooms would have plummeted.

I grabbed the phone to call Leversee to let him know I was leaving town. He appreciates this type of gesture. In fact, he is most curious about my comings and goings, though he seldom informs me of his own. He justifies this inequity on the basis that he has fellow officers to back him up, while I am "floating around out there" all alone. Floating? You'd think I was a dust mote. Well, I happen to like working alone.

I speed-dialed his number. It rang four times and a microsecond before his voice mail would have kicked in, he picked up. "Leversee speaking," he said in his cop voice.

"Hello, Lieutenant."

"Ms. Fisher," he said, warming a good thirty degrees.

"I just called to let you know I'll be out of town a couple of days."

"Business or pleasure?"

"Business. In Shore Haven."

"I'll miss you," he said simply. We'd been keeping company for four months and he still made me dizzy with pleasure. We had spent nights apart, but I certainly preferred sleeping *with* him. This preference was more than sexual. Lying next to him at night, I felt safe and calm. This may seem a contradiction in terms—a cop making a P.I. feel calm—but he usually did. I was tempted to tell him about the process server on my tail, but I knew he wouldn't sympathize. After all, if I'd been desperate enough to accept a scurrilous snoop job, I could take the court appearance along with the money.

"I'll miss you too," I said. "I'll call when I get back."

"Wait—what about a number in Shore Haven?"

"Haven't got one yet. Just call me on my cell."

"All right," he said. "What's the gig?" See what I mean? Most curious about my activities. I told him I'd be investigating a purported suicide, then signed off.

My next stop was the bathroom. This room is a hoot, by the way, with its pedestal sink and claw-foot tub that seems big enough for four. I say seems because I have never tested the hypothesis. Anyway, I buzzed my teeth with an electric toothbrush, washed my freckles, and dabbed on a little makeup—just in case I needed to charm someone. I tugged a comb through my wavy auburn hair, pulled it straight to my shoulders, then let it snap back like a rubber band. The tan pantsuit I had worn to work was wrinkled, but wrinkled is what linen gets, so I left well enough alone. I prefer more intense colors, but beige, taupe, and tan are great to sleuth in: they tend to make the wearer invisible.

I was ready to go but thought I should check the street before leaving. As I peeked out between my bedroom curtains, who should come whistling up the walk but Iggy Phlecks, carrying a big white envelope. *Shit.* Iggy was a colleague, a sort of friend of mine, but he certainly wouldn't let collegiality or friendship stand in the way of the forty bucks he'd make by nailing me with those papers. My doorbell gave an ominous shriek. Shouldering the black bag, I tiptoed out the back door and down the fire escape, where, as fate would have it, I stumbled on that last crooked step.

Pitching forward into the yard, I hit the sidewalk with a loud *smack.* I stifled a yelp, then checked myself for damage. My hands burned from having broken my fall, but I was otherwise unharmed. My black bag was fine, but my purse wasn't: it had vomited half its contents into a patch of dandelions. As I scrambled about to gather comb, pen, keys, and notebook, sweat streamed from every pore of my body. Where the hell was my wallet? I couldn't leave without my wallet. It held my credit cards, my P.I. license, my driver's license, my fake I.D., for chrissake.

Suddenly, I spied the missing item over in the driveway, where any fool—Iggy, for instance—could see it. I crawled over to my precious faux-leather wallet, snatched it up, and jammed it into my purse. Then I crept through the back yards of seven stately Victorians and snuck out to my car. I squinted down the block at Iggy whose finger still poked at my doorbell. I dove into the LeMans, revved it gently, spun around, and sped off toward M-43.

I laughed a satisfied *heh* at having outwitted Iggy. We like to get one another's goat and he had gotten mine the last time around. He had done some surveillance for me and, well, had charged more than what was friendly. You might say that Iggy is the amoral, mischievous younger brother with whom I've never been blessed. Instead I've been saddled with an older sister, Amanda, who is as moral and hardworking as an ant. Guess how that makes *me* look? But I suppose she has to keep her nose clean: she's a church organist and teaches at the Cynthia Blue Conservatory of Music. I really do care for my sis, as well as for her daughter, Rebecca, for whom I have lofty hopes. I firmly anticipate that she will grow up to be a crack shot like her Auntie Gayle.

The trip west on M-43 was full of glory. Summer wheat had gone from green to gold, and tall corn was drying in the fields. Crows swooped down and filled their gullets, disproving the old saw that there's no such thing as a free lunch. Then came Van-Burgen County with grapes heavy on the vine and dwarf trees bowed with apples, peaches, and pears. VanBurgen County is poor in per capita income yet Eden-like, a vast garden with Lake Michigan lapping its western edge.

At 4:35 p.m. I drove into Shore Haven, a tourist trap mostly bereft of tourists. Only the wealthy, elderly, or childless would wander the little town's trinket shops mid-week in September. Shore Haven still attracted weekend visitors of very stripe and would continue to do so through October, when Lake Michigan would grow too cold for even the most devoted sailors to ply. Then would come the long, brutal winter, when no one from outside would dream of visiting, and Shore Haven would reclaim itself—a town full of townies owning the ice, and more power to them.

But winter was still a long way off.

I parked and walked up the street to the Black River B & B. The huge old house was festooned with dormers and balconies, places to await the long-lost sailor or philandering husband, as the case may be. I rang the bell and soon was greeted by a stocky woman about sixty years old. She had the shrewd black eyes of a rodent, a blunt nose, a firm mouth, and coarse white hair chopped off at the jaw. Milady was attired in a snap-down-the-front dress in a dark flower print.

I asked if she had a room available.

"Depends on how long you want to stay," she replied, none too friendly. "Weekend's booked, but I could put you up through Thursday. I have the west room, thirty dollars a night, or the north room for sixty. Bathroom's down the hall, shared by all guests. Breakfast is continental—coffee, tea, rolls, and fruit."

"Sounds great. I'll take the west room, tonight and maybe Thursday."

She beckoned me in and introduced herself as Mrs. Hogoboom. Dutch names are common in West Michigan, as the shoreline was heavily settled by Dutch immigrants of the conservative Christian-Reformed faith. Collingwood boasts many folks of Dutch extraction, such as Mr. DeKats, who is very conservative, indeed for a gambling addict who owns a flophouse.

Mrs. Hogoboom took my cash, wrote a receipt, gave me two keys, and rattled off the house rules: "Come and go as you please, but always make sure the front door is locked." Then she pointed to a door left of the stairs. "This leads to my part of the house. It's off-limits to guests."

The dour Mrs. Hogoboom showed me upstairs to the west room, where floral prints and cascades of ruffles nearly swallowed the furniture: a chaste twin bed, a white wicker chair, and a dresser. She opened the closet to display a mini-fridge, an electric teapot, cups, and a variety of teas. Across the room, French doors opened onto a balcony with an umbrellaed table and chair; I could breakfast there, weather permitting. I stepped outside for a moment to enjoy the view—the Black River leading to the channel and merging with the blue, blue lake.

"There's no telephone," I observed.

"You have one of those calling cards? You can use the phone in the foyer."

Good thing I had my cell phone. I thanked her and said I'd be going out for awhile but didn't know when I'd be back.

"Come and go as you please," she repeated, a tad impatient.

We went downstairs where she tested me on my door-locking skills. After proving my ability to insert and turn a key, I strolled three blocks to the Shore Haven Police Station, which, along with the town's municipal offices, occupied an old stone building. I asked the cop at intake if I might speak with Officer Swinkey.

"I'll see if the sergeant's available," he said. My, my. Swinkey had been promoted since the last time we'd met. The cop sauntered over to Swinkey's desk and muttered a few words. Swinkey looked blank, then recognition dawned on his face.

I smiled.

Grinning in return, he walked over to greet me. "Gayle Fisher, P.I. What brings you to Peach Paradise? Tracking another scammer?"

"Not this time, John. Could we talk?"

He shrugged and led me back to a desk piled high with reports.

"Catching up on paper work?" I asked.

The big cop gave a rueful one-sided grin. He stood a good six feet, with chestnut hair, hazel eyes, and a thick mustache. Ever notice how many cops have mustaches? Must be all the testosterone. He did look natty in his navy uniform, so many toys hanging from his waist, each in its own black-leather case—radio, gun, flashlight, and a few other playthings I could not identify.

Leversee's dress uniform hung in his closet, creases sharp, but I had never seen him wear it. As a detective, he rarely had occasion to do so. Not that he needed a uniform to look like a cop. Even in a gray business suit he aroused comments like "That's not no CPA" from the residents of the DeKats Arms. I scrawled a mental note to ask Leversee to put on his uniform when I got home—just for me.

"So what's up?" asked Swinkey, seemingly unaware that he'd just gotten the once-over.

"A man's hired me to look into the death of his sister," I said. "An apparent suicide by hanging—"

"*Feinstein?* You've got Feinstein for a client?"

"Yes."

"Look, the Montague woman was found in a room bolted from the inside, *and* the dresser was shoved up against the door. No signs of a struggle—it was a textbook suicide. But this Feinstein, he won't buy it. He wants a big investigation."

"And?"

"The chief says no. What the M.E. decides is good enough for him. Case closed."

"Could I see the case file?" I said under my breath.

Swinkey bit his lower lip and chuckled. "I don't think so."

"Come on, John. I got you a good collar last spring. Richard Mason Jason—"

"*Jeffrey* Richard *Mason?*"

"Whatever."

Swinkey rolled his eyes.

"The Montague case is closed," I crooned. "What harm would it do to show me—"

"No harm at all except it could get my ass fired," he hissed.

"Not *your* ass," I said, smiling as fetchingly as I could. Did he notice how nice I looked, unlike the last time we had met, when I was wearing a face full of peach sorbet? The icy goo had been hurled at me by the evil Jeffrey Richard Mason. It was this indignity as much as his having stolen eighty-four thousand dollars from my sister that had prompted me to jam the business end of my Beretta in his ear.

"I bet *you* could do it and not get caught," I said.

Swinkey propped his chin on his hand. He sighed. "Okay. Meet me at the lighthouse, seven o'clock tonight."

"My pleasure," I breathed. "See you later."

I sashayed out to the street then hot-footed it to the little Shore Haven Library. Since I used to toil in a library and practically completed a degree in library science, any library is an open book to me. This one was lodged in a quaint brick building next to an Episcopal Church. I wandered briefly, getting the lay of the place, then snagged a phone book and perched next to a large wall-mounted map of the county. There were three Montagues in the directory and only one, Dennis, lived on the lake. I copied the address and drew myself a route to get there.

Before long I was cruising down the Blue Star Highway, past orchards, farms, and fruit stands. I turned left at Sand Creek Road and continued till I came to a sign: *Stop! Private Beach. Residents and Guests Only.* A sign like that makes a terrible watch dog, all bark and no bite. So I drove on. Sand Creek Road ended at Beach Street, where I turned right. I snailed past houses that looked secluded but not lonely. All were large. Some were summer cottages boarded up for the winter, while others were year-round homes. I passed the Montague residence at 134 Beach Street, then parked by a blue Cape Cod that was shuttered for the season.

I crossed the yard to the breakwall and descended two flights of stairs to a narrow beach, some fifteen feet of sand from breakwall to lapping surf. The wind was whipping my hair, so I secured it with a stretchy band I keep in my wallet for emergencies. Then I donned the poor-girl's disguise: sunglasses. I shed my sandals, dangled them from a finger, and plodded down the sun-soaked beach. Lake Michigan sand is soft and fine, but woe to the sandy foot inside a shoe, for that soft fine sand will grind the skin right off your foot.

One, two, three, four, five houses. I walked and idly gazed about as if I'd been invited, a gawker with a right to gawk. I trained my eyes on the Montague house. It was lovely, probably erected in the twenties. Built of dark red brick, the house stood two stories tall, a one-story porch on each end lending a sense of grace, width, and symmetry. In the middle stood a pair of French doors, accented on either side by a flat false pillar that made me think of Greek tragedy. Nearly half the characters in those old plays kill themselves. Had Eleanor Montague?

The lawn, shaded by huge cottonwoods, was lush green and in need of mowing. Ivy climbed the bricks, and wisteria wove through the arched entry to the back yard. Above the pound and *shhh* of the waves I heard piano music, Rachmaninoff, fast and intense, like a body falling from a bridge. Suddenly, the French doors flew open and the music grew louder. An old man close to eighty, wearing gray sweat clothes and white deck shoes, stepped out into the wind.

Then I did something dumb. Instead of continuing down the beach, I dodged behind the Montagues' metal beach stairs and waited. A moment later the old man came tottering down the steps. A woman called: "Daddy? Daddy, come back in the house!" The man paused, cowering on the steps as I crouched below, wondering how I'd explain my presence if anyone happened to see me.

The old man peered down at my face, his terrified grimace mirroring my own emotion. Then I remembered that he had Alzheimer's disease. I smiled at him and held a finger to my lips. Slowly, he mimicked my gesture, a gnarled finger landing to the right of his mouth. The woman called out again, sounding much closer: "Daddy? Please, let's go in." I saw her arms reach and pull at her father.

"I don't waaaaant to go in," howled the old man.

"Come on, Daddy," the woman begged, her voice quieter.

"There's that girl," he said, pointing at me. I backed closer to the concrete wall, willing myself to vanish in the gloom behind the stairs.

"Eleanor's gone," said the woman.

"Noooo!"

"It's time for dinner."

"Dinner?" repeated the old man. "I just had breakfast."

"You had breakfast this morning."

"I just had the—the round things—"

"Come on, Daddy," she said gently, no longer pulling at him. And all at once he relaxed and walked with her back to the house.

I crept out of my hiding place and hastened down the beach, lest old Mr. Montague should break loose and see me again. I pride myself on being invisible when I do surveillance, and here I'd been caught by an old man with dementia. I was damn lucky he'd taken me for poor dead Eleanor and his daughter had written me off as a hallucination.

I DROVE BACK TO TOWN, my grumbling stomach urging me to find a place to eat. I chose the Black River Inn, whose walls full of nets, ropes, grappling irons, and cat-o'-nine-tails were a bondage fantasy come true. As the place was nearly empty, I was seated by a window that looked out on the Black River. A good many boats were still docked at the marinas nearby, but river traffic had waned since my last visit to Shore Haven. A couple of sailboats trolled upriver, sails furled, their crews as sun black-ened and lean as beef jerky.

As I perused the menu, the image of a burger floated in my mind—a thick, dry, broiled burger, dripping with Heinz Chili Sauce. Unable to sway my desires to something with less cho-lesterol, I ordered steak fries and a burger well done.

After that satisfying meal I returned to the B & B, where I noted that the room next to mine was occupied. A woman's giggles and a man's low laugh floated from under the door.

"Mark, oh, Mark!" gushed the woman.

"Trish, Trish, Trish," sighed the man.

That's right, *The Mark and Trish Show,* emanating from the groin of the Black River B & B.

In the lavatory I scrubbed my face and brushed my teeth, then regarded myself in the mirror. I glowed from my stroll on the beach, I burn that easily. But with auburn hair, what else could I expect? I hauled out my makeup. To tell the truth, I hate the way it feels, and it screws up my skin. I've got freckles already—why encourage spots? Nevertheless, I dusted my face with a little powder and slicked on a coat of lipstick—Guava Stain. Granted, I have never seen a guava, but I was willing to bet that they weren't that color. It looked inedible. I pulled off the elastic band and my hair bounced back to its original shape as though it had never been confined. It was getting a little long. Maybe Leversee would trim it for me. He had before, with that steady hand and keen cop's eye.

After finishing my ablutions, I headed back to my room, again passing the amorous squeals of laughter and sexy low chuckles. Great. Just great. I hoped the program wouldn't last all night. If only Leversee were there and the laughers weren't and I didn't have to meet some other cop in a deserted lighthouse in—I checked my watch—five minutes. Yipe!

Grabbing my bag, I ran downstairs and out to the street and down to the beach and jogged the rest of the way to the lighthouse. I was sweating, my hair was flailing in the breeze, and I'd left the elastic band in the sink at the B & B. I must have looked like a banshee.

THREE

A WAVE SMACKED against the rocks, splashing me with spray. As I shivered in the wind, I thought of the long history of drownings attached to this locale. Three boys had been swept into the lake and drowned just this past June. Why had Swinkey chosen such a spot for a meeting? And where was he? The place looked deserted.

Just then, the big cop circled around from the far side of the little lighthouse. He was smoking a cigarette, one hand shielding it from the breeze. He wore civilian garb—jeans, a plaid shirt, and a lightweight tan jacket. A sizable gun bulged in his pocket, surely not a regulation way to carry a sidearm, but hey, it had to go somewhere. A jacket pocket happens to be my favorite place to stash a gun. When I'm carrying. Otherwise my dainty Beretta reposes in my underpants drawer.

Swinkey said, "Hi" and "Let's go inside."

I nodded my head. He hauled out a jangling bunch of keys, opened the door, and we squeezed into the small round room. "How'd you get keys to the lighthouse?" I inquired.

Swinkey smirked. "I have my ways."

Typical cop answer. Well, enough with the niceties. "Did you bring the file?"

"Have a seat." He motioned toward the bottom step of a stairway that spiraled up to a blinking computer screen and a swiveling lamp. I sat and he joined me—hip to hip on the cold metal—then he pulled a plump interoffice envelope from inside his jacket.

Eagerly, I unwound the string that secured the envelope and

slid the file onto my lap. The file opened to a shiny color photo, eight by ten, of Eleanor Montague, hanging. Her bloodshot eyes bulged, her tongue protruded dark and swollen; her whole head was inflated and red. Color photography—what a boon. I closed my eyes, but there she hung, behind the lids.

So I opened them to see what, besides horror, the picture had to offer. She was in a bedroom, its double bed disheveled. A hole had been knocked in the ceiling and a sheet knotted around a beam. She appeared to have tied a corner of the sheet around her neck, then jumped off the bed. Her bare feet dangled a few inches above a rug littered with plaster and dust. A sheer white shift, sleeveless and embroidered, shrouded her thin body, and heavy black hair hung loose to her waist. To her left, a huge mahogany dresser had been shoved against the door.

"Nice picture," I said. "How'd you guys get in to take it?"

"Through the window."

"First floor?"

"Second," he said. "Fire crew brought a ladder."

"Window locked?"

"Yep. They had to smash the glass to get in."

"And there's no other way into the room?"

"Nope."

I studied the picture again. A nice bedroom, if you could overlook the dangling corpse. Dark oriental carpet, mahogany furniture, a couple of Matisses on the wall—reproductions, I assumed—a bedside table with a lamp, an empty glass, and a red enameled pillbox. "What kind of pills?" I asked.

"Seconal."

"She have a scrip?"

He scratched his cheek. "Not so far as the husband knew."

"So she gets herself good and drowsy, moves a huge dresser, punches a hole in the ceiling, rigs up a make-shift noose, and jumps."

He nodded. An expressive man.

"She's not very big," I pointed out.

"Oh, big enough. The M.E. found abrasions and plaster imbedded in the knuckles of her right hand."

"Anyone check for prints on the glass, the pillbox, the dresser?"

"Uh-uh."

"Really?" I said, restraining my incredulity. "And why no autopsy? Isn't it mandatory for suicides?"

"Maybe in Collingwood County but not over here." The way he said this, you'd think our counties were spinning in separate galaxies.

"Why's that?"

This time he made the gimme gesture, fingers rubbing thumb. "Autopsies cost a thousand bucks. There's nothing fishy. M.E. has every right to declare a death a suicide, case closed."

"How soon?"

"Right away if he wants."

"Jeeze. Is that what he did in this case?"

"Uh huh. The body went straight to the funeral home, cremated the next day." He dragged on his cigarette, then crushed it, sizzling, on the damp cement floor. "Who'd want an open casket with a face like that? The mortician's a man, not a magician."

"Cremated, you say?"

"Yeah. Feinstein found out, he went ballistic. Said his sister was Jewish and never should've been burnt up, hadn't Hitler and his crew already burnt up enough Jews? Feinstein and Sean Montague don't get along too well." At that, he gave a dry, humorless laugh.

I took a few minutes to review the rest of the file while Swinkey fired up another smoke. The room was silent except for the motor that turned the light up above, the flipping of pages, and the suck and blow and eventual crushing out of Swinkey's second cigarette. The file revealed little more than the big cop had. Fiona, Sean, and Dennis Montague had gone out for their nightly soft serve at the Ice Princess at 6:00 p.m. on Tuesday, September 1. Eleanor had stayed home, ostensibly to practice her flute. I glanced at the photo again, saw no flute. At 7:00 p.m., the family returned home. Around 7:30, Sean found the door to his and Eleanor's bedroom locked. She failed to respond to his calls. Alarmed, he phoned the police who, along with the Fire Department Rescue Squad, arrived at 7:42 p.m. They entered the room via the window. The Medical Examiner placed the time of death at 6:30 p.m.

In the file was included a note scrawled on half a sheet of cheap paper. *I'm sorry. You're better off without me. Eleanor.* The note was barely legible. I closed the file, handed it back to Swinkey. I said, "Thanks."

Then he scootched a little closer and kissed me. Except for the taste of cigarettes and couple of prickles from his mustache, it was a nice kiss—soft and warm and a little wet.

"Sergeant Swinkey," I said, disengaging myself from his lips. "What makes you think you can steal a kiss?"

"Steal? Didn't feel like a theft to me. I thought—"

"What's that on your left hand?" I interrupted.

"What?"

I pointed at the gold band encircling his ring finger. "A wedding ring?"

"Come on—"

"Besides which, I've already got a cop."

"Where's that? Collingwood?" Again, he spoke as if my home were light-years away.

"This is not a jurisdictional issue," I explained. "No matter if I'm in Collingwood, Shore Haven, or Beans Creek, Tennessee. He's my cop, wherever I go."

Swinkey held up his hands in surrender. "Okay, okay—"

I did feel guilty, though, using Guava Stain on the poor man just to get facts about Eleanor Montague. I suppose it's possible he would have given me the info anyway, but what was done was done. "Thanks a lot, Swinkey, for sharing the file. You're a nice guy. A little impulsive, but nice."

He was absorbed in lighting yet another cigarette as I made this speech. "Getting late," he replied. "I better go home, tuck in the wife." He rose and pulled me to my feet, then we left the shelter of the lighthouse for the cutting wind and the dark of night.

I trudged back to the B & B, the picture of dead Eleanor etched on my brain. Horrible. Pitiful. What bothered me most was the rush to cremation. What if the M.E. had changed his mind? What if he had ordered an autopsy and checked for Seconal? He might have found that she was too drugged to have hanged herself. Ah, but someone else could have done it for her.

All that aside, Sean had been damned insensitive to cremate Eleanor without first consulting her brother. Bill had said that the Montagues were short on cash. If Sean had too little money to bury her, wouldn't Bill have chipped in? Bill, who had refused to give Eleanor money to move back to Chicago and now felt guilty as hell? From the sound of it, he would have paid a lot to avoid cremation.

As I crossed the threshold at the B & B, Mrs. Hogoboom bustled through the portal that led from her part of the house. "I have a complaint against you," she said, aiming a finger at my head. "You ran out of here and neglected to bolt the door behind you. It may seem trivial to you, but it's vital to me to keep this house safe. What if a rapist broke in because *you* forgot to bolt the door?"

I reddened for the third time that day. I was on a streak, but what could I expect coming from a family like mine, subject to such fierce blushes that we had named the phenomenon: the McKenzie flush. Gramma McKenzie, Mom, and my sister Amanda all endured the worst form of the condition. Fierce reddening of the chest, neck, face, and ears; perspiration; and acute embarrassment two to three times a day. I had inherited the milder form and usually suffered the blush no more than two or three times a week.

And there I stood, my face painted the color of guilt. "I'm sorry, Mrs. Hogoboom. Really. It won't happen again."

"See that it doesn't," she snapped.

Cowed, I mounted the stairs, dreading the explosion of flowers that awaited me. After that bawling out I yearned for a soothing monochromatic décor—cream, pale yellow, or pale green. I locked myself in my room and shut my eyes against the gaudy ruffles, feeling lonely and sorry for myself. My neighbors, by contrast, were still giggling and mumbling and emitting sporadic cries of ecstasy. Shit.

I missed Leversee. I would call Leversee. I fished through my purse for my cell phone but failed to find it. I fished once more with the same results: no phone. With mounting dread, I inverted the purse and shook its contents onto the coverlet. There lay all the miscellany that weighs down a purse…but no cell phone. Where was it?

With a jolt I recalled my "trip" down the fire escape and my purse disgorging itself into the weeds. In my anxiety over the wallet, I'd forgotten the cell phone. I could envision the neighborhood raccoon carrying it off, the little bandit.

Well. At least I had my wallet and my long-distance calling card. Though I hated the thought of running into Mrs. Hogoboom again, I stole downstairs to the foyer phone and dialed Leversee's home number. The phone rang once, twice. "Come on," I muttered. It rang again and finally he answered.

"It's me," I whispered.

"I can hardly hear you," he said.

"I can't talk any louder."

"Why's that?" That's Leversee: always prying.

"I'm calling from a place that's not very private."

"Why not go someplace private and call me on your cell phone?" he suggested, ever so reasonably.

"I lost my cell phone," I replied. "So how's it going?" I said, attempting to change the subject.

"Lost your phone, eh?"

"Yes. *So how's it going?*" I repeated, in exasperation.

"All right. Can't complain. Say, your friend Iggy dropped by a half hour ago."

"Iggy?"

"Yeah. He said he had a report for you, but he couldn't find you at the office or at home and he thought you might be at my place."

"Damn!" Just then, I heard a rustling. Someone was spying on me. Mrs. Hogoboom? The nerve of the woman. I said a loud, "God dammit," for her benefit, then pulled the phone cord as far upstairs as it would stretch and cupped a hand around the mouthpiece of the receiver. "Iggy's trying to serve me with papers to testify in a divorce case," I whispered.

"What are you?" asked Leversee. "Co-respondent?"

"Very funny. It's the Naylor case. I did some surveillance for the husband and now he wants me to put a hand on the Bible and unload about his wife and her lover."

"Didn't you anticipate that this might happen?" he asked, as though to a slow learner.

"Of course, I did. What I need from you now is sympathy, not logic."

"I feel so sorry for you," he said in a mechanical voice.

"What did you tell Iggy?"

"I said you'd be in Shore Haven a couple of days—"

"Oh, no—"

"Hasn't he done work for you before?"

"Yes, indeed. In fact, he worked for me on the Naylor case. I paid him the big buck and this is the thanks I get." I had subcontracted Iggy to take over surveillance of Mrs. Naylor for two days, Iggy demanding and getting more pay per hour than *I* got, so I ended up losing a hundred dollars on the deal.

After a pause, Leversee said, "So, what's happening in Shore Haven?"

"Nothing much." Then, stupidly, I angled for sympathy again. "A cop I sort of know gave me some background on the case I'm working, and he seemed to feel entitled to a kiss."

"What did you do to make him think that?" said Leversee, accusingly.

"Nothing. I got this officer a good collar last spring. I figured he owed me one."

"One what?"

"Jesus, Leversee."

"Look," he said, "I know how you operate."

"What's that supposed to mean?"

"I know from personal experience. How you get information."

"I never made a pass at that guy."

"You made one at me," he said.

"First of all, I never make a pass unless I absolutely have to, and second, I absolutely had to in your case, and third, it had nothing to do with getting information."

"But you got some all the same."

"What information?" I said. "That a certain killer might have been right handed? That and fifty-five cents'll get you a raisin bagel at Stein's."

"It was information," he insisted.

"Most people *are* right handed."

"Information I should never have given you."

"So what are you getting at?" I said.

"You know how to manipulate men."

"What? I have about as much talent in that area as a radish."

"You have tons of talent, Ms. Fisher."

How was I to respond to that? Thank him for the compliment or say fuck you?

Besides, I *had* tried to charm Swinkey, if only a little. But that wasn't making a pass; it was flirting. Making a pass is an attempt to get someone into bed, while flirting is a natural, normal part of communication between the sexes. But I didn't say so because Leversee would have fought the notion all the way to the World Court. I blurted, "I have to go now," and hung up. *Then* I said, "Fuck you," prompting Mrs. Hogoboom to pop her door open and glare at me.

"This is a *decent* house, young lady. I do not appreciate your nasty language."

"What kind of language do you appreciate, Mrs. Hogoboom? 'Oh, baby, oh, baby, oh, baby'?"

"What?"

"That's what my neighbors have uttered all afternoon and into the night. Can you imagine what sweaty images those words conjure in my mind? Excuse me, Mrs. Hogoboom, but are you running a bordello?"

The woman gaped at me and I forestalled further argument by tromping upstairs to my room. A few minutes later, Mrs. Hogoboom scaled the stairs and knocked at my neighbors' door. Their love-mumbles ceased and the door creaked open.

"Mark, you're going to have to keep it down in there," said Mrs. Hogoboom.

Keep it *down?* I thought. Fat chance.

"I've had a complaint," continued the sanctimonious old bat.

"Come on, Aunt Karen," came the man's low voice. "It's just the TV."

"I mean it, Mark."

The door creaked shut and Mrs. Hogoboom's footfalls receded down the stairs. Then came an eruption from Mount St. Giggles next door.

I fumed over my neighbors, Mrs. Hogoboom, Leversee, and Iggy for half an hour, then shucked my clothes and crawled in among the ruffles. When the panting and squeaking died down, I killed the light and closed my eyes, only to be treated to the image of Eleanor Montague's hideous dead face. I opened my eyes, closed them to horror, opened them again, and eventually drifted off.

THE NEXT A.M., I woke to renewed moaning and shuffling next door. Early risers. Although I was awed by their ability to wring so much pleasure from their rented bed, I wished Mrs. H. would march upstairs and sweep them out with her witch's broom. Their amorous activity made me feel worse about my fight with Leversee, not to mention sexually destitute.

With my neighbors thus occupied, I felt free to hog the lavatory. I took a long shower and blow-dried my hair before the mirror. I decided to skip the lipstick and powder lest I turn too many men's heads, then I said, "This is bullshit," and drew a defiant streak of Guava Stain across my mouth. Then I felt stupid for wearing makeup that I hate merely to spite Leversee, so I wiped a tissue across my lips and threw it in the trash. Men.

Out in the hallway I spied the morning meal. Mrs. Hogoboom had set out breakfast rolls, fresh fruit, and paper plates on a narrow table. Perhaps she had gotten a lewd earful when she dropped off the goodies. I chose a cheese Danish and an orange, then ducked into my room.

While water heated in the electric teapot, I sorted through the teas, finally choosing Minty Mist. I exchanged my bathrobe for a linen pantsuit, a taupe twin of the one I'd worn the day before, then carried my breakfast out to the balcony. The sun shone from the east and had already warmed the air to about sixty degrees. The river below was oily and black, while to the west, waves rolled in like molten silver.

My peace was destroyed by the nubile Trish, who in pink shorts and baby-blue tee-shirt padded out to the balcony. She ruffled her very short, very blond hair and sat at a small table, munching Danish, a stupefied expression on her face. I directed my thoughts to what I would do that day. I would use the straight-forward approach: I'd call on the Montague family and learn their story—if they would tell it to me. And I'd try their neighbors. It's amazing how many people are willing to blab all they know about folks they've lived next to for years and years.

Then I packed, preparing to decamp. I wouldn't miss Mrs. Hogoboom. To put it delicately, we hadn't hit it off. If my investigation warranted my staying another night in Shore Haven, I intended to check into a motel. I trundled my bag downstairs, opened the door, nipped outside, locked the deadbolt behind me, then tossed the keys through the mail slot onto the foyer floor. There.

Twenty minutes later I was driving up Beach Street. I parked opposite the Montague home, near a creek. Sand Creek, I supposed. I picked up my purse and advanced on the house.

FOUR

EQUALLY ATTRACTIVE FROM THE STREET as from the beach, the
Montague home was surrounded by gardens. Herbs grew along
the north side of the house, while wild flowers abounded on the
west, and zinnias, snapdragons, pansies, petunias, and mari-
golds bloomed on the east. I stepped up to the door and rang the
bell. Someone inside was playing piano but more quietly and
gently than on the day before. Was it a song by Schumann? Yes.
My sister had played it as a child while I still fumbled with "Tune
of the Tuna Fish." A woman shouted, "Sean, get the door!"

A couple of minutes later, a young man flung open the portal.
He had frizzy red hair, pale skin, and a slender body. He was
about six-two with a slight stoop—born, no doubt, of thousands
of hours at the keyboard. His shoulders and arms were well developed, his hands massive. He wore a white Oxford shirt, open
at the neck, and baggy brown corduroys. I took him to be the
widower, Sean Montague. "You from the agency?" he asked in
a flat voice.

From the agency, eh? I could take a cue. "Yes."

"Have you ever cared for someone with dementia?"

"Is this an interview?" I asked, glancing about the yard.

"Sorry," he said, without feeling. "Come in." I followed him
down a shadowy foyer to a large room with several long windows
looking out onto the lake. In the center of the windows stood the
French doors through which the elder Mr. Montague had escaped
the day before. Sean swept a hand to indicate that I should sit

on a worn leather couch. "I'll tell my sister you're here," he said, then vanished up the stairs.

The room, though appealing, could have used a good cleaning. The yellow walls were faded with a big block of brighter yellow above the brick hearth. Artwork out for reframing? Sold off, more like. I squared up a stack of *Music Magazines* then examined a tiny gold piano on the coffee table.

All the while, the pianist played on. How unlike the previous day's performance when the music was pounded from the keys. Today's tune was wooed. It drew me to another pair of French doors, these leading to the north porch. A grand piano nearly filled the messy room, and old Dennis Montague was running expert fingers along the keys, with nary a false note. The music was sweet and wistful, like an old love letter that makes you want to cry.

There came a patter of feet on stairs, and I turned to see Sean and a tall young woman. She seemed vaguely the elder of the two, perhaps twenty-six to Sean's twenty-four. She had the same frizzy red hair, but it was much longer and partially tamed by a tortoise-shell clip. Both sister and brother bore the marks of the past week—bruised-looking eyes, tension in their gaze—as though they had endured a disaster and expected more to come.

The siblings differed mainly in demeanor. While he was cold and silent, she was warm and high-strung. A snake and a bird. Beyond this, she had an artsy flavor. She wore a purple shirt, a teal jumper, and handmade sandals—but no makeup or jewelry.

"Your father plays beautifully," I said.

Brother and sister shared a glance that seemed to say, *What an ignoramus.*

I shrugged. "It's pretty."

At that, Fiona Montague introduced herself and her brother.

"Pleased to meet you," I said.

"And your name?" she asked.

"Betty Jo Bialosky." I'd given her my favorite fake name, one for which I actually have false I.D. The name came from an old Firesign Theatre album. I was willing to bet that this pair had never heard of the Firesign foursome, much less listened to them riff.

"Have you ever taken care of a person with Alzheimer's disease?" Fiona asked.

"Some," I lied.

Fiona's green eyes turned bereft. "Oh, we were hoping for someone with lots of experience."

"I've got experience," I said in a rush. "I'm very good at watching people who, uh, need to be watched. And I can assist with bathing and dressing and keeping an invalid amused." This was all true. I excelled at surveillance, plus I had helped my mother nurse Gramma McKenzie when she broke both legs in a car accident awhile back.

Fiona and Sean telegraphed one another looks of doubt.

"Why not give me a try?" I said, selling myself with the confident smile of a Fuller Brush man. "I like old folks and they like me. That should count for something."

"Yes," agreed Fiona. "It should."

Sean cleared his throat.

Fiona said, "Excuse us a moment," and the siblings adjourned to the kitchen. A murmur of words issued forth, but I couldn't make them out till the old man suddenly stopped playing.

Sean was saying, "—hate her. Why can't—"

"Shhh," hissed his sister.

Presently, Fiona returned to the living room. "Tell you what," she said. "We'll try you for a week, see how it goes. Hours are nine to six, plus the occasional evening if Sean and I both have to go out. And emergencies. Can you do that?"

"Sure. No problem."

"The pay is five an hour," she said in a faltering voice. "Two hundred a week."

"That's less than minimum wage," I mumbled. I didn't really care, yet it would look fishy if I failed to complain.

"I'm sorry it's not more. But we can give you a place to stay while you're caring for our dad."

I smiled. My sleuth side hoped to be lodged in the room where Eleanor had been found, while the rest of me shuddered at the prospect.

"It's a small trailer," continued Fiona. "At Sunnyside Park at the end of the street. About a quarter mile away—an easy walk."

"Sure," I said. "Sounds fine."

"All that remains is the question of who pays the agency fee," said Fiona.

I said, "I do," and she relaxed a notch or two, visibly glad to be relieved of the responsibility.

"When can you start?" she asked.

"How about this afternoon? I can work from one till six."

"Great," said Fiona. "And then I'll take you out to Sunnyside and get you settled in."

We warmly shook hands while Sean hulked in the kitchen archway like a block of ice, freezing me with his eyes.

As I walked out to the LeMans, an old Pinto drove up, oily smoke streaming from its exhaust. A strapping blonde in a pink uniform unfolded herself from this rustmobile.

"Here for an interview?" I asked.

"Hey, sorry I'm late. My car—"

"Well, we've decided against hiring anyone."

"What? I drove all the way out here, almost to Denton, and you're not hiring? West Care just called this morning." She looked ready to thump me.

"I'm sorry. Really. Here, let me give you something for your time." I snatched a twenty from my purse and handed it to the woman.

She held it up to the light as though it might be counterfeit, then she shoved it in her pocket. She dug her white nurse's shoe into the gravel, grumbled, "Okay," and left as she'd come, in a petroleum haze. Not very patient, that one. Better I should take care of the old man—for a couple days at least. I checked my watch: 9:40 a.m. I had three hours to turn myself into Betty Jo Bialosky, health-care aide.

I floored it all the way back to town where I parked directly in front of the library, raring to begin the transformation. Lacking local I.D., I knew better than to apply for a library card. Instead I asked the librarian if she had a file on Alzheimer's disease.

"Oh, yes." She was slim, past fifty, with blue eyes and short ginger hair. She was so vibrant, she reminded me of a thousand little bells tinkling all at once, albeit silently; this was a library, after all. She quickly found the file, whose pamphlets and articles I skimmed, setting aside several that might prove useful in my new "career." I copied them on the library's Xerox machine at fifteen cents a sheet—overpriced enough to warrant a citizen's arrest! But I needed the information, so I swallowed my gripes and kept dropping coins into the hungry little slot. Afterwards, I asked the librarian for the location of the nearest used-clothing store.

She gazed upward for a moment—listening to a distant choir? Then she said, "The Second Reformed Resale Shop, just down the block."

I thanked her and zipped down the street to the resale shop. There I purchased a creditable used uniform: pale green pants and a short-sleeved tunic made of a plasticky material that repels stains, rinses out in the sink, and never needs ironing. Not badly worn, this ensemble ran me four bucks. I imagined that the Montagues would approve of my thrift. In addition, I bought a used white cotton cardigan for two dollars and some slightly worn white walking shoes for seventy-five cents. The shoes were a size too big, but a pair of thick white socks, for an extra quarter, took up the slack.

The woman who stepped out of the First Reformed Resale Shop looked every bit the experienced heath-care aide. Or hairdresser. Or waitress.

Since my cell phone had gone AWOL, I needed to locate a pay phone. It's so hard to find a good one these days. You know, the old kind that closes for privacy and silence? I finally found a drive-up phone station that was about as private and silent as the Moose Lodge on Bingo Night. I had taken the precaution to look up West Care's phone number while at the library, as phone-booth directories tend to be sodden, hanging in shreds, or entirely absent—as in the present case. I dialed and a woman answered with a cry of, "Good morning, West Care!"

"Hello," I said, raising my voice to Fiona's register. "This is Fiona Montague. My brother and I have decided against hiring a health-care aide at this time. My cousin Nancy's helping out. So please, don't send anyone else for an interview."

"Hmph!" came the huffy reply. "It's kind of a nuisance for us to screen the applicants, then you turn around and get a relative."

"We're just not ready yet," I sighed. "But I'll call back when we are."

"Very well, Miss Montague. We'll be happy to help you when you're…*ready*."

My next call was to my sister in Montrose, on the opposite side of the state. Mandy, as I have mentioned, is a church organist, all the family genes for music having been dealt to her lucky chromosomes. While I had struggled with the old upright, Mandy had showed great skill, eventually switching to the organ, with its ridiculously complex keyboards, stops, pedals, and pumps.

On the other hand I can fire a gun with uncanny speed and accuracy, while Mandy was knocked flat on her ass the only time she tried to shoot. We all have our talents—or so Gramma

McKenzie likes to say. If a killer comes after me at least I'll have a chance. What can Mandy do? Throw an organ at him? But I still think she got the better genetic mix. I could sympathize with Bill Feinstein: he and I would never be one of them, the elite, the musicians.

The phone rang twice before my sister answered with a well modulated, "Hello, Amanda speaking."

"Mandy, it's me," I said. "Got a question for you."

"I'm fine. How are you?" she said in one of her smarmy attempts to improve my manners.

"Me? A-OK. I was wondering if you had any info on a piano player named Montague."

"I heard him play once when I was a child. Mrs. Drury took me."

"Let's see here. You must have been all of eight years old when you had Mrs. Dreary for a teacher. Sean would have been an infant then, or possibly *in utero*."

"I'm talking about Dennis Montague," said Mandy. "I've never heard of Sean."

"Sean is the son of Dennis. So Dennis is—was—a big-time piano player?"

"I'll say. He won the Berlinger Prize when he was twenty-one, toured internationally, performed with all the great orchestras. Then about ten years ago, he dropped out of sight."

"Well, he's got Alzheimer's."

"Poor man! And he's got a son who plays?"

"Sean's a 'great pianist' hopeful, I guess. Can you sniff around, see what you can find out about the clan? Mother, father, sister, brother. And Sean's wife, Eleanor Feinstein Montague. A flautist." I had never before had occasion to speak the word, so I said it again: "Flautist."

"I heard you the first time," said Mandy. "'Sniff around'? What am I? A bloodhound?"

"No. Yeah. Use your contacts, get the skinny. It's fun, you'll like it."

"'Get the skinny'? You sound like a thug. Musicians don't get the skinny—they dish."

I guffawed. Mandy's all right. "Okay," I said. "See what you can dish up."

"You're welcome," she replied.

"Same to you but more of it. Talk to ya later." And I hung up. Mandy and I had been getting along much better since I'd begun to subvert her civilizing ploys. It gave me great satisfaction to cut through the crap—at least with my own sister whom I'd know since we were both in diapers. If you remember the diaper part, it's easy to prick an elder sib's bombastic balloon.

Starving, I did a drive-through at Chix Max, opting for a grilled chicken sandwich and fries, then I sped to the parking lot at the public beach, rolled down my windows, and ate. The eating took all of five minutes, during which time I amused myself with the notion that Iggy would have a devil of a time trying to deliver a subpoena to Gayle Fisher in Shore Haven. Let him try, I thought magnanimously. All the while I'd be five miles north disguised as Betty Jo Bialosky, health-care aide, getting paid not only by Bill Feinstein, but also by the Montagues. What better way to spy on them than as a servant in their own home? It was a typical Iggy gig: spying from within. I had out-Iggied Iggy.

I tried to dredge up some pungent quotation about servants leading their masters around by the nose, but it didn't quite come. So I moved on to my postprandial chore of reading about Alzheimer's disease—"A.D." to those in the know. After my hilarious noontime mood, the articles were sobering.

The first gave the warning signs of dementia: "memory loss; difficulty performing familiar tasks; problems with language; disorientation of time and place; poor judgment; misplacing things; changes in mood, behavior, or personality; and loss of initiative." I'd seen the confusion of time in Dennis Montague who, at five p.m., thought he had just eaten breakfast.

The second article focused on recent findings. A.D. can be hereditary and linked to heart disease. Vitamin E, aspirin, and ibuprofen may prevent it, and the drugs Aricept, Remnil, and Nemenda can slow it, but there is no cure.

I turned to an article on strategies for calming persons with dementia. Anxiety and pacing are common; restraints only increase the agitation. The best way to communicate is to hunker down, make eye contact, speak slowly in a low voice, and give plenty of time for the A.D. person to process what you've said.

The next essay had to do with memory. People with dementia can't remember what you tell them, so it's pointless to get mad when they forget. A person with A.D. may be unable to recall what occurred a minute ago, but he can tell you every detail of Easter at Gramma's in 1925. Was that why Dennis could play the Schumann so well? He'd learned it as a child?

I read about safety. The greatest danger is for the patient to wander away from caregivers, get lost, and die of exposure. Another danger is injury around the house. Just as small children need child-proof environments, A.D. people need dementia-proof homes. Security…now, that I could relate to. Locks were to be installed out of sight; guns, knives, and mowers stowed away; and smoking supervised. Plants were to be removed because a person with dementia might eat and possibly be poisoned by dirt, bulbs, leaves, and flowers. Fiona was right. Her father would have to be *watched.*

The last article dealt with the progress of the disease. A.D. has stages and can move fast or slow, lasting a couple of years or as many as twenty. Ultimately, the brain becomes so damaged that it can no longer direct the body, and all the organs shut down. Curled in the fetal position, the sufferer dies.

I pitied the old man. He hadn't chosen this ailment nor could he fight or control it. He was no longer Dennis Montague, internationally acclaimed pianist. He was the victim of an incurable disease that had stolen his memory and would eventually steal his life.

At 12:30 I headed back to the Montague house, in no way ready to take on the old man.

FIVE

When I rang the bell, Fiona shouted, "Door's open! Come in!"

I obliged.

"I'm in here!" she called.

I followed her voice across the foyer to a sizable U-shaped kitchen. It was old and not exactly clean, but orderly. Cast-iron pans hung from on high and glass-paned cabinets displayed dishes and glasses—a charming room, but probably unsafe for the old man.

Dennis was slouched in the breakfast nook, a sort of restaurant booth painted pale green. He wore a large bib spotted with food, and Fiona was prodding him to finish his meal. "It's good," she said, pointing at the remnants of a hamburger patty, mashed potatoes, peas, and lettuce on his plate.

"No," complained Dennis. "No more."

"Then drink your water," said Fiona. "It's good for you."

I performed some mental math and concluded that Dennis must have fathered his children in his fifth decade. My own dad was forty-five when I was born, making him as old as most of my classmates' grandparents. If he were still alive, he'd be close to Dennis's age, and though I missed my father every day, I felt a rush of gratitude that he would never have to endure arthritis, cancer, or Alzheimer's disease.

Fiona held a green plastic glass to the old man's lips; he pretended to take a drink, then let the water dribble down his chin.

"Okay," she mumbled. "I guess you're done." To me she said, "There's a washcloth by the sink. Could you rinse it with warm water, wipe his face?"

As I approached with the cloth, he said, "It's that girl."

My heart clenched in my chest. Fiona said, "No, Daddy, this is Betty Jo."

Had he recognized me from the beach or thought I was Eleanor? Forcing a smile, I tried to dab at the old man's mouth, but he seized the cloth and proceeded to clean his whole face, ears, neck, and both hands. "That's good," I encouraged. "You can wash yourself."

Just then, the sound of finger drills swelled into the kitchen. Up and up the keys they climbed—mechanical, emotionless, and incredibly fast. No doubt the drills would have irritated most people, but not me. They took me back to my childhood when fingers were exercised daily, though Sean played with much greater velocity and strength than I or even my sister had ever possessed. His drills were the macho display of a young man.

Next came the trills, fast and hard and regular as machine-gun fire. I had never played them well. Not them or any of the other fancy finger moves—grace notes, mordents, and turns—that ornament the Bach two-part inventions Mandy had mastered but I had not. Oh, well. Despite my lack of talent, I looked upon Sean's and Dennis's piano playing as a bonus to my job.

As Sean continued his trills, the old man grew agitated. He cleaned and recleaned his fingers, one after the other, then suddenly announced, "I've got a performance. Where's my tux?"

I tried to reclaim the washcloth, but he jerked it back and kept scrubbing his big hands. Fiona, at the sink doing dishes, said, "No, you don't have a performance. And give Betty Jo that cloth."

He dropped it and cried, "I'm playing tonight! Where's my tux?"

"You're not performing, Daddy. Not tonight."

A half minute later, he stuttered, "I've got a p-performance, Beethoven, the uh, uh, the Fifth, with, with, with the B-B-Boston Symphony. I need my tuxedo!"

"Daddy, please. Listen to me. There's no performance! You've retired."

"Retired? When?"

"Ten years ago."

"No! How? You canceled my performance?" came his anguished reply.

"Daddy, you've quit."

I took the bib off the old man, then this entire agonizing exchange was repeated five more times. Oh, god, I said to myself, then asked Fiona, "Would your father like a walk? It's nice out. I can take him."

"Yes, that's a good idea, but I'll come too. He can slip away just like that," and she attempted to snap her wet fingers, but they slid noiseless to her soapy palm.

Within five minutes we were ready for our walk. When we stepped out into the warm fall air, Fiona said, "Look at that." She pointed at a fat bumblebee, dusty with pollen, backing out of a red snapdragon. "If only I had my Nikon," she sighed. "The light's perfect."

"Is that what you do?" I asked. "Take pictures?"

"I try. But it's difficult with Daddy so bad. I don't get out much." She kicked a weed, said, "I'm just feeling sorry for myself. Let's walk."

Outdoors, Dennis seemed to forget about his performance and his tux. Hallelujah! He shuffled along with little animation while Fiona and I talked.

"He gets stuck sometimes," she said.

"I see."

"It can go on all day. If he keeps at it, I give him an Ativan.

It soothes his anxiety, but it makes him sleep too much. I don't want him drugged, but sometimes the kindest thing for all of us is to give him his pill and let him relax."

I nodded. The same anxious fragment of conversation repeated all day would drive me mad. How it had affected Eleanor?

"He can never go out by himself. There's water all around—the lake, the creek, the channel, the swamp."

"I don't see how you've managed to care for him all alone—I mean you and Sean."

"Sean?" She laughed mirthlessly. "He's not much help. His wife…"

I asked, "What?" But I knew what.

Fiona pushed back her frizzy red hair. "You might as well know. Sean's wife?" She broke off, eyes brimming with tears. She wiped them on her arm and went on. "Eleanor was helping with Daddy. But she killed herself."

I said, "Oh, my," feigning shock. "That's terrible."

"Eight days ago."

"I'm so sorry." And I was. For Eleanor, Bill, and Fiona as well. She struck me as exhausted, depressed, but not a killer. She had lost a helper and probably a friend. "Was it a surprise?" I ventured.

Her eyes flashed. "Of course, it was! Do you think we'd let—"

"I'm sorry. I just meant that some people who kill themselves have tried before."

"No—never. She had plenty to live for. She was a wonderful flautist, like a gorgeous mezzo soprano. Her warmth and vibrato were exquisite." Fiona paused, then muttered, "I guess she was frustrated, stuck in No-wheres-ville minding a crazy old man."

That seemed a poor reason to kill oneself, especially for someone who'd been at it so briefly. I'm sure Fiona would have preferred to take photos and not tend her dad. But she seemed far from ready to end it all. She was coping. She'd hired me.

We walked along to where the road deadended at a narrow channel. A white post-and-rope barrier warned off cars from taking a dive. A few of the posts had been marred, as if tapped by a bumper or two; a steel barrier would have been safer. On the other hand, the road was posted with a five-mile-an-hour speed limit and a dead-end sign, so only a drunk or a fool would drive into the creek.

While Dennis peered down at the choppy water, I looked off to the west, where sailboats dotted the distance on the sparkling blue lake. I'd spent time on all the Great Lakes, but none was as beautifully blue as Lake Michigan. I imagined Chicago on the other side, its grand old buildings like an antique clasp on a bracelet of sapphires.

As the lake breeze cooled, Dennis's nose began to run. Fiona dabbed it with a tissue, then steered her quivering father back to the house. Once inside, she parked Dennis in the living room and draped him with a shawl, whereupon he promptly dozed off. Sean was caressing the keys. Something by Chopin, oddly slow and sad. Fiona stretched out on the couch. "I'm exhausted," she moaned. "Daddy was up at four a.m."

"Want me to clean while you rest?" I asked.

She shed a wan smile. "Yes, that would be wonderful. The kitchen needs a good going over."

The kitchen? I wanted to check bedrooms. But if she and Dennis both fell asleep, I could sneak upstairs and snoop.

The next half hour I spent sweeping the kitchen floor and cleaning the stove. Yes, I know how to perform these homely tasks, but I rarely do them for my own pitiful, closet-sized kitchen. My fridge is thirty years old, containing more frost than food. My stove is black enamel, with decades of indelible crust. There are four cupboards, a wooden table, and two chairs. That's all. Most days, I toy with the thought of moving, simply to get a better kitchen, but the rest of the apartment, with its tall windows and mellow hardwood floors, suits me.

Every few minutes, I checked to see if Fiona had fallen asleep. Once, she was sitting up flipping the pages of a *New Yorker;* another time, she was slouching, watching TV. When she was lying down, eyes closed, mouth open, I assumed she was snoozing. Sean was still playing the Chopin, repeating certain passages, but quietly, gently.

I tiptoed across the living room, past Fiona and the snoring Dennis, then up the stairs. The fourth step creaked loudly. I froze, waiting for her to sit bolt upright and demand to know what I was doing. But father and daughter dozed on. I scaled the rest of the stairs on the wall edge of each step—where they're least likely to squeak. A hall bisected the upstairs, with two doors on the street side and three on the lake. The first room on the lake was tiny with a single bed. Stacked on a table were dog-eared copies of *International Piano,* CD's, cassette tapes, and items of men's clothing. Sean's digs? He had probably shared a room with Eleanor until her unseemly demise, but who could sleep there after that? I was amazed he could stay in the house at all.

Next came a bathroom—smaller than mine, but most are. Then the master bedroom, which boasted a double bed, a worn burgundy bedspread and curtains, a Persian carpet, an exquisite view of the lake, and a wall full of photos. All were of Dennis as a younger man. In each picture he stood before a different grand piano, a different conductor, a different orchestra. In each he wore a tuxedo and the passionate expression of a man with a new mistress. Dennis Montague had led a romantic, nomadic life. No wonder he had waited so long to have children. But what had happened to his wife?

I tried a door on the opposite side of the hall, but it refused to open. Hunkering down to examine the keyhole, I noted a simple warded lock. When I jiggled the knob, something rattled on the other side, most likely a cheap bolt. This had to be the room where Eleanor killed herself. Or was killed. I longed to break in and scrutinize the place, but I restrained myself. I'd wait until I had little chance of getting caught.

The last room was done up in faded girlish frills—Fiona's childhood room, I surmised. Framed photographs lined the walls, mostly nature studies and portraits, all quite good. The mahogany wardrobe, dresser, and double bed seemed identical to those in the police photo of the hanging Eleanor.

"What are you doing?" demanded Sean, who had silently climbed the stairs and now stood a scant two feet behind me.

A jolt of surprise ran up my spine to my head. "Your sister asked me to clean," I blurted. "I finished the kitchen and thought I'd straighten the upstairs."

"If it needs straightening, Fiona will do it," he coldly replied. A sweet boyo was our Sean.

"Then what would you like me to do?" I asked, all innocence.

He frowned, plainly at a loss. "Well…you could clean the bathrooms. Upstairs and downstairs. But leave the bedrooms alone."

"Yes, sir."

"You'll find cleaning supplies under the sink." Then he slunk into his own room, leaving the door ajar—to monitor my behavior, I presumed.

I hated to be treated as a lackey and a drudge, but that's what I had signed on for, so who was I to complain? As for Sean, he had every right to be in a rotten mood if his wife had actually killed herself. I felt awful after my father had died, and losing a wife to suicide had to be worse. The stigma. Why had she done it? What had *he* done—or not done? He'd probably be asking himself those questions for a long time to come. *If* he were innocent. If he were guilty, then maybe he *felt* guilty. Or maybe he simply had a lousy personality.

I shut the bathroom door and turned my attention to the medicine cabinet. It was old, with a large mirror whose silvering had pooled into spiders. Inside stood vials of pills. Aha! Ativan for the old man. Aricept for the old man. Parafon forte for Fiona, "for back pain." And a variety of patent nostrums—cold pills, gas pills, laxatives. But no Seconal.

The cupboard beneath the sink held an ordinary stockpile of bathroom necessities—bars of soap, rolls of toilet paper, bottles of shampoo. I wondered which had been Eleanor's. The blue dandruff remover? The herbal stuff? The scientific brand? I reviewed each item, finding nothing untoward. The sink was ordinary, as was the tub, except for a plastic bath bench and heavy-duty grab bars. Wrinkling my nose, I hauled out the toilet brush, toilet cleaner, and antibacterial spray, then started to scrub. Fifteen minutes later, I passed Sean on the way downstairs. He was sitting up in bed, arms folded, bony ankles crossed, glaring at me. I nodded and smiled, then slouched downstairs to clean an even duller bathroom.

At 4:30 p.m. Fiona and Dennis were still mumbling in their dreams, so I returned to the kitchen to survey the contents of the refrigerator. A package of chicken breasts lay thawing on the bottom shelf. I set this on the counter, then made a salad, throwing in lettuce, cucumber, radishes, and homegrown Michigan tomatoes that were plump, juicy, and delicious.

I was scrubbing potatoes when Fiona wandered into the kitchen. "Oh, god, look at the time," she breathed. "I was really zonked. I've been trying to get things done while Daddy sleeps, but I wasn't getting any sleep."

"Were you planning on the chicken for dinner?" I asked.

"Mm-hm."

"I made a salad. Baked potatoes okay?"

"Sure. This is wonderful…god." She puttered about, setting the table, while I stuck three Idahos in the oven at 500 degrees. She went upstairs to wash, then came back all smiles about the clean bathroom. When I put the chicken breasts on to broil, she called Sean and woke her father. Five minutes later, she and Dennis came dragging into the kitchen like invalids, ready to be served a tasty and health-restoring meal. They chatted some, ate well, and their spirits seemed to rise. Sean arrived late. Picking at his food, he said nothing and acted blue.

What was wrong with this picture?

None of them looked like a murderer. But what does a murderer look like? The only one I'd ever known had seemed ordinary enough. As far as I could tell, a murderer could look like anyone. Be anyone.

Fiona apologized for there being only three chicken breasts. I munched a salami sandwich and salad instead—delicious after my half-day as char and cook. Then, while Fiona and I did the dishes, Sean cleaned up the old man and led him in to plunk on the piano. He started in on the Schumann again. I asked Fiona the name of the piece.

"'*Von fremden Lädern und Menschen,*'" she said, her German accent sounding authentic. "'Of Foreign Lands and People.' He's been stuck on that song all week."

"It's pretty."

"It's beautiful, but after the hundredth time, it could drive a person insane. I swear, he'd play that song all day if Sean would let him."

When the last dish had been wiped and put away, Fiona called out to Sean that we were leaving and that he would have to watch the old man. He yelled back that he would.

"I said *watch* him!" she repeated.

"I will!" he impatiently replied.

Fiona shivered with annoyance and we left.

SIX

WE TOOK MY CAR down to Sunnyside, which, as advertised, lay a quarter mile away, at the south end of Beach Street. The park was laid out in loops, rows, and spikes in an asymmetrical, yet balanced pattern, double wides at the periphery, singles and halfs filling the middle.

Fiona took me to a half-sized Airstream, a mini-blimp on wheels. She explained that her parents had kept the trailer for guests. "It's comfortable for one or two," she said, "but sleeps four in a pinch." I thought of Leversee and me sharing the space and how we'd get on one another's nerves P.D.Q. And who would grab the third and fourth spots? Sergeant Swinkey and Iggy Phlecks? Maybe we could all play bridge.

The tiny living room had a pair of built-in mini-couches that made up into a short double bed. "See those boards?" Fiona pointed at three pieces of reinforced plywood tucked close to the door. "You set them across the couches and fit the cushions on top." There was a red princess phone and a small answering machine. "I'll call if there's an emergency with Dad. Go ahead and use the telephone, but, please, no long-distance." Fiona reddened a bit—an amateur blush.

"I'll use a phone card if I have to call out of town."

She bashfully explained how to use the queer little toilet (it had two foot pedals for flushing: one to open a trap door, the other to release water), then she gave me the key and left.

What a relief to finally be on my own! Spying from within

was far more grueling than staking out a suspect from the comfort of a car. This inside job required me to play a role eight hours a day, while outside surveillance demanded nothing more than a low profile and faithful observation. Sure, it was a full-fledged yawn, but it was made bearable by a cozy car, cheese curls, books on tape, and the belief that the dung beetle being watched would eventually screw up and reveal what I wanted to know. I loved the *gotcha!*

I cranked open the jalousies and a breeze poured through, a tingling delight after four hours in an air-conditioned house. What a shame to lock out the lake breeze, but I suppose the humidity would have played havoc with the piano, the center of the Montague universe—the piano.

There's nothing like new digs to excite my sense of snoop. The trailer was equipped with a small fridge, a range top, a microwave, and a sink; cupboards and drawers with utensils, dishes, glasses, and silverware; twin padded benches for sleeping; a closet with bedclothes; a tiny shower; and a cupboard with clean towels.

My curiosity satisfied, I decided to watch the sunset down at the beach. I traded my uniform for chinos and a tee-shirt and climbed down the trailer steps. Just then, a young woman called, "Hey, you're new here, aren't you?" She was swinging one of those Michigan State six-pack coolers—white and green.

"Yep. Just moved in today."

"I'm Patty Winfield—not Wingfield, Winfield," and she spelled it out for me. "What's your name?"

"Betty Jo Bialosky."

"Bialosky? Sounds Polish."

Hmm. Polish? Russian? "It's Prussian," I said.

"Oh." A wrinkle of puzzlement appeared between her brows. Patty looked to be a hundred and forty pounds arranged to perfection on a five-seven frame. Her golden hair was cut in a curly shag, and her eyes were hazel, gold flecked. She wore a clean white sweatshirt, jeans that had been ironed, and a big friendly smile.

"I was just going for a walk," I said.

"Me, too. Where you headed?"

For some unknown reason, I didn't want to tell her. Then I felt silly. Maybe I could elicit some gossip about the Montagues—interrogate her in my own subtle way. So I said, "The lake. Care to come along? We can watch the sunset."

"Sure, let's go."

We took a mossy cinder-block path to the beach stairs, where she asked, "What brings you to Sunnyside?"

"I'm helping out with old Mr. Montague," I replied, descending the steps.

"How do you like it?"

"Fine."

"Getting along with Sean and Fiona?"

"Sure."

"How's old Dennis doing?" she inquired.

"Pretty good."

As we started down the second flight of stairs, I had to ask myself who was interrogating whom? She lacked my subtlety, of course, but she was learning a hell of a lot more about me than vice versa. But then the joke was on Patty. Nearly everything I had told her was a lie. That brought a grin to my lips. Perhaps after she had slaked her curiosity, she'd pour out all she knew, like a primed pump.

We shed our shoes and hunkered down in the warm sand as the sun made its slow dive into the lake.

"See all that purple in the sky?" said Patty.

"Yeah."

"It's pollution. Care for a beer?"

I hate beer but said, "Yes," as part of my pump-priming. I'm a sneaky one.

She handed me a Bud from her cooler. I popped the tab and sipped. Wet. Cold. Bitter. Not my cup of tea. Actually, some chamomile would have hit the spot.

"So what do you do?" I asked.

"I'm an LPN."

"That so? Where do you work?"

"Community Hospital. And I'm part-time at the HSD—"

"The what?"

"The VanBurgen County Human Services Department," she recited. "I'm a visiting nurse."

"Sort of like what I do—except I'm just an aide." I gave a shrug of resignation.

"You ought to go back to school," Patty said. "Pay's a lot better for nurses."

"I know. That job with the county sounds neat. You like it?"

"Well, it's hard work, lifting people, bathing them. But the money's good. How d'you like it at the Montague's?" she asked again. "Truly."

"It's all right."

"This is none of my business," she admitted, "but how do they seem to you?"

I drew a couple of spirals in the sand before responding. "Tired."

"Huh?"

"They slept this afternoon. All three of them."

"My God, it's no wonder, after what's happened. You know about Sean's wife, of course."

"What do you mean?" I blandly inquired, readying my brain cells for a gush of information.

"She killed herself."

"She what?" I dropped my jaw—conveying amazement, I hoped.

"She hung herself right in that house. Last week. Look, I don't know about you, but if my significant other killed himself right in our house, I sure wouldn't want to be in it, much less sleep in it."

"Maybe they've no place else to go."

"Is that what they told you?" she asked.

"No. They haven't mentioned it at all."

"Well, it's not true. They may not have a lot of cash, but they could sell that house and get a pretty penny. It's worth four hundred thousand if it's worth a cent. They could go someplace else if they wanted."

"Four hundred thousand," I breathed. "That's a lot."

"Lake property. Bunch of high rollers from Chicago come up here, think they're getting a bargain at that price. Shoot. I live at Sunnyside year round, two-fifty a month, and enjoy the heck of out of the lake."

"It's hard to figure," I said, obliquely. "So, does anyone know why Sean's wife, uh, killed herself?"

Patty swallowed some beer, then let out a sigh. "It's not a nice place over there, Betty Jo."

"What do you mean?"

"I'd rather not say."

Coy. She finished her beer in silence.

When the purple and gold had faded from the sky, we dusted the sand from our behinds and trudged back up the stairs. Lights were twinkling in trailers here and there, enough to illuminate our way. Patty mentioned that her trailer was a single. "I'm lucky to be up by the road," she said. "I'm one of the few who can stay here year round."

"Why's that?"

"Snow. The trailers are so close together, it's impossible to plow the park. Besides, most of the folks here have real houses somewhere else—Grand Rapids, Lansing, Collingwood. My trailer's been in the family for years. I'd invite you over, but it's kind of a mess." She pursed her lips in a sheepish smile.

"That's okay," I said, sincerely doubting that Miss Ironed Jeans would have a sloppy home.

"Can you find your way back to your place?" she asked. I assured her that I could and we said good night.

The evening had gone chilly, so I was glad to get back in my little trailer, where I cranked all the jalousies shut. While I rinsed out my uniform, I reviewed my chat with Patty. My pump-priming approach had worked—but only to a point: *"It's not a nice place over there, Betty Jo."* That's what she had said. And then she had stemmed the flow. I hung my uniform in the shower to drip dry, making a mental note to pump Patty again real soon.

As I took off my chinos, sand poured from the cuffs to the floor. I hate tracking sand all around, especially into bed where it could pass for an invasion of fire ants. So I slid my chinos back on and swept the sand out the door. Then I wriggled into my nightgown and lazily claimed the padded bench next to the red phone. I called to check my answering machines. Zilch. I rang up Leversee, but he was out. I left a message with my new phone number, adding, "Don't leave any messages 'cause I'm under-cover and the answering machine's not secure. Well, you can leave a message, but nothing specific. Something like, 'This is Steve, give me a—'"…then his machine cut me off.

I had been shorted on sleep the previous night, then I'd worked hard for the Montagues and taken two walks. I was as drained as Patty's beer can. So I washed up, switched off the lights, and wrapped myself in a comforter on the padded bench, where a few grains of sand grated on my tender derriere. Talk about the princess and the pea! I groaned in resignation.

By and by my thoughts returned to Eleanor. Would she have killed herself simply because the Montague home was not a nice place? Perhaps. But that still left the problem of little Eleanor pushing around that humongous dresser and punching a hole in the ceiling, using a hand hardened and roughened by what? Flute playing? Perhaps if she were horribly angry...

But something else had been bothering me. Women had their ways of killing themselves. Pills, gas, carbon monoxide—slashed wrists if they were feeling especially violent. But hanging, like shooting, was more the province of men. Not that women never strayed into that province—Mary Pfeiffer, for instance. But it was uncommon. So here was tiny Eleanor Montague, a flautist, for chrissake, in her white nighty with the embroidery, not only bashing a hole in the ceiling and hauling around heavy mahogany furniture, but also stringing herself up like a desperate con in a jail cell.

It didn't fit.

And what about the door? It had been bolted from the inside, so the rescue squad had to enter the room through the window. But they wouldn't have removed Eleanor's body that way. They would have moved the dresser, unbolted the door, and taken her out through the house. Yet the door had been rebolted. Who had done it, and how had he or she left the room?

Patty had said, *"It's not a nice place over there, Betty Jo."* Could *not nice* mean that a person could get killed? Had Eleanor been murdered?

SEVEN

THE COMFORTER CREPT AWAY sometime in the night, leaving me to shiver in the cold and wake two hours early, at six a.m. I got up and peed, then made a cup of Tetley tea and huddled under the comforter, sipping the hot brew. Leversee had failed to call back, probably out late on a case. Well, he's a homicide detective, and people do bump one another off at night. He gets the beep, he goes.

At sunrise I pulled on a sweater and chinos, then walked down to the beach. The lake was quiet, soft waves lapping the sand. A fringe of dry foam marked the high water level of the night before, a mere ten feet from the bluff where the trailer park stands.

The Great Lakes shoreline had been eroding for years, ever since the Saint Lawrence Seaway had been "improved" for international traffic in the 1950's. The St. Lawrence River had been dredged, new locks built, and the waters of the Great Lakes artificially raised to make them navigable for huge freighters. This traffic was making money for someone, but the environment had paid the bill.

The ocean-going vessels had brought a variety of hitchhikers—sea lampreys, zebra mussels, and infinitesimal organisms—who out-competed native species and lacked predators within the Great Lakes. Fish numbers were down and native freshwater mussels all but extinct.

The sun gleamed on wet rocks at the water's edge. I squatted to retrieve a large fossil, a conglomerate. Along with bits of pre-historic debris was imbedded what looked to be an enormous antique tooth, two inches long, with a round grinding surface and a pointed root. "What d'you know," I said. "The lake still has teeth." I pocketed the fossil and strolled along the shore, chilly water licking at my feet.

I was glad to have this time alone. Time to be myself and not Betty Jo. Time to relax my guard against Fiona, for I did have to guard against her. As pitiful as she seemed, she might have killed her sister-in-law. Fiona might have done it, or Sean, or both of them together, so I had to be careful.

Then I ran. I ran as though running from the whole lot of them. I ran until my lungs burned and my legs ached, and then I slowed to a jog. The beach ended, as beaches do, at a small creek that crawled across sand and soft green seaweed into the lake.

Back at the trailer I showered and wriggled into my clammy uniform, then I drove eight miles south to the DeMuntt Gas and Eat—an uninspiring name, yet imagine the reverse. Unsure which meals Fiona intended me to share with the family, I purchased orange juice, raisin bread, rye bread, cream cheese, cottage cheese, boiled ham, and a squeeze bottle of mustard. One of those huge cookies laden with chocolate chunks whispered my name. I bought it.

Back at the trailer, I drank a glass each of water and orange juice, then ate a ham on rye with mustard. Not an elegant breakfast, but at least I was stoked and ready to spy. I strode down to the Montague house, arriving at nine sharp. Sean was chopping away at the piano, while Fiona nursed a cup of coffee and the old man slept.

"Up at four a.m. yesterday, but who knows when he'll rise today? I try to get him up at eight each morning, but if he doesn't want to get up, I can't make him." Fiona sighed and sipped her brew. "Want something to eat?"

"Oh, no thanks, I've already had breakfast."

"Cup of coffee?"

"I'm not much of a coffee drinker," I said, Tetley's tiny little tea leaves having provided an ample caffeine buzz. "But herb tea would be good, if you have some."

She rummaged in a cupboard, producing a tea called Strawberry Fields. She got out a mug and put the kettle on to boil. When it whistled, I completed the chore and sat with her, sniffing the sweet strawberry scent of the tea. "What's on for today?" I asked. Giving her no time to answer, I said, "I could clean some more while your dad's asleep."

A look of pathetic gratitude swept her pale face. "Would you? I know you weren't hired to clean, but…" and her green eyes began to tear.

I handed her a napkin, which she held to her face. "What's wrong?" I asked.

"Something horrible happened last week," she mumbled.

"You mean Eleanor?"

"Yes."

My skin prickled with alarm, a surprisingly intense response. "It must be awful."

"You don't know how awful." She covered her eyes with the napkin and wept it to a pulp. I tore a couple sheets from a roll of paper towels, handed them to her. When the deluge was over, she wiped her face and blew her nose.

"I'm sorry," she hiccupped. "It's the Rachmaninoff—it intensifies the emotions. Besides which, this house has the *worst* aura…."

"Aura?"

"Can't you feel it? The violence? Suicide is *murder,*" she whispered. "The murder of oneself."

"No," I admitted, "I don't feel it. All I feel is that you and Sean have been under a brutal strain and you both need rest. Can't you go somewhere for awhile?"

"I'd love to. But what about Daddy? How could we go anywhere with him?"

"Couldn't you put him in a nursing home?" I ventured.

"No! Absolutely not."

"I mean for a week or two, so you can get away—"

"Look, Betty Jo, you can't stick a sick old man in a nursing home like a dog in a kennel."

Clearly, Fiona was dead set against being separated from her dad, so I let the matter drop. It was none of my business anyway. No. My business was to ferret out the truth about Eleanor's death. So I said, "How about if I clean upstairs? Maybe my bustling around'll wake him."

"I doubt it," she said with a wry smile. "If the Rach hasn't woken him, nothing will. The sun's out. Let's work in the garden. It's a four-star mess."

"I'm not much of a gardener," I protested.

"It's easy. Come on, let's breathe some fresh air."

As we stepped outside, I noted that workmen were putting storm shutters on the house next door. "Expecting a hurricane?" I asked Fiona.

She laughed. "The owner's a surgeon from Chicago—Dr. Krevitz. He likes his place boarded up by mid-September."

We went to the brick garage for tools and gloves, then returned to the garden. A red cardinal flew up from the lawn, drawing my gaze to the window of the locked room. For the first time, I realized that its glass was entirely gone. No one had replaced it after the fire department had knocked it out. I said, "Fiona, you've got a broken window up there."

"I know."

"Is someone going to fix it?"

"No. Sean doesn't want anyone up there."

"But what about damage? You know—rain, insects, squirrels, thieves?"

Fiona frowned.

"I can nail a piece of plywood across the window if your brother doesn't want a glazier—"

"I'll talk to him about it later," she said evasively.

"Do you have a ladder?"

"What?"

"A ladder, so I could put up the plywood—if Sean says it's okay," I explained.

"We've got a stepladder, I guess, out in the garage."

I could check that out when I returned my tools. No point in being too obvious about wanting to see the ladder. Fiona and I knelt by the petunias, she pointing at weeds, both of us pulling them out. After we had worked a few minutes, I said, "That's terrible about your sister-in-law."

"It's all so unreal," she replied. "Actually, it's worse than murder. With a murder, you've got someone to blame. With suicide, you can only blame yourself."

Hmmm. Fiona blamed herself. "What do you mean?" I asked.

"What did you do? What didn't you do? Or maybe she was depressed, and we didn't see—"

"She was depressed?"

Fiona yanked a cottonwood seedling out of the soil, its taproot pitiful and thin. "No more than the rest of us! It's tough being stuck here with a demented old man." Then her tone softened. "Eleanor was a wonderful musician. She gave up a lot to help with Daddy."

A stipend of twelve thousand a year wasn't my idea of a lot, but I nodded as if in agreement.

Fiona wiped her damp face on her shirtsleeve then fell silent. For the next two hours, she preened the herb garden while I weeded the annuals. My neck felt as if it were being pinched by a giant crab, so I consoled myself with the thought that I was getting thirty-seven fifty an hour from Bill Feinstein in addition to the five dollars an hour from the Montagues. I suppose that Iggy consoled himself the same way when he labored in an auto-parts plant, watching his co-workers for laziness, sabotage, and theft. But he'd be earning fifty an hour for spying and another twenty for making crankshafts. Such chutzpah!

Still, I was making a total of forty-two fifty an hour. At that rate, I'd gladly pull weeds all day—except that I wasn't getting any closer to the truth about Eleanor.

At 11:30 Sean came out to announce that the old man was up. Fiona asked me to dump the weeds, put away the tools, and water the flower beds. She indicated a garden hose that lay in a heap next to a tap. Inside the garage I found an aluminum step-ladder that was far too short to reach a second-floor window. But Sean or Fiona could have borrowed or rented a ladder and used it to leave the bedroom after having bolted the door from the inside.

The rest of my garden chores busied me until noon, when the sky grew dark and darker still, ready to pour down rain. My uniform was smeared black around the knees, my hair stringy, and my face running with sweat. I washed in the downstairs lavatory, then took off my pants and rinsed the knees until they were grimy gray. I patted them damp dry on a towel and slid them back on.

When I joined the family in the kitchen, Dennis was clad in the same gray sweats he'd worn the day before, but his face had been washed and his white hair combed. He was wearing a bib and eating hot dogs and baked beans with his children. "Get some food and join us," said Fiona.

I dished up a plateful of the humble provender and sat next to her. Sean cast me a dark look, then asked his father if he wanted anything.

"Some of those, those—uh, round things."

Sean frowned in puzzlement. "A slice of bread," said Fiona.

"Put a little butter on it." Sean fetched a slice of Italian bread, which actually was round, or at least oval. The old man carefully wiped his plate with the bread, then consumed it, bite by bite.

"He does a good job with his eating," I said, just to break the silence.

"Oh, Daddy's good as gold," said Fiona. "Would you clean up the kitchen, Betty? Daddy can play piano awhile, till the visiting nurse arrives. She usually gets here at one. You can take your break then and come back at two." Her voice inflected up at the end, as if she were asking a question rather than giving an order. That was her way and it made me like her, despite my suspicions.

"Sure," I said. "Then maybe you can take a nap and I can clean." I was picturing myself inside Eleanor's room. Just how I would get there, I didn't know.

"Sounds grand," said Fiona. "I'm wiped."

"If you sleep, sleep upstairs," said Sean. "Betty can watch You-Know-Who and clean the living room. It's a mess."

Good old Sean. I nodded, said, "What about the window?"

Fiona nudged me under the table.

"What window?" demanded Sean.

"The broken window upstairs. It's about to rain. You ought—"

"That window's none of your goddamn business," spat Sean.

At that, the sky lit up, hesitated, then boomed with thunder. Dennis threw his hands over his head, crying out in terror. Wind howled and the clouds let loose a downpour.

BECAUSE OF THE DELUGE I worked through my break, with plans to leave at five instead of six. The rain had tapered off by one, when the visiting nurse arrived: Patty Winfield, from Sunnyside. I couldn't help wondering why she had neglected to tell me that Dennis was one of her patients. When Fiona started to introduce us, Patty said, "We've met."

Her golden shag was pulled into a ponytail, her sturdy limbs clothed in a uniform like mine, except it was pink. And clean. She squatted next to Dennis, gazed into his pale blue eyes, and talked slowly in a low voice—exactly what the Alzheimer's articles had recommended. Dennis liked her. He grinned when she took his temperature and blood pressure. But when she suggested a bath, he said, "No."

"Daddy hates to bathe," Fiona explained. "He's afraid of the water. But he needs a bath. He hasn't had a good wash all week. And he needs clean clothes."

"Okay," said Patty. "Betty Jo can help."

I was about to protest, but thought better of it. I was, after all, a health-care aide. Certainly I would know how to give a bath. "I've helped older folks bathe before, but not anyone with—" and I mouthed A.D. "It's different, isn't it?"

"Oh, yes," said Patty, charming me with her eyes. "Just follow my lead and you'll be fine." She turned back to the old man. "Dennis?"

After a pause, he said, "What?"

"Let's go upstairs and give you a bath."

Pause. "What for?"

"That's a good question," said Patty to Fiona and me, with a laugh. To Dennis she said, "It'll make you feel better."

Pause. "You want me to take my clothes off?"

"Yes," said Patty.

"Would you like to have a baby?" asked Dennis.

"Hmm?"

"I could give you a baby." And he grinned like a five year old who's uttered something awful and precocious and funny— and knows it.

"Never mind him," said Fiona, turning red.

"That kind of talk's pretty common," replied Patty. "People say all kinds of things." People with dementia.

"I could give you a baby," the old man repeated in a singsong voice.

"Well, I don't need one," said Patty, and we all burst out laughing, Dennis included.

"But you need a bath. Let's go up and get you washed." She put out her hand and waited for Dennis to reach out to her, then she helped him to his feet. Patty and the old man took a slow walk upstairs, Fiona and I trailing behind. The practical nurse parked Dennis on the toilet, lid down, then whispered to Fiona and me, "I'm sure he doesn't want an audience. But you two stick close by, in case I need help."

We nodded in agreement. I grinned in relief and Patty closed the door.

Fiona said, "Let's clean Daddy's room." She tugged some sheets from a cupboard in the hall, and we changed the old man's bed. Then I stood before the black-and-white photos of the younger Dennis. Forty, fifty, sixty years old, hair fading from dark to white over the years, but always side parted and combed back. He looked sleek in his tuxedo, his hands huge on the pianos, commanding the keys.

"These pictures are wonderful," I said.

"Mother took them," said Fiona, sounding wistful.

"You have your mother's talent?"

"I hope so."

"What happened to her?"

"Stroke."

I nodded. "My dad died of a heart attack. Sometimes it's better to go fast."

"She didn't. She was in a nursing home for six years. I guess that's—"

Just then, the shower was turned on, and the old man cried, "You're killing meeee!"

Great, I thought. Murder by shower.

Patty soothed, "It's all right, it's just water."

Fiona was halfway to the bathroom when the yelling subsided. Patty was saying, "That's fine, Dennis. You wash yourself."

"Patty's so good with Daddy," sighed Fiona. "And a big help to Sean and me. She's the one who suggested we call West Care."

I nodded again, feeling guilty because I had helped so little with the old man. On the other hand, I had scrubbed a mile of grout and yanked a ton of weeds. Besides, I planned to vanish in a day or two, and they could find someone better.

We straightened and dusted the old man's room, then Patty called for towels and clean clothes, and Fiona brought them. Together they dried and dressed the old man and helped him shave and brush his teeth. I stood in the hall by Fiona's room, glanced in, saw nothing damning, and wondered if I had time to dash in and search it. People keep all kinds of incriminating goodies in their drawers.

Fiona put the kibosh on my search plans by opening the bathroom door. Patty was saying, "You should let him perform as much of his own personal care as possible. It's good for him." I peered into the bathroom where Dennis was standing before the mirror, raking a comb across his head.

"I know," said Fiona, as if she'd heard this a hundred times before. "And he needs a haircut, but he pitched a fit last time I took him to the barber."

"Cut it at home," advised Patty, stripping off her latex gloves. "It's much easier that way."

At last the old man's toilette was complete. Despite the excess hair, he looked great. His eyes sparkled, and he smiled as though glad to be alive. Fiona led him downstairs, Patty and I following, like ladies-in-waiting to an ancient king. Midway down the steps, Fiona said, "Oh, Betty, would you go get Daddy's sheets and towels? We'll throw them in the washer."

I said, "Sure!" and ran back upstairs to Fiona's room.

This would have to be the world's fastest search. I opened her bedside table and stirred a finger through a battered collection of paperbacks—plays mostly, by Sophocles, Shakespeare, and Eugene O'Neill—remnants, it would appear, of college days. I peeked under the mattress at nothing but box springs, glanced through the wardrobe at nothing but clothes. I was on a roll. I tried the bureau, starting at the top, where Fiona kept hosiery and underwear. After giving these items a cursory search, I proceeded to sift through the second and third drawers, where she stored cotton sweaters and blue jeans, respectively. Then I moved to the bottom drawer: a scattering of photographs on the left, a Nikon camera in the middle, and a pink jewelry box on the right. I picked through the photos, mostly of Dennis, Sean, and Eleanor. Near the bottom of the pile lay a duplicate of the picture that Bill Feinstein had given me—Eleanor and her flute.

I opened the jewelry box upon a tangle of necklaces, earrings, and pins. A rosary was mixed in. I suppose the family was Catholic, but not very. Music was their true religion. I closed the box, then lifted it out to see if anything was squirreled away behind it.

Bingo.

In the back right corner of the drawer lay a baggie full of pills—red, white, and yellow, all jumbled together. With a thrill of discovery, I grabbed the baggie to inspect it more closely. Just then, Fiona yelled, "Betty?" and started up the stairs.

EIGHT

"JUST A MINUTE!" I CALLED. Then I did something foolish: on impulse, I jammed the bag of pills into my pants pocket where it bulged like cellulite on a 300-pound woman. I frantically tried to extract the bag, but the more I tugged, the tighter it wedged against my hip. Fiona's footfalls were growing ever closer, so I shoved the jewelry box back in the drawer and shut it. Then I scurried about, snatching up sheets and pillowcases and towels, a pile so high that it blocked my vision. And that's how I happened to knock Fiona from the top of the stairs down three steps to the landing. Dropping the bundle, I cried, "Fiona, are you okay?"

Shakily, she struggled to her feet, saying, "Yes…I guess so." We regathered the dirty laundry and carefully trod downstairs, I mumbling apologies and Fiona assuring me that she was all right. I hoped she hadn't noticed my protruding pocket.

After Patty left, I did the laundry and scoured the kitchen. Occasionally, I'd pat the package of pills, trying to flatten it, but my efforts were useless: the capsules remained etched beneath my cheap polyester uniform. Meanwhile, Sean tinkered with some Chopin, Dennis snored on the recliner, and Fiona snoozed in her room. At five she padded barefoot into the kitchen to *oo* and *ah* over my work. The stove and refrigerator gleamed like showroom models. I felt like an idiot.

"I'll drive you home," she yawned. "Sean'll watch Daddy."

"You don't have to take me," I said, holding a dishtowel against the telltale bulge. "The rain's stopped."

"Well, if you don't mind. See you Monday."

"Call if you have an emergency," I said, then took my leave, grateful to escape. After a full day on the job, I understood what Fiona meant about the "aura"—anxiety clotted the air. Part of the tension came from Sean's piano playing: it was beautiful but relentless. Whether fierce or subdued, it was racked with emotion. Sean was clearly in agony. But as what? Widower or guilt-twisted wife killer?

Fiona added to the angst. She was worn down, frustrated from tending her father night and day, and seemingly appalled by Eleanor's death. I added in my own drop of anxiety, blocked as I was from my goal of searching the place. As for the pills, what they might reveal, I did not know. I just hoped that Fiona wouldn't notice they were missing.

BACK AT THE TRAILER I stripped off my polyester pants, then eased the bag from the pocket and poured the pills onto the kitchen counter. There were a dozen white tablets imprinted *TYLENOL CODEINE 3,* three yellow tablets, two yellow capsules, and twenty red capsules marked *Lilly F-40.* Could those be Seconal? A quick browse through the *Physicians' Desk Reference* would confirm or refute my guess. Surely, the Shore Haven Public Library would own a copy.

Why had Fiona hidden the pills? Was it because she was appalled by the suicide? Or because she suspected that Eleanor had been murdered? Or because she had killed Eleanor? As I rebagged the pills and zipped them into my black travel bag, I weighed the pros and cons of trying to return them to Fiona's drawer. I decided that the risk was too great. If Fiona noticed that they were gone and accused me of taking them, I'd simply deny having done so.

Then I thought to check the answering machine. The red message light was blinking. Leversee had called, asking me to phone him at work or at home. I tried him at Public Safety and he answered right away. Glad to hear his voice, I asked if he had missed me, and he gave the verbal equivalent of a shrug. I said, "Are you coming out here to visit me or what?"

"Where's 'out here'?" he asked in his cop voice, just to tick me off.

But I didn't take the bait. "A few miles north of Shore Haven. I'm staying in a trailer park called Sunnyside. It's right on the lake. I miss you. Are you coming to visit?"

He rattled some papers, then said, "Yes, of course I am."

I gave him directions and asked for his E.T.A.

"Around eight," he said.

"*That* late?"

"I have some work to finish."

"Fine. See you at eight."

I hated his acting that way but surmised that he was still sore over Swinkey's loose lips. An evening of bliss would take the rigidity out of Leversee's attitude. Or so I assumed.

With nearly three hours to kill before he arrived, believe me, I would have given them a speedy death if I could have. But I couldn't, so I got down to work. I checked my answering machines at work and at home. Nothing. For a paranoid moment, I wondered if Iggy had weaseled his way into my office and apartment, then played and erased my messages. He could have. I certainly might fiddle with his answering machine if I were tracking him. Then I laughed at my silly fears. Why would Iggy put such energy into serving a piddling subpoena? No matter how much time he spent, Marty Klein would never pay more than fifty bucks.

I made myself a sandwich, stacking the ham high and applying a flourish of mustard. After devouring this creation and draining a glass of o.j., I chased the delightful meal with the chocolate-chunk cookie. Presently, that warm, relaxed feeling came over me. It's how puppies and kittens must feel after a good meal, ready to flop down and snooze the night away. But not I. I put on my chinos and sweatshirt and went looking for Patty the practical nurse.

After wandering around the trailer park for five minutes, I asked a girl sitting on the concrete steps of a double wide if she knew Patty.

"She's my neighbor," responded the girl. "But she's gone right now."

The girl was about eighteen years old, blond with pale golden skin and blue eyes. Her hair was rickracked—probably dried in little braids, then unfurled. She was stunning but seemed not to know it, which made her all the more appealing. She invited me to join her. I sat on the steps and introduced myself. She said, "Patty told me about you. You work for the Montagues."

"That's right."

"My name's Debby—Debby Fenton. I work for Dr. Coulter—he's a dentist. I'm his receptionist, but sometimes I help in the *operatory*."

I had to smile. Debby had the unguarded charm of a little girl, eight or nine years old. She smoothed her hands over her tight jeans and straightened the tube top that stretched across small, firm breasts. A strand of toothfloss was draped around her neck, a rare accessory. Did I mention she had perfectly straight teeth? Perhaps they had landed her the job.

We got to chatting, and she gushed forth a veritable flood of facts. "I helped with an extraction today. I got to run the suction machine—you know, sucking up the blood? Doctor's assistant handled the laughing gas—ha!—nitrous oxide, I mean. That's what Dr. Coulter uses to knock 'em out. Not the teeth—the patients."

"Sounds…grisly."

"It can be. Depends on how many teeth get yanked. If it's just one, there isn't much blood. If it's a bunch—"

"I see."

"Today was a full-mouth extraction. Plus if he uses the nitrous, there's more blood. Xylocaine's safer, but some people like to be knocked out for an extraction, and I don't blame 'em."

"What do you do with the blood?" I had to ask. "After you suck it up."

"It all goes in a bottle. Afterwards, I empty it out."

"What about HIV?"

She frowned as if offended. "We all wear masks and gloves. It's totally safe." After a brief silence, Debby got back to work: "We had a robbery last month."

"Really?"

"Yeah. Doctor and his wife were on vacation, not that you need to go on vacation living in Shore Haven, if you know what I mean."

"It's a resort."

"Right. Anyway, we had a robbery. The police saw a broken window in the office, and they investigated."

"Uh-huh."

"They wanted Doctor to come right in and tell them what was missing."

"But he was on vacation," I said.

"Yeah. But Officer Voight, he knew I worked for Dr. Coulter, so he phoned me to come in and help. It was 6 a.m. on a Sunday morning. So I said, 'Okay.' When I got there, Officer Voight and his partner were waiting—"

"You mean Sergeant Swinkey?"

"I don't know. He was a tall guy with dark hair and a mustache. First, they wanted to know about cash, and I said there wasn't any 'cause Doctor takes it home every night. Besides, he was in Hawaii. A file drawer was half open, like the robber had searched it or something, so the cops pulled it out all the way. Officer Voight's partner, he sticks a pencil in there and flips out a rubber."

"A condom?"

"Yeah. One of those 'ribbed for her pleasure,' like they sell at DeMuntt's. I was so embarrassed. Then he says, 'What's this?' Well, it was obvious, so I didn't say. It was in a package and all, but I'd just as soon not yak about it."

"You think Dr. Coulter was playing around?"

"I donno. Anyway, we kept searching. Doctor's got three operatories and a jillion tools in each one. Some of the drawers were open, but I couldn't tell what was missing." She paused to run the floss between her central incisors, a contemplative gesture. "Well, the third operatory is where Doctor keeps drugs, and that room was trashed."

"Drugs?"

"Yeah. The drug cabinet was broken and the pills were all gone."

My whole body perked up like a giant ear. "What kind of drugs?"

"Nembutal, Tylenol 3's, Percodans. Mostly Seconal. Doctor had a great big bottle of Seconal, like red jellybeans. He uses 'em to relax his patients before an extraction."

Stolen Seconal. I wondered if this robbery had anything to do with Eleanor Montague's death. Sean had told the police that Eleanor didn't have a prescription. "Say, did you happen to know Eleanor Montague?"

"The girl who…?" and she hoisted an imaginary noose to pantomime hanging herself.

"That's the one."

"I met her a few times. She was…kinda weird, ya know?"

"How so?"

"Well, she'd go to that same trailer you're staying in, and she'd play a flute. Sometimes for hours."

I scratched my earlobe. "She was a professional flute player."

"Huh. I didn't know that. Anyway, she was on the outs with

her husband, Sean, and who can blame her, what with his relationship with his sister and all?"

"What do you mean?" I asked, barely keeping a squeak of excitement out of my voice.

Debby shrugged.

"They fought?" I asked.

She shook her head no.

"They were a little too close?"

"Using the same toothbrush is a little too close," she said, pointedly. "They were worse."

"So why didn't Eleanor just leave?"

"I guess she did. You can't leave any further than what she did."

"Yeah."

Suddenly, Debby asked what time it was.

I said, "Ten till six."

"Hey, gotta go. I got a date tonight with this guy named Mark. He's kinda cute." She leapt to her feet and ran into the trailer. And that was it. Of course, I was disappointed, but consoled myself with the thought that I could come back another day and tap into the flood.

Back at the Airstream I gussied up, then sat down next to the red princess phone. I was thinking about calling Swinkey to ask about the drug robbery. Maybe he'd tell me something. I plucked his old business card from my wallet and dialed his number on the off chance that he was still at work. He wasn't. So I left my number with the dispatcher, adding that there was no emergency, that the sergeant could call back Monday, but not to leave a message if I wasn't in.

Then I called Bill Feinstein. An answering machine clicked on after five rings. I started to leave a message, but Bill picked up the phone.

"I'm here," he said. "I just didn't feel like talking to anyone," and he added in a rush, "except you."

I swallowed. "Bill, I think you've got reason to be suspicious about Eleanor's death. Was she any kind of a fitness buff—you know, runner, weight lifter, that sort of thing?"

"No, not at all. When we were kids, our parents wanted us to swim, play tennis, golf—all that. But we refused. Eleanor played the flute and I drew cars."

"That photo you showed me—Eleanor looked thin, not particularly strong. Yet, according to the police report, she moved heavy furniture and punched a hole in the ceiling. It's possible, but not likely."

"Is that it?" he asked. "Is that all you've got?"

"No. Did your sister ever take sleeping pills?"

"Not that I'm aware of."

"Okay. And what about Sean? I've gathered that you don't like him, but what else can you tell me about him and his family?"

"He's a selfish prick. He lived off my sister, and now he's living off a senile old man."

Not a whole lot of objectivity there. "What about Fiona?"

"What do you mean?"

"Anything strange about her relationship with Sean?"

"Strange? I don't know. I only met her once, at the funeral, and we were all upset. Except Sean. He's a cold one all right."

"Can you think of any reason why Fiona might want your sister dead?"

"No. It was Sean."

"What motive would he have? Did Eleanor have money?"

"I told you before. She had a small inheritance and made a little cash playing with the chamber orchestra and teaching flute. She used it to support *him*."

"Could there have been another woman? Another man?"

Bill took his time answering. "All I can say is that Eleanor was miserable with that jerk. He's—pathologically self-centered."

I sighed. Listening to Bill's vague rational for the so-called murder made me doubt my own suspicions. "I'll stay on it couple more days, see if anything materializes."

"A couple more days? I hired you to find out what happened. I don't care how long it takes."

"Believe me, I'm trying. I just don't want to waste your money."

"I don't care about the money."

We said our good-byes and I hung up the phone.

I lay there thinking of how the murder—if it were a murder—might have occurred. If Sean were the killer, he could have persuaded Eleanor to take Seconal: *"Take one of these, honey, it'll help you nap. I know it's hard to sleep around here with me banging on the piano all day and Dad shuffling around at night."* Then after fifteen, twenty minutes, when Eleanor was feeling weak and boneless, Sean could have gotten Fiona out of the house on some pretext—maybe taking a walk with the old man—so she wouldn't hear Eleanor's protests or the furniture scraping around. Then Sean could have moved the dresser to block the door, climbed on the bed, and knocked the hole in the ceiling. But not with his hands; he'd want to keep them safe. How clever to seek out a rafter that way—I would never have thought of it. Then he would have had to grind some of the plaster into Eleanor's knuckles. He was certainly strong enough to string up a small woman who was woozy from barbiturates. Then he would have exited the murder scene—somehow. Then he would have rounded up Fiona and Dennis for their nightly trip to the ice-cream stand. Except for the fact that there was no way out of the locked room, the murder was definitely doable. But why? Insurance? Most insurance policies have a suicide exclusion, not to mention that Sean and Eleanor seemed too poor to invest in insurance. Why would he have killed her?

Or had Fiona murdered Eleanor? Was she physically strong

enough? The old man couldn't have done it; he lacked the mental capacity to see the crime through. Or had the killer been Eleanor herself, strengthened by the insane resolve to commit suicide, able to move tall bureaus, punch holes in plaster, and take that last leap into space?

I chewed at this problem as though chewing a tough piece of steak, unsure whether to keep chewing, swallow, or spit it out.

AROUND EIGHT, brisk steps approached the trailer, then two taps sounded at the door. I knelt on the padded bench to peer through the louvered window, but my caller was too close to the Airstream for me to see. I went to the door and asked, "Who is it?"

Leversee answered, "Who are you expecting?" and I threw open the door and pulled him in. Actually, this wasn't the brightest move because he hit his head with a fierce rattle on the top of the doorway, which is plenty tall enough for a five-foot-four woman like me, but not for a six-foot guy like Leversee. He clapped one hand to his forehead and used the other to stave off my murmurs and ministrations. After a full minute, he allowed me to sit him on one of the little couches in the "living room."

"Honey, are you all right?" I babbled.

"Just stunned. I wasn't expecting an assault." His green eyes glared at the offending doorway, then scanned the rest of the trailer. "It's small," he said.

I bent to kiss his forehead. "It's insights like those that make you the best detective in the whole wide world."

"So how's life in Shore Haven?" he asked, ignoring my flattery.

"Couldn't be better," I said, stroking his wavy blond hair. "Let's see. I scoured bathrooms yesterday. I weeded a garden and cleaned a kitchen today."

"Sounds like you're close to solving the case."

"Close? I've solved it. Mr. Plumber did it with a spatula in the flower bed."

"Seriously, what are you working on?"

"You always have to know what I'm doing," I pointed out, not for the first time. Or the second or third.

"Yes, I do."

"But you never tell me—"

"Sometimes I tell you too much."

"Okay," I said. "It's an apparent suicide—remember? Maybe a murder."

"You taking precautions?"

"What are you talking about? Birth control or a gun?"

At that, he swept me down into his arms and pressed his lips to my mouth. Now, I had been a star pupil in all three self-defense classes I'd taken at the YWCA, so I could easily have broken his hold. But why buck the flow?

NINE

EVER THE MASTERFUL ONE, Leversee showed considerable ingenuity in coping with the cramped environment. Forty minutes later, we clung together, glazed eyed, in the "bedroom," a trail of discarded clothing marking special points of interest along the way. Shirts lay on the little couches, shoes and slacks on the floor, panties and BVD's on the stove, my bra in the sink, and Leversee and I on a padded bench, in a miracle of physical compression—on his part, at least, given his height. "You'd be a natural as a yogi," I murmured in his ear.

"A what?"

"A yogi. A practitioner of yoga."

"Oh, one of those."

"In fact, I believe I've seen this position in a book on Kundalini yoga."

"Isn't that some kind of sex manual?"

"I suppose it could be looked upon—"

Leversee interrupted my evasion with a slow wet kiss.

"You know," I said awhile later, "those little couches in the other room?"

"Yes?"

"They somehow turn into a king-sized bed."

"They may turn into a bed…but king sized? I doubt it."

"Let's check it out."

We extricated ourselves from the padded bench and went to

investigate. "Sand on the floor," noted Leversee as he retrieved his gray slacks from the linoleum.

"That's keen detection," I said to be nice, but really, I was absorbed in the mystery of the king-sized bed. I removed the cushions from the couches, then pulled out the three boards. "These go across the couches somehow."

Exhibiting all his manly cleverness, Leversee swiftly arranged the boards—incidentally giving me a breathtaking view of his posterior. Then we covered the boards with couch cushions, a comforter, and a pale blue sheet from the closet. "Voila," I said.

"It's not king sized," he said.

THE NEXT MORNING found us luxuriating, then showering one at a time because the shower was too tiny for two. In Leversee's case, too tiny for one: he complained that he had to crouch the whole while and the water came out in a trickle. "You'd get more water from a soup can with two holes punched in it," said he.

"I thought you liked camping out," I replied.

"I do. But this isn't real camping. It's some girl version of camping."

Men.

We prepared breakfast, Leversee manning the skillet to fry up six anorexic slices of boiled ham. Now, he's a very masculine guy, yet graceful for a cop, but the space was so small he kept bumping into the fridge or the closet or the stove. At last, we spread our meal on the little kitchen counter. Ham, orange juice, raisin-bread toast, and kiwi yogurt.

Stirring a spoon in his yogurt, Leversee asked if I had seen Iggy.

I nearly choked on a raisin. "No, knock wood," and I rapped knuckles on the cabinet above my head. "But how's he gonna find me here? I'm five miles north of Shore Haven proper. And I'm using a fake name—Betty Jo Bialosky."

"Sounds foolproof," Leversee said. "But Iggy's no fool." That remained to be seen.

As I started to dismantle the bed, Leversee asked to use the phone, and I said use a calling card if he was phoning long-distance, and he said he was planning to—meaning he's not a mooch. He went to make his call, then returned almost immediately to stick a white card beneath my nose.

"What's this?" he demanded.

"Huh? Looks like a business card." I pushed his hand six inches away so I could read the damn thing: *Officer John Swinkey, Shore Haven Police.* "It is a business card. What of it?" But I knew what of it. Leversee was about to make a stink.

"I thought you were done with this guy."

"I am."

"Then why's his card next to your bed?"

"Well, he left it there the last time we copulated—you know, so I won't forget his name—"

"Gayle—"

"I left his card by the phone in the event I had to contact him regarding the case."

"So you're *not* done with him."

"'Done with'? You make it sound as if we had some tragic affair."

"Are you planning to see more of him?" asked Leversee.

"You—you green-eyed monster!"

"Are you?"

"No! We were exchanging information, not DNA."

"But he wanted to."

I sighed heavily. "Maybe he thought I'd be offended if he didn't—make the gesture."

"What?"

"He was just trying to be polite," I said.

"What is this? Reverse-reverse sexism?"

"I never heard of that," I said.

"And I never heard of man making a pass just to be polite."

"Oh, yeah? Happens all the time—to other women, I mean, not me."

"Polite, my ass," muttered Leversee.

"Look, like I told him, I already have a cop, and one's plenty enough for me."

"Good."

"Way plenty enough." I stacked the three boards and shoved them back by the door with a *clunk*. "You ought to learn to trust me."

He said, "I do trust you."

I cast him a sidelong glance. "You do?"

"As much as I trust anyone."

"Is that high praise for me or low praise for humanity?"

He began to organize the couch cushions. "A little of each."

"Leversee…"

"Gayle…"

It was a truce. Or possibly a standoff. Leversee made his phone call, I folded the sheets, and we exited the trailer. By then it was ten o'clock and the sun had warmed the air to seventy degrees—or so indicated the weathered thermometer next to the door. Leversee and I strolled arm in arm down to the beach. He started to head north, toward the Montague home, but I quickly steered him the other way with the promise of seeing a "cute little crick."

We shuffled through the sand till we reached the creek and, being the only souls around, stopped to touch lips before turning back. Then we raced to the beach stairs and flopped onto the sand, the sun warming our backs as we watched the waves roll in and break into foam. A pack of sailboats were scudding across the waves, and a speedboat bounced and hummed in the distance.

I loved being with Leversee, except when he acted like a

jealous jackass. And sometimes I wished that we weren't P.I. and cop, for we had more or less agreed never to discuss our cases until mine were solved or his had gone to court. Even then, I left out juicy bits and I'm sure he did too. I inched a little closer to him, as if to bridge the gap.

"Okay," I said, "now that you trust me so much, you can tell me a little about what you've been doing in Collingwood, and I'll tell you a little about what I'm doing in beautiful Shore Haven."

"You go first," he said.

"No, you," I countered.

"Don't you trust me?"

I sniffed. "All right, I'll go first. The 'suicide' I'm investigating? Maybe it really was a murder. But dig this: the M.E. declared it a suicide immediately. There was no autopsy and the body was cremated the next day."

Leversee frowned. "No autopsy? This county's got a cash-flow problem."

"Now you," I said.

"Meth Dealer A was gunned down by Meth Dealer B. This occurred yesterday at 3:03 p.m., outside Mr. Lavonne's Bar and Grill."

"Witnesses?"

"Sure. But no one saw anything."

"Frustrating. But at least you know it wasn't suicide."

At that, he applied fingers to my ticklish ribs and made me shriek.

I jumped up and said, "I'm starving."

"But we just had breakfast."

"I can't help it. I'm hungry."

So we drove north to the tourist town of Denton, where it would be unlikely in the extreme for Iggy to seek me out. We stopped at a fake English pub where Leversee chewed on a char-broiled burger and cottage fries, while I gobbled down turkey, lettuce, and tomato on whole-wheat.

"That's right," he said. "Keep up your strength."

"What do you have in mind?"

"What do you think?"

"I thought you had to work this afternoon," I said.

He caressed my thigh under the table. "It's noon. I'm not on duty until three forty-five."

"Oh."

We finished our meal, then hied back to Sunnyside. Upon entering the trailer, Leversee cracked his head again, whereupon we repaired to the padded bench so I could kiss it better.

Some time later, we found ourselves in another yoga pose. There's nothing like a new setting to spark one's ingenuity. This time one of my legs was folded under and the other outstretched like a cat's, pointing at the North Star—well, you get the picture. Eventually, I hit my crescendo, and Leversee his, and a moment later he cried, "Good god, my ankle, I think I've sprained it!"

I nuzzled his ankle, then we lay close together (how else can two adults lie on a narrow bench?) drowsing until two-fifteen, when my swain rose to dress for work. Then the phone rang, and I reached to pick it up. It was Swinkey.

"Oh, hi," I said in a flat voice.

"You wanted to talk about something?" he asked.

"Not just now. I'm a tad busy. Mind if I call you latter?"

"Sure. I'm on duty till four."

And we signed off.

You would have thought that Leversee and I were both too full of endorphins to raise our quills, but, no, that was not the case. The way Leversee stared at the phone, it might have been a scorpion. "Who was that?" he inquired in an officious voice.

"Who do you think it was?" I replied. That's what's called "answering a question with a question," a potentially annoying response, but Leversee's question didn't deserve an answer. After all, the call was harmless.

"Was it John Swinkey?"

"Who?" There, I did it again.

"The guy you were making out with," he said, jamming his legs into his slacks.

It's amazing how quickly the pulse of anger will clear one's mind and body of those mellow post-coital hormones. "I can't believe you just said that."

He snatched up his shirt. "You're screwing this guy? This *officer?*"

"He's a sergeant now," I corrected. "He got a promotion."

"You're screwing this *sergeant!*"

"Of course, I am. We get it on five, six times a day. I'm surprised he hasn't stopped by since you got here. You want me to invite him over right now? I will."

I hopped off the bench, grabbed the phone, and commenced dialing. Meanwhile, Leversee put on his shoes and stalked out of the trailer, slamming the door behind him. "You shit!" I yelled, but too late for him to hear.

I was so angry, all I could do was drop the phone and feverishly straighten the trailer. In the midst of this frenzy I found his socks and BVD's on the bathroom floor; without remorse, I dropped them in the trash. A few minutes later there came a rapping at the door. Leversee. He had seen the error of his ways and come back to apologize. I shouted, "Go away!" The knocking continued, until at last I relented. I *would* let him apologize, *then* I'd tell him to go to hell. Wrapping myself haphazardly in a sheet, I dashed to the door and flung it open. The next thing I knew, I was holding a fat white envelope.

Iggy Phlecks stood before me, a look of profound satisfaction twinkling in his eyes and twitching at his lips. Was it because he had finally delivered that despicable subpoena? Or was it

because I was draped in nothing but a light blue sheet? I threw
the cursed envelope in his face and attempted to slam the trailer
door, but he had stuck one black, steel-toed boot into the
doorway, and slam as I might, the boot wouldn't budge.

Though Iggy is like an annoying younger brother, he's
actually older than I—in his early thirties. He's about five-eleven,
with a lean, muscular body and a bit of a crouch. He has angular
features, dark blond hair, and glacier blue eyes. On that day, he
was wearing jeans and a black sleeveless tee-shirt, exposing his
right shoulder and its home-made wolf's-head tattoo.

"Son of a bitch," I seethed, tightening the sheet around me.

"Hey, don't bad mouth the messenger. You wanna bitch at
someone, call Marty. These papers are from him," and he shoved
them at me once more.

"I know who they're from." I grabbed the envelope. No point
in scorning it: there's no such thing as undelivering a subpoena.
It's like trying to undeliver a baby. I *suppose* I should have
stepped inside to rip open the envelope, but no one seemed to be
about, so I did it right then and there. Glancing through the
papers, I said, "Hmm. Naylor vs. Naylor. Sounds like a boxing
match."

"I think the technical term is 'knock-down, drag-out
divorce.'"

"September 30th, Collingwood County Courthouse, Judge
Baumann."

"Well, so long. Guess I'll mosey on back to Collingwood."

"Wait a minute," I said. "I have a job for you, if you're interested."

"Sure," he said, leaning in close.

I held out my hand like a traffic cop. "Let me get dressed
first." Once again I tried to close the door, but Iggy's boot
remained firmly in the way, and, unbeknownst to me, firmly atop
the hem of my sheet. Therefore, when I jumped back from the

door, preparing to kick his boot away, my toga was dragged down a very critical six inches. Iggy threw back his head in wild guffaws while I shrieked in dismay and ran for the bathroom, grabbing my clothes en route.

When I had finished buttoning my blouse and zipping my chinos, I opened the bathroom door upon Iggy, who lay sprawled, uninvited, on the padded bench where Leversee and I had so recently enjoyed our yoga session.

"You idiot," I said.

He made some *tch-tch* noises. "Is that any way to hire a detective?"

"Get up," I said. "We can talk outside."

"I like it here. It has a certain flavor—or should I say aroma?"

I usually refrain from physically attacking my business associates, but Iggy is more of a scrapping litter mate than a colleague. Besides, I had just had a really lousy ten minutes. So I leveled a kick at him. Unfortunately, he caught my foot and flipped me onto the bench opposite. My head banged against the aluminum wall, rattling the entire trailer like a giant maraca. Little sparkles jittered before my eyes and red hot pain radiated from my crown, while a flush of rage zoomed up my chest to my neck, face, and ears. I'd long had a yen to grapple with Iggy, and I'm not talking about sex. Pure and simple, I wanted to kick his ass. Usually in a friendly sort of way, but that day, I wanted to inflict pain.

Iggy, showing a heretofore unknown chivalry, extended his hand to pull me to my feet. I clasped his paw, swung him into a half nelson, and trapped him in a head lock—one, two, three. Then I ran my thumb from behind his ear to the point of his jaw, halfway back up again, and pressed.

Hard.

Iggy squinched his eyes shut and sniffed against the pain.

"How'd you find me, Iggy?"

"I made a good guess," he said between clenched teeth.

I pressed my thumb a little harder. "I think you'll feel better if you told the truth."

"I followed your cop boyfriend," he hissed.

"You followed him last night?"

"Yeah. Now, what was that you said about feeling better?"

"Oh, sure." And I let up the pressure on his mandibular angle. "You followed him all the way from Collingwood, and he never noticed you once?"

"Guess he had dancing fairies on his mind. Ha!"

I pressed my thumb a bit harder. "You certain about that, Iggy?"

"Yeah."

I pressed harder still.

"Come on, Gayle, fun's fun, but you don't have to get carried away—"

I gave my thumb a little twist.

"I put a remote GPS on his Ford!"

"Why you—"

"What would you do in my place? Suppose you had a perfectly good subpoena to deliver to a very good friend, and she's trying to duck you? It was a challenge," he said.

"So you wasted two days trailing around after Leversee, trying to get to me? For fifty bucks?"

"Hell, no. That's chump change. Marty's giving me fifty-five."

"You must not have anything to do with your time."

"Well, no, Gayle, I don't. Y' know how it is."

I did. And what he had told me made sense…if you knew Iggy.

The stubble on his jaw, chin, and neck was beginning to irritate my arm. His skin was greasy and he stank from his night in the car. I heaved a sigh. "I'm going to let you go, but don't try anything stupid, or Mama will spank." I let him out of the head lock, and he shook himself like a wet dog. I said, "Are you really interested in work?"

"Sure."

"Let's go outside and we'll talk—and if we see anyone, I'm Betty."

I slipped my feet into sandals, then followed him out of the trailer. Like I said, Iggy and I are friends, but I wasn't about to let him get behind me.

We headed down to the beach, then ditched our footgear to wade in chilly water. The wind caught our shirts, flapping them like sails. I laughed. "You really bugged his car?"

"It's not a bug," he said with disdain. "It's an RGPS—Remote Global Positioning System." He extracted from his jeans pocket an object about half the size of a spool of thread. In an excess of Igginess, he tossed it into the air and caught it, then held it out for me to view. "It's got a magnet on one side, transmitter on the other. It sends a signal to a satellite, which relays the transmitter's exact location to a hand-held locator device."

"Say, don't they have these things in Cadillacs and like that?"

"Those are non-remote GPS's," he said, as if embarrassed by my ignorance.

"Where'd you get it?" I asked.

"Internet."

"You better hope Leversee never finds out what you did." Of course, I was the only person liable to tell him. If I ever spoke to him again.

Iggy pulled a Camel from his shirt pocket and fired it up with a Bic lighter, his hands sheltering both flame and cigarette from the wind. He took a deep drag, then coughed, expelling a stream of smoke. "It was worth it," he said.

"Yeah?"

"That look on your face when you opened the door, that look

when I threw you the subpoena, that look when you accidentally showed me your—"

"Shut up, Iggy."

"I suspected you had a fine body. But ya never actually know till it's stripped bare." He sculpted in the air an impossibly zaftig female form, lingering salaciously over the curves.

I said nothing.

"The way that tin can was rattling last night, you woulda thought Leversee was getting a connubial visit at the state pen."

"It's not *connubial*," I morosely replied. "It's conjugal."

"Only if you're married. You and the lieutenant aren't, so I guess I'd call your visit *convivial*. That's Latin for 'living with.'"

"I'd have never taken you for a prude," I said.

"I'm not. But my old man is. He'd call your arrangement with Stevie-boy 'sinful.'"

"And what about you, Iggy? You ever do anything sinful?"

"Every chance I get."

"Which is probably never. I bet you spent your entire youth learning Latin in some Jesuit school, and you never got over it."

Iggy sucked on his cigarette plaintively, then let the smoke out his nose. "What's this about a job?"

"I'd like you to follow Alex Naylor, see if he's getting any action on the side."

"I don't think so, Gayle."

"Why not? I'll pay the going rate—thirty-eight ninety-five an hour."

"I'm gonna ignore that insulting monetary offer and get right to the core of the boil. Last May, Marty Klein hired you to spy on Mrs. Naylor, and you subcontracted me to watch her for two days. This week, Marty hired me to deliver you a subpoena to testify against *Mrs.* Naylor in a divorce case. Now *you* want to hire me to watch *Mr.* Naylor. See what I mean? It's unsanitary."

"'Sinless and Sanitary.' You ought to have that tattooed on your dick."

"Now, if *Mrs.* Naylor wanted to hire me, that would be fine."

"It would?" Talk about hair-splitting morality.

"Hell, yes. What else've I got to do? Lie around Shore Haven all day watching you and your boyfriend shake a trailer?"

"Enough with the trailer, Iggy."

"Say, did I tell you? He didn't look any too happy when he got in his car to go home. Anything wrong, Gayle? Anything you want to share? I'm here for you, Gayle—"

I muttered, "Shut up."

Iggy flicked the butt end of his cigarette in a long arc into the cold blue lake.

"Tell you what I'll do," I said. "I'll call Mrs. Naylor and ask her to phone you, so you can get started."

"Sure, that's fine. I have only one question."

"Ye-esss?"

"If the husband's goofing around, why hasn't she put a P.I. on him before?"

"It's a long, boring story, Iggy, and I'm not going to waste your time telling it to you."

"I'll ask her," he said.

"Good luck," I said.

Iggy snickered.

"And remember: not one word to Marty or I'll have to tell 'Stevie-boy' about the RGPS," I said.

Iggy's face puckered as if at a bad smell, though I sincerely doubt that a bad smell would bother him. More like, he's a connoisseur of bad smells. A collector. He mumbled, "Okay."

We walked back to the trailer, shaking hands at the door. "No hard feelings?" he asked.

"No, I guess not. If I had to get those stupid papers, there's no one I'd rather beat up for having given them to me."

"You bet," he said. And off he swaggered to his car.

I watched Iggy until he was out of sight. Bug Leversee, would he? Life was getting complicated. I locked the trailer door, then sat cross-legged on the padded bench next to the phone. I got Therese Naylor's number from information, then dialed. The phone gargled twice before a man picked up. Probably not Alex—he'd moved out of the family home in June. I asked to speak to Mrs. Naylor. The man said she was out but would return in a couple of hours, could he take a message? I replied, "No, thanks. I'll call back."

TEN

As I have said so many times, VanBurgen is a poor county. But not everyone in it or from it is poor. Topping the not-poor list would have to be Therese Naylor and her brother, Bobby Defresnes. Heirs to the Defresnes Winery millions and owners of thousands of acres of prime fruit-growing land, they were the modern-day nobility of VanBurgen County. Bobby oversaw the winery, which produced wine, schnapps, brandy, cordials, and juice. In addition, he owned Pauling Pasta, a far tonier restaurant than one might expect to find in a dot like Pauling, and he had piles of investments. Therese co-owned a flower shop in Collingwood and was married to Alex Naylor, who ran an investment firm. She had belatedly realized not merely that she hated her husband, but that she loved a woman.

When she had asked Alex for a divorce, he hired Marty Klein to sic a P.I. (me) on her, in hopes that she would be found in the arms of another man, thereby gaining Alex an advantage in the split of marital cash, most of which had come from Therese's trust fund. After a grueling investigation that required me to sit for hours watching Therese do little or nothing, I learned the identity of her lover: the charismatic Lynne Jeffers, a recently murdered radio talk-show host. As was my duty, I shared this information with Marty, but I urged him to withhold it from Naylor. And now Marty had had me subpoenaed to blab what I knew in court. My testimony would enrich Alex Naylor, a fortune hunter *par excellence,* as well as sap money from and humiliate Therese, whom I sort of liked.

I re-read the subpoena that Iggy had given me, then reclined on the padded bench, growing drowsier and drowsier. Well, why not? I'd taken two walks that day and engaged in two grappling matches, albeit of very different types. I was exhausted. That comforter would feel so comforting, I thought. Therefore, I wrapped it around me and slept.

TWO HOURS LATER I awoke in accordance with my usual nap timetable. I'm not one of those forty-winkers who bounces up from a brief snooze ready to thrash the world. I require two hours to take the damn nap, then an hour or so to recover from having taken it. Nevertheless, I find it hard to resist a nap: indeed, I am a nap-alcoholic who swills down sleep, then wakes with a horrendous hangover.

I was in no great hurry that day so performed none of the recovery shortcuts, such as shivering under a cold shower or thrusting my head into a bowl full of ice cubes. Instead, I stuck with the slow strategy: I washed my face, flossed and brushed my teeth, scrubbed my tongue for good measure, dropped two ibuprofen, and took a brief stroll around the trailer park. By the time I approached Debby's trailer, I was feeling sharp enough to take on more of her free-flowing data. I rapped on her cheap screen door, but no one answered. In fact, the place looked vacant—windows dark, no voices, no music, no TV. Likewise, no one was home chez Patty. So I went back to the Airstream to call Therese Naylor.

This time no one answered the phone, a message machine kicking in on the seventh ring. I was in a quandary. Should I leave a message or just hang up? After the recorded greeting and the beep, I said, "Therese, this is Gayle Fisher—" whereupon she picked up, saying, "Gayle, this, uh, line may not be secure." Therese was getting wiser. Being trailed and nailed by a P.I. will do that to a person.

I said, "Could we meet?"

"Sure. What about Pauling Pasta—around 8:30?"

I checked my watch. Seven-thirty already. "That'll be fine."

We said our farewells, then I rummaged through my pitiful collection of duds for something decent to wear. I ended up re-ironing my chinos and camp shirt with an itty-bitty travel iron on one of the boards that make up the bed. Actually, my clothes didn't look or smell that bad. Or so I told myself. I combed the snarls out of my hair, then trotted out to the car. I gazed at it speculatively, recalling Iggy's RGPS. Even a little car like mine had so many places to hide a bug, it would take a psychic to find it. It could be attached to the undercarriage, the engine, the trunk, or the underside of the seats, like some hideous metal-sucking alien. Fortunately, no one had reason to put a signal sender on my car. I got in and headed out to the highway, wracking my brain over how to get to Pauling from Shore Haven.

Maybe a GPS would come in handy, making it unnecessary to possess map-reading skills. But I *like* to have skills. For instance, I can do my taxes without a calculator. So I turned on the overhead light and unfolded my ragged map of Michigan as I drove along, planning a route to Pauling. I'd take M-43 to M-40 and turn south.

It was shocking to see the distance I'd have to cover in—I checked my watch again—forty minutes! Turning east on M-43, I put on some speed. As long as I slowed down for the three little burgs I'd pass through on the way to Pauling, I could speed with impunity the rest of the time. In Collingwood County, you'd get busted for that kind of driving, but VanBurgen is—well—poor, so it's short on cops. The State Boys help out as much as possible in counties like VanBurgen, but all in all, you can pretty much pick your own speed between towns. I chose seventy-five, about right for the interstate, but twenty miles over for M-43.

I MADE IT TO Pauling Pasta at 8:35 p.m. By then I was famished and thought that a drink and dinner, perhaps Chicken Alfredo, would make the trip especially worthwhile. When I inquired if

Mrs. Naylor had arrived, the hostess led me to a booth in the bar. Unfortunately, Therese was not alone; she was with her hot-headed brother, Bobby. I had interviewed him when I was investigating Lynne Jeffers' murder, but I doubted that he knew I had interviewed his sister as well. Or that she and Lynne had been lovers.

Bobby and Therese were in their late twenties, Bobby vaguely the younger of the two. Both were French to the core, with heavy black hair, black eyes, proud noses, and subtle chins. Bobby crossed his legs at the knee, then brushed non-existent lint from his navy slacks and v-neck sweater. Therese was elegant in a navy-and-red knit dress, but visibly jittery.

I sat down. Bobby flicked the hostess a "get-lost" look and she withdrew. I surmised that drinks and dinner were not on the agenda. "What do you want with my sister?" he demanded.

"I just want to help—"

"By blackmailing her?" he blurted.

Therese said, "I'm sorry, Gayle. I told him I didn't want him here, but he insisted."

I shot her a tight smile. "Back in May, I was hired to do surveillance on Therese." I paused, then asked, "Is it all right if I tell your brother what I learned?"

She nodded, a look of misery on her face.

"Your sister was having an affair with a person who died shortly after I started surveillance. I never caught them together, but your sister told me that she'd had the affair—"

"Oh Christ, Teri! Never confirm?"

"Bobby, please, be quiet," begged Therese.

"I like your sister," I said, "but the ethics of my profession require that I give my employer any information I've gotten on his behalf."

At the word *ethics*, Bobby had barked a laugh. He sounded like a conceited seal.

"I urged my employer not to tell Therese's husband," I said. "But he did. And now I've been subpoenaed to testify—"

"And you want *money,*" accused Bobby.

At that, I shot him the grim eye. We were all silent a few tense seconds, then I continued. "If I refuse to testify, my employer could still submit my report as evidence. But there *is* something that Therese can do. She can have Alex followed."

Therese whispered, "No."

"What?" demanded Bobby. "You haven't—"

"No, I—"

"You've got to, Teri. What the hell kind of lawyer have you got anyway?"

"Wes is a very capable man," she said. "He thinks he can save my trust."

"He *thinks,*" complained Bobby. "This is incredible."

"You've got eighteen days," I said. "You need to hire someone to watch your husband day and night. If he's been unfaithful, you'll have more bargaining power."

Therese shook her head. "What he's got on me—it's far worse than anything I could get on him."

"Maybe not. Has your husband made investments for you?" I asked.

"Yes."

"Get an independent auditor to review your account," I suggested. "See what he can come up with."

Therese nodded. Her eyes held a glimmer of hope, while Bobby's seemed a little less hostile.

"We'll review the account first thing Monday morning," said Bobby, taking charge once again. "And we'll get someone to watch Alex."

"Would you do it?" asked Therese.

I said, "No. It's unethical for me investigate both spouses. But I do have a colleague, who, provided there's anything to sniff, will sniff it out." I wrote Iggy's name and phone number on a cocktail napkin and passed it to Therese. "Good luck," I told her. "I think you can nail Alex, one way or the other."

As I started to rise, Bobby grabbed my wrist. "What's in this for you?" he asked.

I recalled my surveillance of his sister, all the times I'd seen Alex raging at her. "Your brother-in-law's a bully and a prick," I said. "Think about it." I broke his grip and made for the door, leaving one big question unasked and unanswered: What if, after Iggy's investigation, I still had to testify?

On my way out, I glanced back at the siblings. Therese was crying into a hankie, and Bobby looked as though a seven-point earthquake had just hit. Had she revealed to him the identity of her lover? The beautiful, the vibrant, the promiscuous, the bisexual Lynne Jeffers. She had been Bobby's lover, too.

Yes, a P.I. picks up all kinds of hush-hush tidbits in the course of a snoop job. Not that Lynne's simultaneous affairs with Bobby and Therese had been a complete secret. Therese knew, Lynne's husband knew, her sister knew, and I knew. And now, I surmised, the Count of VanBurgen County knew.

OUT IN THE parking lot, I hesitated. I was starved. I craved the succulent morsels of chicken, the garlic-kissed mushrooms, the sherried sauce, the steaming linguini. But after a stunning exit like that, I could hardly pop back into Pauling Pasta and order dinner. I stared balefully up and down the street at the town's other late-night eateries—fast-food shops that fell oh so short of the mark. I thought, Hell, Iggy's already given me the damn subpoena. Why not go back to Collingwood, eat a good meal, sleep in my own sand-free bed, and drive back to Shore Haven in the morning?

So instead of wending my way back to the lake, I picked up the expressway, shot east to Collingwood, and stopped at

Ipolito's, Collingwood's own overpriced answer to Pauling Pasta.
I guess Ipolito's rational is that if it costs more, it must be better.
Actually it is better, but not in equal measure to the jacked-up
price.

A lone woman, I was seated near the clatter of the kitchen at
a table the size of a middling tree stump. Accepting my fate with
good grace, I ordered Chicken Linguini—Ipolito's version of
Chicken Alfredo—then amused myself with crispy Italian bread
daubed with extra virgin olive oil and freshly grated parmesan.
I was content…until thoughts of Leversee invaded my mind: *If
he hadn't acted like such a jerk, I could be dining with him now
and sleeping with him later.*

In the fullness of time, a salad arrived, then the main course,
which drove away all those plaguey thoughts, as well as satisfied all my gustatory hopes and desires. I'm not one of these
dainty types who becomes full mid-dinner and has to take the
rest of the meal home in some sissy foam box. No, I just keep
chewing and it hasn't hurt me yet. But as they say, prevention is
the best cure, so I decided to stick around Collingwood long
enough Sunday to catch a swim at the Y.

Sated at last, I skipped the spumoni and went home, where I
pried two day's worth of mail from its box and mounted the stairs
to my cozy apartment. Then I took a long soaking bubble bath,
for to tell the truth, I was a little achy—as much from my en-
counter with Leversee as from my wrestle with Iggy. I relaxed,
let my mind float back to Bill Feinstein, dead Eleanor, Sergeant
Swinkey, the Montague clan, Debby the dental assistant,
Leversee, Iggy, Bobby Defresnes, Therese Naylor…

I HAVE A BAD HABIT of falling asleep in the bathtub, then waking
up in the middle of the night, staring at the high ceiling of my
bathroom. In the summer it's okay—I don't have air condition-
ing. But with fall coming on, nights were down in the fifties. By

law, the landlord isn't required to stoke the boiler until October 1, so of course he hadn't. I stepped blue-lipped and shivering from the tub, then toweled off, put on flannel jammies, slid under the covers, and slept.

CONSCIOUSNESS NEXT ARRIVED at nine-fifteen—late-ish for me. I threw on an old muumuu and flipflops, then picked my way down that evil fire escape, hot on the trail of my errant cell phone. A search of the dandelions produced nothing but a pitiful dead mouse, so I got down on hands and knees and scoured the dewy grass, getting my muumuu all soggy.

Then I saw a glint of light—the morning sun reflecting off a cell phone otherwise hidden in a froth of chickweed. As I seized the damp apparatus I recalled the warning of Cordless Cal, the cell-phone sales whiz: "Never get the phone wet." I had the squeemy feeling that I was about to find out why.

Up in my tiny kitchen, I used a clean dish towel to pat the phone dry. It was so cute, hardly bigger than a credit card, shiny blue with chrome trim. But did it still work? I pressed the *on* button and got no response—except a rise in my blood pressure. Maybe all that the device needed was a charge. So I stuck one end of the charger into a wall socket and the other into the phone. There came a horrible *snapping* sound. As I tore the charger from the wall, the phone jerked and hissed, then lay smoking and inert. Good lord! I had electrocuted my own cell phone.

I knew from previous cell-phone disasters that Cordless Cal didn't work on Sundays. Well, I'd been getting along all right without it...

After that inauspicious start to the day, I tidied my apartment, then went through the mail. Nothing important. Literally *nothing*. It all got torn in half and dropped into the trash. I had been thinking about getting a shredder, so no trash-stealing criminal could utilize one of the dozens of offers for credit cards

I receive and discard each year. Think that doesn't happen? I've had three clients—one rich, two on fixed incomes—whose identities have been swiped. After a moment's contemplation, I tore my trash into confetti and mixed the bits with a fly swatter. If an identity thief stalked me, I'd at least make it difficult for him. Or her.

Presently, I checked my answering machine. More nothing, except for a call from my mother, announcing that she and Grandma McKenzie planned to visit my sister in Montrose, and I should drive over to see them if I had "a chance."

"*Fat* chance," I said, erasing the message. It's not that I hate my mother, but she's so exacting. She doesn't mind that I'm a P.I.; she merely minds that I'm a worse P.I. than my father was. Well, maybe I'll be his equal in another twenty years. What's that they say about experience? It's a great teacher? Besides, I don't think I'd be bragging to say that I'm already a pretty good P.I. When an old lady comes to me complaining that her lap dog is missing, I can generally find it.

ELEVEN

Aᴛᴇʀ ᴡᴀsʜɪɴɢ ᴀɴᴅ ᴅʀᴇssɪɴɢ, I hoisted my gym bag and trotted down to the car. The sun beamed down through a blue sky—a perfect September day. I drove to the DeKats Arms and entered the lobby. There were the queasy sea-green walls, the slouching couches, the balding carpet, the butt-filled ashtrays. There was the big sign: *ROOMS FOR RENT, Daily, Weekly, Monthly.* There were the dozing denizens, men of indeterminate age. Home, sweet, home away from home.

I unlocked my office door and scooped up the postman's offering—all junk mail. I tossed it in the trash, then checked my message machine. The little red light was blinking, so I gave the replay button a careless push. Out poured the voice of Marty Klein. He was "concerned" that Iggy had been unable to find me to deliver the subpoena. I guess he hadn't gotten the good news that I'd been nailed. I jabbed the erase button and made a crude remark, then felt guilty, as though I had said, "Fuck off," to my own dead dad.

Marty had been a long-time business associate and pal of my father. He had urged me to get a P.I. license. He had written me a reference so glowing, it was practically radioactive. He threw me snoop jobs whenever he could. He had every right to expect me to play ball.

My father had specialized in taking photos of cheating spouses, so he'd had no qualms about going to court and revealing what he'd seen. If he had learned that Therese Naylor had committed adultery with Lynne Jeffers, he would have mounted the stand and spewed the whole story, no matter how many people got hurt—because it was his job to do so.

I realized, in that moment, that I would never be the investigator my father had been. It mattered little that he had taught me the techniques of surveillance, or how to pick a lock, wield a camera, or shoot a gun. I was a different person; ergo, my results would be different.

Still feeling guilty, I plopped into my father's ancient swivel chair and revved up the venerable Mac, whose hum and percolation lightened my mood. My father had never mastered a word-processing program, while I could use one well enough to turn out razor-sharp reports.

I typed up what I had done for Bill Feinstein in the previous two days, managing to stretch it to a page. Oh, lord. Working on the inside had turned out to be far less productive than I had hoped. I printed the paltry page, stuck it in a manila folder marked *Feinstein, Bill,* and filed it in a cabinet crammed with my father's successfully completed cases. Oh, yes, he and I differed. He had been successful; I was not.

I motored to the Bagel Shop, intending to buy a bottle of orange juice and a pumpernickel bagel, but decided that food I had never consumed before (papaya nectar and a jalapeño-cheddar bialy) might lift my spirits. It didn't. Then I drove to the YMCA to sweat out my negativity. I got in line for the Universal machine—no, I don't use free weights—and for the first time since June, I did a few reps.

Next, I hied off to the locker room, wriggled my sweaty body into a tank suit, took the obligatory shower, padded out to the pool, and slid into the medium lane. Stroke, stroke, breathe. Stroke, stroke, breath. Stroke, stroke, etc. I swam until the black feeling that had gripped me dissolved, and then I pulled myself dripping from the pool, limbs as heavy and slow as a hippo's.

Back at home, I packed a grocery bag with three days worth of clean clothes—just in case. While choosing underwear, I retrieved my gun. It was wrapped in a dishtowel and a plastic bag to keep my panties from picking up the scent of gun oil. I balanced the .22 caliber Beretta on my knee. The previous spring I had resolved to carry it at all times, which had made sense since I was tracking a killer. But once I had returned to the world of background checks and surveillance, the gun seemed an unnecessary weight that dragged at my jacket pocket, making it look bad for no good reason. I mean, the most I've ever pulled a firearm on a background check is never. But now? If, indeed, Eleanor Montague had been murdered, the perp might get wind of my sleuthing and try to kill me. So I tucked the gun in my bag.

If I hadn't been furious with Leversee, I would have given him a jingle. But what did I have to share? That Iggy had stuck a bug on his car, delivered the dreaded subpoena, and accidentally stripped me bare? Or that I'd held Iggy in headlock on the same padded bench where Leversee and I had enjoyed the most recent version of the time of our lives?

Screw it.

I marched my bag out to the car and made for Shore Haven. At the Blue Star Highway, traffic slowed to a crawl, the unmistakable sign of a "festival" in progress. Just what was being celebrated I hadn't the faintest idea. Shore Haven lauded everything from porcupines to pineapples, all to attract those breathlessly desired yet barely tolerated tourists. If only they'd mail in their money and stay home.

I followed the crowd to the little town's heart, a three-dollar-a-day parking lot for sightseers. Still feeling a languor in my limbs, I strolled down to the public beach, which was wide and deep, its sand soft, clean, and nearly white. Due to the festival, the beach was packed. There were Frisbee-playing boys in knee-length shorts, plump mothers, tots who squatted by the shore throwing gobs of damp sand, and young lovers sunning themselves in Speedos and bikinis. It must have been eighty degrees, but hardly a soul had the courage to enter the bracing lake. Those who did advanced slowly through icy water, bodies rigid, arms poised in the manner of Frankenstein's monster. Or else they ran, hectic and screaming, into the blue. Whether walkers or runners, all bathers scurried back to the hot beach soon after having penetrated the frigid lake.

For a few days each year, after a week of ninety-degree weather, Lake Michigan is the best place in the world to swim. The water warms to seventy degrees, at least near the shore, and bathers frolic in fresh water. It rolls in like blue gelatin, with neither chlorine nor salt to offend hair, skin, eyes, or nose.

A policeman was patrolling the beach, swinging his baton with the air of a man who wanted to do something else with his hands. I deduced that he yearned to hold a cigarette. Actually, he was too far away for me to detect the nicotine hunger in his eyes, but close enough for me to identify him as the ubiquitous Sergeant Swinkey. And he would want a smoke.

The observant Swinkey saw me just then, waved and sauntered over to chat. He took off his cap and wiped his sweaty forehead on a darkly tanned wrist.

"Looks like you do everything around here," I said.

"Oh, a little this, a little that," he modestly replied. "We've only got fifteen cops on the force, including Chief Glenn, and he sure as hell isn't gonna haul ass out to patrol the beach on a Sunday."

We nattered awhile about the purpose of this gathering. The Pear Festival. The day's events would include the picking of pears in local orchards, competitions between bakers of pear pies and pressers of pear wine, displays of dried pear art—whatever the Shore Haven Chamber of Commerce could dream up for the big-hipped fruit.

This topic at last wrung dry, Swinkey inquired why I hadn't called back.

"Oh, gosh, I've been so busy, I forgot."

"Busy? You mean you got something?"

"Not exactly. I met a girl who told me about a robbery, a whole lot of Seconal stolen from a dentist named Coulter?"

"Yeah. That happened, oh, let's see here—"

"Back in August," I prompted.

"Right, it was four, five weeks ago."

"*Seconal*, Swinkey."

"Oh, I get it. Eleanor Montague."

"Right."

"God dammit, I sure would like a smoke."

"Don't let me stop you," I said.

"Chief Glenn doesn't like us to use tobacco on foot patrol. No smoking, no chewing, no spitting."

"Thank god about the spitting," I declared. "It breeds rats."

Swinkey chuckled. "Rats breed the same way as humans. Spit's got nothing to do with it."

I was about to say it could, then decided against swapping ideas on sexual practice. "So, what d'you make of the Seconal robbery?"

"Voight and I took the call. Four kinds of drugs were stolen, mostly Seconal. Most likely, some kid did it, a patient of Coulter. Saw those drugs, decided to score some for personal use."

"Or to sell?"

"Maybe to friends. But to a person like Eleanor Montague? I doubt it."

"What about Sean or Fiona?" Fiona had got hold of those pills somehow—either stole them or bought them.

"I double doubt it. They're different, the Montagues?"

"A cut above?"

He snorted. "That's a matter of opinion. What I mean is, they keep to themselves. They're not the type to hang out with the local drug crowd."

"Well, thanks for the info," I said, hoping to conclude our talk.

He stepped a little closer. "You still hooked up with that Collingwood cop?"

"Swinkey," I cooed, pointing at his ring finger.

The big cop patted his mustache, then headed back out to the beach.

After five minutes in the sun, I felt sweaty and parched, so I walked two blocks to *I Know Your Vice,* Shore Haven's very own sorbet/coffee-bean shop. Much to my pleasure, Keith Laughton was handling the scoop. I had met the teen back in May, when he had helped me nab Jeffrey Richard Mason, the scammer who had stolen those eighty-four thousand dollars from my sister, Amanda. For capturing the criminal, I had received a one-hundred-thousand-dollar reward. Originally, I had hoped to give Amanda eighty-four grand and Keith five grand (for school at Grand Valley State U.), but when I learned I'd be taxed on the windfall, I trimmed the gifts to sixty for Amanda and five for Keith, leaving five for me, half of which I spent on the LeMans. Once Mason has been tried and convicted, Amanda has a chance of recouping part of her cash, and I sincerely hope that it's more than twenty-four thousand—so I get some too.

I glanced through bags of fancy coffee beans until the busy store had cleared out, then I headed to the counter and greeted Keith. He was smallish and skinny, with sharp features, intelligent black eyes, and definite black brows. His frizzy black hair was pulled back into a knot, and he was dressed all in white, including a long white apron.

He smiled broadly. "Hey, man, whatcha doing in Shore Haven? Chasing another crook?"

"I suppose. How's school?" I asked.

"Great. Started last week of August."

"So why aren't you *at* school?"

He shrugged. "I come home to work weekends, see my folks and some friends. I study all day Mondays and Wednesdays. My classes are Tuesday-Thursday."

"And Friday, you goof off?"

"Yeah. But don't worry, you'll get your money's worth."

I laughed. "That's good to know. Say, I bet your folks are glad to see you weekends."

"They were last week. This week they're gone, took the RV out to California to visit my sister Sally."

I asked for some black-raspberry sorbet in a waffle cone.

"Sorry, black raspberry's long gone. Try pear—it's special for the festival."

I agreed to this and he scooped me a hefty cone full. I paid with a ten and told him to keep the change. He grinned, said, "Need any help with what you're working on now?"

I thought a moment. "Know anything about that dentist getting ripped off last month?"

"Dr. Coulter?"

"Yeah. Someone broke in, stole Seconal, Nembutal, Percodan, and Tylenol 4's."

"I can ask around," he said, "maybe have the scoop by tonight."

"Really?" I said with enthusiasm.

"Sure."

"Why, you little dickens." I gave him my phone number at the trailer, then said not to leave a message if I was out. "By the way," I added, lowering my voice, "I'm going by the name of Betty Jo Bialosky this week."

"Yeah?"

"So don't call me Gayle. Call me Betty Jo."

He squinted. "Okay."

I thanked him and stepped back out into the sunny street. I nibbled the pear sorbet…. Black raspberry is better.

On the way back to Sunnyside I stopped at Billy's Shop-Rite for groceries. I was meandering along the dairy aisle when who should round the corner but Mrs. Hogoboom. I said, "Hi," but she pushed past, a nasty look on her face. Maybe she still held a grudge about my having failed to lock her door. Or perhaps she had resented my having called her establishment a brothel. Oh, well.

Back at the trailer I loaded food into the fridge, then sauntered over to Debby's trailer in hopes of picking up some more gossip about the Montagues. Sure enough, the dental assistant was out on the steps, putzing around with her tooth floss. She wore turquoise short-shorts, a turquoise-and-white checked halter, and four silver ear cuffs on her left ear. I hailed her and she waved me over for a chat.

When I inquired how her date had gone, she said, "It was okay. We went to this kegger way down the beach, then he wanted to go to his apartment. Well, it turns out he lives in a B & B—that's bed and breakfast—with his aunt, Miss Hogoboom. So I say, 'No, thanks, I had her for study hall and she's kind of a'—and I started to say bitch, but since she's his aunt and all, I said, 'battle ax.' That's what my dad calls my great-aunt Dawn. It's kinda mean, but it's nicer than bitch."

"So you made an early night of it?"

"Ummm, not exactly. He came over here." She giggled.

"And you say he's a cop?"

"Yeah. Officer Mark VanDee."

I filed that wet bit of gossip under "Oh, baby, oh baby, oh baby," and cross referenced it with "Trish." It never hurts to have some dirt on the local constabulary.

"How's your weekend going?" she asked.

"Oh, I washed my uniform and walked the beach a couple times. Nothing hectic. I've been thinking a lot about the Montagues, of course. Sean and Fiona." With Debby it wasn't so much a matter of priming the pump as directing the spray.

"Oh, jeeze," she said. "Those two."

"I was just wondering, well, how you learned about their, uh, relationship."

"Someone told me in strictest confidence."

"Eleanor?"

"No, someone else."

"And what did this person—"

"She told me she'd known Sean and Fiona since they were little kids. They all used to play together. But Sean and Fiona had always been way too close. Closer than a brother and sister should be. Know what I mean?"

I played dumb. "No. What *do* you mean?"

"I mean sex, Betty Jo."

"Oh, god."

"Yeah. Eleanor got wind of it, you know?"

"You mean, they—"

"That's exactly what I mean. Eleanor walked in on 'em. Caught 'em right in her and Sean's bed." She ran the floss around a bicuspid, then flicked away a tiny morsel of food. "After that, she stayed down at the trailer most nights. That's how I met her."

"And she said nothing about it?"

"Nuh-uh. She was the shy type."

"I wonder why she didn't just leave."

"No money."

"Didn't she have family?"

"A brother in Detroit. He said, 'You made your own bed, now lie in it.' Then he kicked up a hullabaloo at the funeral."

I thought of Bill's agony, his passion to spend every cent to find a killer. Bill had to feel like a monster for having turned his sister away when she needed him. And truly, if he had helped her, she might still be alive.

"How terrible," I mused, "her walking in on Sean and Fiona that way."

"I'll say. But, see, this friend of mine had the same experience? oh, gosh—years ago."

"The same friend who told you about Eleanor?"

"Yeah. She was having a sleep over with Fiona, and they stayed up kinda late, till Mrs. Montague said quiet down and go to sleep. So they did. At least, my friend did. Then there was a noise. She woke up. The wardrobe was open, and my friend thought Fiona was in there playing. So she crept out of bed and peeked inside. Well, back behind the clothes was a secret passage into Sean's wardrobe next door. They were both in his bed, bare naked, doing what my friend knew was wrong wrong wrong for children, not to mention brother and sister, to do."

"Did they see her?"

"No. She backed right out of there, got into bed, and pretended to sleep. Along toward sunrise, there was a rustling in the wardrobe, and out came Fiona. She closed the door, dropped her nighty over her head, and climbed into bed. When Mrs. Montague came in to wake 'em, my friend said she felt sick and had to go home."

"That's some story," I said. "So you think Eleanor killed herself because she saw Sean and Fiona—"

"—doing it. Yes. That's what I think. Look, she was cheesed out. Who wouldn't—"

Debby's phone chose that moment to ring. She said, "Be right back," and went to answer it. Five minutes later, I guessed she wasn't returning. I wandered down to the beach, wondering if Sean and Fiona actually had an incestuous relationship. I hadn't picked up any sex-vibes between them, and I'm pretty good at spotting that sort of thing. Even on opposite sides of a room, lovers exert a pull on one another, like magnets. On the other hand, lovers breaking the incest taboo might have developed a strong shield against detection. If the incest story were true, Sean and Fiona might each have a reason to get rid of

Eleanor. The idea of the secret passage appealed to me in a big way. It would explain not merely how a murderer could create the impression of a locked-room suicide, but also how the door to the death room remained bolted from the inside. I'd look for that passage next chance I got.

I returned to my trailer, antsy with anticipation. Casting about for a distraction, I ended up rereading the Alzheimer's materials from the library. Then, like the addict I am, I took a nap.

WHEN THE PHONE RANG I was dreaming of blue gelatin. I reached out, knocked the phone to the floor, picked it up, and mumbled, "Hello."

"Betty?" The voice was so far away, a tinny little whisper.

"Yeah?"

"I can hardly hear you," said the distant voice.

"I can hardly hear you," I replied. I peered at the phone, thinking I'd broken it, then realized I'd been speaking into the earpiece. I rotated the receiver 180 degrees and tried again. "Hello?"

"That's better." It was Keith.

"Have any luck?"

"I think so. There's a guy says he's got information. Can you pick me up at work—around nine?"

I stared at my watch. The little hand was already on the eight, leaving me an hour to pull myself together and drive to town. I said, "See ya," and hung up. One hour. Oh, god. I stumbled to the fridge and pulled out the ice trays.

AT NINE SHARP I parked in front of *I Know Your Vice* and waited for Keith to emerge. I could see him within, carefully wiping the counter. When he saw me he grinned, then ditched his cleaning rag. He bopped out the door, locked up, and hopped into my car.

"What's the word?" I inquired.

"Guy's s'posed to meet us on Hill Street, nine-fifteen. He's the one s'posed to know who robbed the dentist."

"Okay. How do we get there?" Now, Shore Haven is a tiny town, small as a wallet, and Hill Street had to be just around the corner; I'd probably driven on it many times, but I tend to ignore names of streets unless I'm tailing someone. Keith told me to turn left at the end of the block, then we climbed a surprisingly steep hill. I say surprisingly because ninety-five percent of Michigan is dead flat.

"Turn right," he said. "Pull over to the curb and wait."

I complied. "So this is Hill Street?"

"Yeah. Actually, it's not a hill. It's a glacial moraine."

"You into geology?"

He gave a shy smile. "Some."

I recognized where we were: on that houseless street that rushes down a short block toward a wooden barrier and the Black River channel, then at the last minute swoops to the right past a brick office building, the Black River Inn, and the Black River B & B. That street.

While we waited, engine idling, Keith pulled the rubber band off his short knot of hair and ran a hand through the dark frizz. "I hope he's on time."

"Me, too," I said. "This place gives me the creeps."

Keith laughed. "There's nothing creepy about Shore Haven. I lived here all my life, and it's about as scary as Mr. Magoo."

Nevertheless, I was glad I'd brought along Ms. Beretta, who was still swathed in her towel and plastic bag. As I opened my purse to take her out, I heard a car approaching from behind. It was driving without lights.

"That's our boy," I said, as the car pulled toward the curb. It was going a little too fast, then suddenly, it sped up and rammed us from behind. Glass tinkled and Keith and I were jolted within our seat belts. My heart squeezed into a fist and began to batter my ribs.

What I saw in the rearview mirror seemed to be a big old beater, but the street was so dark, I couldn't make out the color, model, or driver's face. I pulled away from the curb, whereupon the beater rammed us again. Once more came a jingle of fractured glass, and Keith and I were whiplashed in our seats. On our left a chain-link fence ran all the way down to the Hill Street curve. On our right rose a stone retaining wall. In essence, we were trapped, skidding down a short chute to the channel. Our only chance to avoid the cold black water was a sharp curve to the right. But the heavy old beater had slammed us with ample force, and my car was running, in gear, and pointed down a steep incline, so it offered no resistance. We were halfway to the channel, flying so fast, that if we tried to turn right, we'd run smack into the brick building.

Keith jammed his hands against the dashboard and his feet against the floor, terror freezing his face. I jerked the steering wheel to the right, hoping the retaining wall would slow us, and as we flew downhill, Keith's side of the car scraped against the wall, giving rise to a comet's tail of sparks. Unfortunately, the red needle on the speedometer hadn't declined; no, it had jumped from fifty to sixty to seventy miles an hour. In a split second, I weighed my choices: channel or brick building?

"Don't turn!" shouted Keith.

In the end, the beater chose for us: it rammed us one last time. With a deafening *craaaakkkk,* we smashed through the barrier, which was huge and white with three enormous black arrows pointing right. Keith covered his head with his hands, moaning, "Oh, shit, oh, shit, oh, shit—"

I stomped the brakes, no avail. We skidded across the damp lawn and took flight over black water—

TWELVE

TIME SLOWED. I thought of last spring when three shotgun-toting goons in a truck had tried to run my car into a lake. On that occasion I had lucked out. I'd veered right and they'd landed in the soup. But now my luck was all used up: this time I'd be making the grand splash. I mean we. Keith and I. Delighted for once that my car lacked power accessories, I cried, "Roll down your window!"

And we hit.

The impact of car against river was brutal, but far less so than had we crashed into the brick building. Though restrained by a seat belt, I bounced upward and smacked my head on the roof of the car. Simultaneously, a vast splash came up around us, as from a boulder tossed into a sea. Adrenaline raced through my veins.

We were floating.

I yelled, "Keith—your window!" then I cranked down my own. When I turned to undo my seat belt, Keith was lolling on his door, unconscious. I shook him and his head dropped toward me. Along the right side of his face spread a dark streak, which, if night vision came in color, would have shown red. His window was cracked, most likely by his head when we landed. I fumbled my own seat belt loose, then pressed the release on his, but it stuck. I pushed and tugged as water flowed in around our feet. Leversee had given me a Swiss Army knife for my birthday the month before. I tore it from my purse, jabbed a thumbnail into the biggest notch, pulled out a sharp blade, and began to saw at the strap. By this time, the frigid water was lapping our knees, which I guess was better than kneeing our—oh, hell. Sawing the seat belt seemed to take hours as the water played around our hips, then our ribs. I was three-quarters of the way through when black water drowned my chin. I gave five fierce underwater thrusts of the blade and at last the belt gave way. With my purse strap looped around my neck, I pulled the latch on my door and shoved.

It wouldn't budge.

A pocket of air remained in the car, up by the roof. I raised my face to suck a deep breath, then struggled through the window into the opaque river where it was impossible to tell which way was up, down, or sideways. But thanks to my recent lungful, I rose through the water, popping corkwise into the cool evening air. I gasped and sputtered, spat water that tasted of iron, and tried to orient myself. The current had drawn the foundering car to the middle of the channel and was bearing it west toward the lake.

I dolphined over the roof to the passenger side, breathed deeply, and resubmerged. I yanked and yanked at Keith's door. Finally, it pulled open, slowly, maddeningly so, and Keith floated toward me. Lungs burning, I grabbed him under an armpit and swam him to the surface, where I drank in the cool air and began towing him north—away from Hill Street and our attacker.

Three people had gathered on the north bank. The thin voices of elderly women floated above the channel, beckoning: "Come on, honey! You can make it!"

I can make it!? Right, I'm a great swimmer.

But the current was dragging at my feet, and I was towing an unconscious, possibly dead young man behind me, and my arm felt ready to break off at the biceps. The weight lifting and swimming I'd done that morning had burnt me out and all that remained was persistence.

Behind us the LeMans sank with a lurid slurp.

The current kept pulling us downstream, even as I tried to swim directly across the channel. But at length, we made it to the corrugated iron wall. One of the ladies yelled to me, "A little further downstream—there's a ladder!"

Yes, of course! Iron ladders had been welded to the channel walls, every twenty feet or so, for emergencies just like this. I let the current carry Keith and me to the nearest ladder, then I seized hold of a rung with my free arm. The sudden stop wrenched me, ripped at my shoulder, but I refused to let go. One of the three old women was on her hands and knees, her pale face peering down at me, like the moon. "We've called 911!" she puffed. "Hang on! They're on their way!"

I did hang, trembling with cold. But really, I preferred hanging in frigid water to swimming in it. If only I could tell if Keith were breathing. "We need to get my friend out of this water—*now*," I called. "It's too cold and he's knocked out. Can you get a rope? I could loop it around him—you could pull him up."

The three ladies fussed a bit. "Rope? Who's got a rope?" twittered the one on her knees.

Another knelt next to her. "I'm wearing pantyhose!" she called. "Will they do?"

I said, "Sure, why not? Please, hurry."

The woman shucked her shoes and tugged at her hose.

"Pixie, speed it up!" cried the third lady, and she yanked at the pantyhose, ripping them off. She tossed them down to me.

I caught them with my teeth. Drawing Keith close, I was able to wrap and knot the pantyhose around his pitifully thin chest. I hoped he was skinny enough for these old gals to hoist. "Now, reach down and grab these ends," I gasped, passing the feet of the pantyhose up to Pixie. I told her to wrap the ends around her hands; when she had, I called, "The three of you—pull!"

The two other ladies lined up behind Pixie and pulled while I shoved from below with my aching right arm. Inch by inch, the women backed away from the channel, like a brave little team of burros with a backbreaking load. A siren howled in the distance. My heart leapt.

Pixie shouted, "Heave ho!" and at last the women had pulled Keith up onto the cement walkway. "He's just a boy!" cried one.

"Look!" wailed another. "His face—it's bleeding!"

Though weak, shivering, and sore, I managed to climb the ladder. "Oh, god…." I fell to my knees next to Keith, held my fingers to his neck, felt a weak pulse. But he wasn't breathing. I screamed his name and shook him.

No response.

Though I'd taken a life-saving course at the Y ten years before, I had never used what I'd learned on an injured person. I paused a moment to review the steps. Then I wiped two fingers through his mouth to clear it, tilted his head back, pinched his nostrils and blew into his cold mouth. I pulled away to see if his chest rose.

"My lord, he's dead!" sobbed one of the ladies. She reminded me of a stork, she was so tall and narrow.

"Ruby, shut up!" This remark had come from Pixie, who was white haired and horsy. The third woman fluttered behind her, a moth flirting with fire.

I pinched Keith's nose again, blowing and pausing until his stomach contracted with such violence that sour water and half-digested food gushed from his mouth. His chest rose, taking in precious air, and he coughed several times yet remained unconscious. Quickly I turned his head and recleared his mouth so he wouldn't choke on the vomit. The siren, meanwhile, had grown loud enough to rupture an eardrum, then stopped, and two men in green jumpsuits loped towards us. An EMT pushed me away and attached an oxygen mask to Keith's face.

The other EMT asked if I were injured. "I'm f-fine," I said, between chattering teeth. "J-j-just c-cold."

He draped me with a flannel sheet, then asked about Keith. I told what I knew—damned little. He was a freshman at Grand Valley and worked weekends at the sorbet shop. "Try his wallet," I tactfully suggested. "Maybe there's an address." A moment later, the EMT's loaded Keith onto a stretcher and carried him away.

Two uniformed cops arrived, introducing themselves as Bigalow and VanDee. Before me stood Mark VanDee, nephew of Mrs. Hogoboom, and sex machine to "Oh-baby" Trish and Debby the dental assistant. VanDee was about thirty, tall and muscular, with dark blond hair, blue eyes, broad nose, and full lips. Compared to Leversee, another tall blond man, VanDee seemed heavy, crude, and slow. Bigalow was Mr. Medium— medium age, medium height, medium weight, medium face— the kind of guy who could get away with murder.

VanDee interviewed the old ladies while Bigalow spoke with me. When he learned I had been driving he asked for my driver's license, registration, and proof of insurance. I unlooped the sopping purse from my neck, dug out my sodden wallet, and began picking through it. I started to pull out the ersatz I.D. for Betty Jo Bialosky, then quickly shoved it back in. To give the police false identification would be the epitome of idiocy. A quick check with the DMV in Lansing would reveal that the license was counterfeit, landing me in an even sloppier mess. So I kept looking until I found a license for Gayle Marie Fisher. I offered it to Bigalow. "Registration and proof of insurance are in my glove box—at the bottom of the channel."

He gave a stiff nod. "So what happened?"

I said I was a private detective from Collingwood, that Keith and I had been parked on Hill Street waiting to meet a snitch who claimed to know details of the robbery at Dr. Coulter's office, when out of the blue, a large unlit car rammed us from behind, forcing us into the channel. The truth.

"P.I.," said Bigalow. He might have been saying, "P.U." Naturally, he requested my investigator's license. I fished it out and displayed it. He stared at it, then handed it back. "Who's your employer? The dentist?"

"I'm not at liberty to say."

He snorted. "You know who was driving the other car?"

"No. Keith might—"

"He's unconscious." Bigalow sighed. "Look, miss, we're gonna have to take you to the station and get this cleared up."

I groaned.

Bigalow led me to the police car. Though he didn't cuff me, he made me sit in back behind a steel-mesh partition (where the doors lack releases and the windows lack cranks), while he and VanDee rode up front in style. I was feeling a couple of degrees warmer under the flannel sheet, but would have kissed a lizard for a hot shower and dry clothes.

I ventured to say, "I know Sergeant Swinkey. Maybe he could help."

"He's off duty," said VanDee.

"We could call him at home," I suggested.

This raised no response. We drove to the little police station, which was so close by, we could have walked there nearly as fast. Bigalow told me to sit in the reception area. Shaking and woozy, I swept the sheet around me, knocking over a chair. I wobbled it back into place and finally got seated, Bigalow eyeing me all the while. He traded whispers with VanDee, then asked if I'd be willing to take a blood-alcohol test.

"I'm not drunk," I declared.

"Then you have no objection."

"Christ—listen to me. Someone just rammed my car into the river—nearly killed my friend!"

"You sure about that?" VanDee's lips curled with contempt. "Weren't you under the influence, joyriding down Hill Street, and you couldn't make the turn?"

"But the women on the walkway—they saw the whole thing," I said.

Bigalow shrugged. "They saw a car in the river. That's all."

"Oh."

"If some vehicle rammed you, how come no one saw it?" asked VanDee.

Anger stiffened my body. "I guess there were no witnesses. If I were you, I'd check for skidmarks. There ought to be two sets," and I silently added *you moron*. VanDee and Bigalow crossed the room to gab some more. At length they returned. "We'd still like you to take a blood-alcohol test," said VanDee.

"Why? Do you smell something suspicious on my breath?"

"Could be vodka," VanDee conjectured. "You know what they say—kisses but doesn't tell?"

"If you refuse," added Bigalow, "we can suspend your license right now. It's up to you."

"What is this?" I demanded. "A police state?"

"Nah, a police station." VanDee snickered at his own lame joke.

Jeckle and Heckle had put me in a such a lousy mood, I could have chewed their guns to pulp and spit bullets through the wall. "Okay," I said, with exaggerated patience. "Give me the goddamn test."

I was led to the mechanical soul of the Shore Haven Police Department, a BAC Datameter—better known as a breathalyzer. This instrument was equipped with a twenty-inch long rubber tube leading to a large word processor, complete with keyboard and LED display. VanDee took what I hoped was a clean mouthpiece from a drawer and attached it to the plastic tube. "Take a deep breath and blow. Keep blowing till I tell you to quit."

Blow? As my tired brain labored at an obscene reply that, even if I could have formulated it, I knew better than to utter, I took a deep breath and blew into the mouthpiece.

"Keep blowing, keep blowing, keep blowing"—VanDee repeated this as if it were his personal mantra—"keep blowing, keep blowing…."

I ran out of air.

VanDee reviewed the LED display, mumbled, "Blood alcohol content, zero-point-zero."

I could have told them that. I'd had one drink that year—in May. You know, drunk drivers are the most dangerous people around, and I would never dream of being one. "May I go now?" I asked. I wanted to find Keith.

"I'm afraid not, ma'am," said Bigalow. "We're going to have to cite you for reckless driving."

"I wasn't driving recklessly."

Nevertheless, VanDee wrote the ticket. I turned over my copy, checked the box that indicated I wanted to contest the citation in court, then handed it back to him.

"I don't want this," he said, thrusting it at me. "Send it to the address on the back. You've got five business days to reply."

Bigalow added, "We'll also have to keep you in a holding cell, unless you can post a one-hundred-dollar bond."

"What!?"

"And we'll have to keep your driver's license. But we'll issue you a temporary permit," Bigalow said.

"Will you take a check?" I asked.

"No," Bigalow said.

"Visa?"

"Cash," said VanDee.

All I had was seventy bucks and some change, but the idea of being locked up in that gerbil cage struck me as completely unacceptable. "Do I get a phone call?"

"Yes."

"What's Swinkey's home number?"

VanDee threw me a tiny Shore-Haven phone book, pointed at a pay phone in the reception area and went to stand by the exit, in case I tried to bolt, I suppose. I found the number, deposited wet coins, dialed, and a few rings later, he answered.

"Swinkey, this is Gayle Fisher. A couple of your buddies are about to jail me for reckless driving—"

"Huh?"

I told him the whole story.

"I know Keith," said Swinkey. "He's a nice kid."

"So your pals here have given me a blood-alcohol test with zero-point-zero results, charged me with reckless driving, and now they want to lock me up 'cause I don't have a hundred bucks bond."

"Hm."

"I suggested they check for skidmarks over on Hill Street. There should be two sets, mine and the other car's. Whoever was driving must have been damn skillful not to plunge into the river behind us."

"What those two know about forensics would just about fill an empty shell casing. Lemme talk to V.D."

I called VanDee to the phone. He listened awhile, said, "Look, the town council's tired of this shit. You know what a pain in the butt it is, not to mention how costly, to haul a car up outta the channel?" After listening again he said, "Yes, sir," then slammed the receiver into the cradle. "He'll be here in five minutes."

Bigalow trusted me to go to the lavatory alone.

I stood at the sink, aghast at my image in the mirror. Medusa—wet hair hanging in tangled snakes, face filthy from black water. The sink had no hot-water tap, an economy measure forced, no doubt, by the town having to fish so many cars out of the channel. Undaunted, I washed my face with cold water and a cracked bar of Lava, then I patted dry with a brown paper towel.

Next, I dumped the sopping contents of my purse onto the counter, my bagged gun landing with a *thunk*. I shook off the water and peeked inside. Amazingly, the plastic bag had kept the towel and gun dry. I rewrapped the Beretta—along with the traffic citation—and tucked them in the bottom of my purse.

I poked a finger through the rest of the flotsam. A recipe for pear pie had turned into sodden gop. I gingerly dropped it in the trash. My wallet and notepad were dripping, so I squeezed them between paper towels and tucked them back in the purse. Barely used powder, lipstick, and mascara were ruined, so I tossed them in the trash. My watch? Dripping. I peered at the tiny writing on its face: *Water Resistant*. It had resisted none too zealously as far as I could tell. Into the trash it went.

I located my comb and began to tug at my hair. I was still unknotting snarls when the door opened a crack and someone called, "Yoo hoo?"

Swinkey.

"Just a minute," I said, giving my hair one last desperate tug. I stuffed my damp comb into my purse and stepped out the lavatory door.

One look at Swinkey's face told me that I had made little improvement in my appearance. I don't know—maybe I should have shed the damp and dirty flannel sheet. Swinkey, on the other hand, looked spiffy. He wore jeans, a plaid sports shirt, and a lightweight tan jacket. "Let's get out of here," he said, petting his mustache.

"Is this a jail break?"

"Very funny." He seized my elbow and steered me out to the street. "You can give me a check for a hundred and we'll call it even."

I wrote him one right away—on a wet check with a damp ballpoint pen. He folded the clammy paper and stuck it in his jacket pocket.

"This is for you." He held out a temporary driver's permit.

"Swinkey, I have no place not wet to put it."

He frowned, and when I didn't take it, he tucked it in his pocket.

"You know," I said, "ever since my car plunged into the Black River, life's been extra complex. Are there any rental cars in this tourist trap?"

Swinkey said, "Ha."

"Cabs?"

"One, but it's off duty."

I moaned. "Swinkey, would you take me over to the hospital so I can check on Keith? Then drive me out to Sunnyside?"

The big cop lit a cigarette, took a drag. "Yeah, okay. But don't screw up."

"What do you mean? Don't make a scene in the hospital? Don't throw a wild party at the trailer? What?"

"Whatever."

THIRTEEN

WE GOT INTO SWINKEY'S Chevy—it was red—and drove over to the Shore Haven Community Hospital, an old brick building, two stories tall and sprawling. At Emergency, the intake desk was overseen by a pert young brunette with a turned-up nose, her nametag identifying her as Ryanne Dailey. She greeted Swinkey with such warmth, I wondered if she was one of his extramarital play pals.

Ryanne told us that Keith had been moved upstairs to ICU. He was breathing on his own but remained unconscious. She had tried without success to notify his parents.

"They're on vacation," I explained. "Driving an RV to California."

"That complicates things," mused the nurse.

"May I see him?" I asked.

Nurse Ryanne eyed me dubiously. I stood up straight, tried to look respectable, trustworthy, yes, even professional beneath my wet hair and soggy shawl. "Are you a relative?" she inquired.

"Sort of."

"Come on, Ryanne." Swinkey's lips spread into a persuasive smile.

Ryanne tipped her head to one side. "All right, John, seeing it's you. But just for a minute."

In the elevator Swinkey said, "Let me do all the talking," to which I could not help snidely replying, "All right, John, seeing it's you."

We met a Dr. Rama in intensive care. She was a petite woman with a vaguely British accent and a silver braid hanging down her back. Beneath a white smock, she wore a turquoise and silver sari, the fabric's pattern intricately beautiful. According to Dr. Rama, Keith had sustained a concussion and was still unconscious. Although his lungs were fairly clear, he had received a large dose of antibiotic to counteract the effects of inhaling even a small amount of rusty, e-coli-ridden channel water.

"Will he be all right?" I asked.

"I certainly hope so," responded the doctor.

When we asked if we could look in on him, she said just for a minute. By that time, we had exceeded Ryanne's minute by five. Keith lay in a semi-private room, wired to an alarming number of blipping machines. He looked young and fragile, eyes closed, skin blanched, damp hair spread like a frizzy halo on the clean white pillow. He had a bandage taped to the right side of his face and an I.V. needle attached to his left hand. I felt like an A-#1 parasite for having dragged the poor kid into such a mess.

I gave his right hand a squeeze, then bent down and murmured in his ear: "Hey, Keith. Please, come back."

Doctor Rama motioned us out of the room, and Swinkey and I returned to the elevator. He punched the button for Floor 1.

"What do you make of that car running Keith and me into the channel?" I asked.

"Could be someone doesn't want the Coulter job looked in to. Or maybe the attack was random."

"You have a lot of that in Shore Haven? Random attacks?"

"No. What we have a lot of is drunks driving too fast down Hill Street, missing the turn, and flying into the channel. Takes a tugboat, barge, and crane to dredge up a car. Got any idea how much that costs?"

"A bunch?"

"A *whole* bunch. The magistrate finds you at fault, *you* pay the bill."

"Well, Swinkey, maybe you'll do me a big favor and examine Hill Street for skid marks."

"I'd be glad to. But what you really need is the accident reconstructionist from the Sheriff's Department. I'll see if we can get him."

"Thanks."

"And a witness would be great."

"What about Keith?"

Swinkey raised an eyebrow. "Someone conscious."

"He's going to be conscious!" I more or less shouted—trying to convince myself, I suppose. The elevator slowed and my stomach gave a weird flop that felt like pure anxiety.

SHORTLY THEREAFTER, my hero delivered me to Sunnyside where I offered a profusion of thanks. He passed me my temporary license and sped off, plainly relieved to be rid of me. And truth be told, I was equally relieved to be alone. My first stop was the shower, where I squandered every drop of hot water available: five minutes under light spray. Clean and warm at last, I toweled dry and put on my sleeping gear. Then I made dinner, mushroom soup and a ham and Swiss on rye. After eating I felt at least 489 percent better.

I lay on my favorite padded bench thinking of Keith in the hospital; the narrow escape I'd had; my car sunk in the channel; the expense to someone, maybe me, of having it hauled out; my having to go before the magistrate; my possibly being convicted of reckless driving; and my current lack of wheels.

Yes, I had had car trouble before, notably when some guy blasted my Pontiac 6000 with a shotgun while I was driving it. Luckily, none of the buckshot had hit me, and the damage had been easy to fix; all I'd had to do was shake the glass out of my hair and get the windows replaced. But my current situation was far worse. I mean, would a drowned car ever run again? And if it did, would it stink of mildew? I hate mildew.

I needed a car, but how could I get one? I reviewed the options. Leversee? He'd probably bawl me out for getting suckered into a trap. Iggy? He was trailing Alex Naylor night and day. That left only one choice: Mom and Amanda.

Mom had lived in Collingwood all her married life, but after Dad died, she sold the family split-level and moved back to Swago Ridge in Southern Ohio. It's either within spitting distance of Raccoon Creek or hawking distance of Hocking Hills—I can never remember which. Anyway, I thought Mom had lost her mind. But she still has a lot of friends down there, and she and Gramma get along tolerably well, so it really was a good move.

Mom and Gramma McKenzie were currently visiting Amanda in Montrose, a mere three and a half hours away. Maybe less, the way Mom drives. She had never harped on the dangers of my job, and Amanda owed me, major big time.

So I gave my sister a jingle. Ten-year-old Rebecca answered. I asked, "Aren't you up kind of late?"

"Oh, Aunt Gayle. I'm not a baby."

"How goes it with the visitors?"

"They're playing Scrabble."

I come from a great Scrabble-playing clan, for whom the word *zephyrs* on a triple word score is the apex of glory. "Honey, would you ask Gramma to come to the phone?"

"Gramma McKenzie or Gramma Fisher?"

"Gramma Fisher."

Rebecca shouted, "Gramma Fisher! Telephone!" then klunked down the receiver on a hard surface.

After a short pause, my mother picked up the phone. "Gayle?"

"Hi, Mom. Up for an adventure?"

"What kind?"

"I need a car. Could you and Amanda tool over to Colling-wood tomorrow morning, pick up a rental at the airport, and drive it to Shore Haven? I'd really, really appreciate it."

"Let me think. I don't believe we can get back before Amanda has to go to work." As if the earth would crack in two if Amanda missed one afternoon at the Cynthia Blue Conservatory of Music.

"Come on, Mom. Mandy can cancel just this once. I need a car."

"Look, Gayle, it's different for Amanda. She's not like you. She has responsibilities."

Oh, sure, she did. My acquisitive yet foolhardy sister had nearly lost her house, her IRA, and everything else to a scammer in a get-rich-quick scheme the previous spring, and I was the one who'd gotten most of it back for her. But I resisted letting my mother pit me against my sister. I sweetly said, "Mom, let me talk to Mandy."

After an extended pause, my sister came on the line. I explained what I wanted and she told me all about her responsibilities (i.e., Rebecca's need for food, shelter, transportation, higher education, and Hello-Kitty accessories) and how seriously she took them. I said, "Great. Now what about your responsibility to your one and only sister who dropped everything when you needed help?"

"You didn't drop everything."

"But I *did* help."

"Yes, you did," she acknowledged.

"How much would you lose if you missed work tomorrow?"

"Oh, let me see…. thirty dollars."

"I'll *give* you thirty dollars. It's a valid business expense," I said.

"Very well, I will be happy to bring you a car."

That's just the way Amanda is. When it comes to haggling, she's Iggy's peer, then has the nerve to act holier-than-thou about it. She drives me nuts, but she's my sister…and I love her.

I asked if she had anything on the Montagues yet, and she replied, somewhat haughtily, "No, but I'll let you know when I do." Then she and Mom conferred and said they could be in Shore Haven at noon. I gave them directions to Sunnyside and told them to "stay calm" and "talk to no one" if I they arrived before me—I'd be along shortly. I gave my phone number in case they absolutely had to reach me.

Satisfied with the outcome of my call, I hung my damp clothes over the shower rod and dumped the flannel sheet outside the trailer, intending to return it to the hospital the next day. Then I spread the contents of my shoulder bag on a towel to dry. I checked the gun again: still free of moisture. Leaving its plastic bag out to dry, I stuck the gun in the closet. The traffic citation went into my black travel bag, next to the pills. And since I had to be Betty Jo in the morning, I set out my uniform and white shoes. At long last, I brushed my teeth and went to bed.

THE NEXT DAY I WOKE before the alarm. In the foggy dawn, I chided myself for having involved Keith in my investigation. He had been hurt—doing what? Prying into a crime that most likely had nothing to do with Eleanor's death. Hugging the comforter around me, I called the hospital to check on my young friend. The nurse in intensive care said he was still unconscious. Heartsick, I hung up the phone.

What's more, I ached all over, my arms, right shoulder, and whiplashed neck especially sore. And I was cold. The trailer, heaterless, was as damp and chilly as misery. I shrugged off the bedclothes and headed for the shower to warm up.

After dressing I examined my purse. It remained damp and stiff but would have to do. I rewrapped my gun and placed it on the bottom of the bag. My wallet, notebook, checkbook, and I.D. hadn't quite dried, but I loaded them as well.

Breakfast consisted of two ibuprofen. I was beginning to feel like an ibuprofen junky, but it sure terminated the pain. Having a few minutes to spare, I sat on my padded bench and sipped a cup of tea. Then the phone shrilled and I jerked in surprise, slopping the hot liquid onto the bed. With a shriek, I shrank from the puddle and grabbed the phone, only to hear my mother's merry voice. She and Amanda were about to set out and they'd see me at noon.

I said a terse, "Thanks," and hung up.

Silently cursing my mother, I seized the comforter and bunched it over the shower rod. The tea had soaked into the mattress, which I slid off the bench and tipped on its side to air out. That's when I noticed that the bench doubled as a storage area.

I'd already snooped through all the cupboards and closets? that's my way. But here was a place I'd foolishly missed. I opened the lid and found old magazines, sandy flip-flops, an antique bottle of Coppertone, and a small, rusted beach umbrella. Pitiful pickings, but at least they prompted me to look beneath the padded bench opposite. I took off the mattress, exposing a second storage area, whose lid opened upon a hodgepodge of old swimsuits. I dug through these to a layer of vintage beach towels, beneath which lay a miniature cedar chest. Locked. I set it on the kitchen counter to inspect: compact, simple and smooth. When I shook it, it rattled. What did it hold? Jewels? Drugs? Mementos?

According to my travel alarm it was eight-fifty already and work started at nine. The box could wait, but with Mom and Amanda coming, I had to straighten the place right away. I did so and departed.

Due to the fog I couldn't see five steps before me, yet I

managed to find Beach Street, which I followed to my destination. As I stepped up to the door, I belatedly recalled the pills. Damn. I hoped that Fiona hadn't noticed that they were missing, and I steeled myself for a possible row. Yet when I rang the bell, she answered not with an accusation, but with a big frantic smile. Her purple tee-shirt and slacks were rumpled and rank with sweat. "Oh, my," she breathed. "Your hair's all studded with dew. I wish—oh, sorry, please, come in!" and she pulled me into the house.

Since Friday, the place had shrugged off its air of cleanliness and order. Blankets and pillows were strewn on couches, dirty dishes piled high in the kitchen sink. Dennis slumped in the breakfast nook, toying with his Cheerios, while Sean played some quirky tune by Erik Satie, managing to make it sound bleak. Fiona said, "Daddy got up at three a.m. I was awake all night."

"Go take a nap," I urged. "I'll watch your dad."

"I don't know. I can't fall asleep just anytime. It's—I'm so scared about Daddy. He got out and wandered over to the creek last night."

"Fiona, I've got an article—it's about security for people with dementia."

"Really?"

"Yeah. I'll bring it over after lunch."

"Oh, yes, please do."

I persuaded her to go relax while I watched Dennis and cleaned the kitchen. By the time I was done, the old man had told me several times about his toy piano falling down the stairs on Christmas eve. "And it broke all to little…." he intoned for the fifth time.

"That's sad," I chimed in.

"I got a new one the next, next…." he said, suddenly all smiles.

"The next Christmas?" I asked, wiping his hands with a damp washcloth.

"A nice one."

Granted, this conversation had gone nowhere, yet it made me think that Dennis might be able to talk a bit about Eleanor, if prompted. I squatted and looked into his eyes as Patty had done. "Dennis, do you remember Eleanor?"

"Eleanor?"

"With the long dark hair? Sean's wife? She played the flute."

"The flute," he said, seeming to catch on.

"Yes. Do you remember the day she died?"

"She played the flute," he repeated, smiling. "Too-too-too-tooooo."

Kneeling, I took his huge hands in my own. "Dennis, please try to remember."

At the word *remember,* his playful smile transformed to a tragic grimace. I squeezed his fingers. "Dennis, please try. Eleanor. She had long dark hair—"

"Nooo."

"Please, Dennis, I need your help. Do you remember what happened to her?"

"Nooooo!" Tears welled in his eyes, then streamed down his cheeks—he wept like a toddler. I hugged him then. He couldn't help me—he couldn't help himself—and I'd been pestering the poor soul about memories too painful or elusive to bear.

"I'm sorry, Dennis, so sorry." When at last the weeping had subsided, I gave him a napkin to wipe his face and blow his nose, which he did with impeccable thoroughness. "That's good, Dennis." He brightened at my praise, as though he'd completely forgotten his storm of tears. "Let's go watch TV," I said, holding out my hand.

Several seconds passed before Dennis said, "All right."

He grasped my hand and we walked to the living room, where

he settled into the recliner and stared at a PBS show on the life cycle of the newt. Meanwhile, I swept the floor and Sean played on. By and by, I snuck upstairs to check on Fiona. She was in bed, snoring lightly. Searching the wardrobe with her in the room would be a little risky, but taking risks is part of my job. So I started to open the door, whereupon it emitted a mournful *eeeeee*. Fiona groaned, and I nipped out to the hall and down the stairs, my heart banging like a Chinese drum. Hadn't these people ever heard of WD-40?

As the morning advanced, the sun burnt off the fog, and by eleven the sky was clear. I hoped that the fog hadn't blanketed the state, for if it had, Mom and Amanda would be tardy. At 11:55 I served chili and peanut butter sandwiches to father and son, then said I'd be back by one p.m. Sean acknowledged my leaving in his surly way, as if I were a lackey, which I was, but I still hated it. Then he helped Dennis dip up a spoonful of chili. I had to give Sean this much credit: he was kind to his dad.

I JOGGED BACK TO Sunnyside, arriving with a quick pulse and a damp brow. There in the parking lot, lounging against a navy Ford Taurus and a white Buick Century were my mother, Amanda, Gramma McKenzie, and little Rebecca. The family that sleuths together…drives me batty.

Mom cried, "Gayle!" and proffered a hug. I held up my hands for silence, then beckoned the gang to follow me to the trailer. Thank god, they obeyed. As I ushered them into the Airstream, they marveled at its compactness, and not a one cracked her head. I'm the tallest of our bunch.

Eventually, I got them settled on the padded benches. My sister was sitting prim, slender, and natty in a white middy blouse and navy slacks. Her auburn hair hung in a sleek bob and her makeup was flawless—no sweat, no oil, and certainly no freckles. But I knew they were there, under the Corn Silk. Mom was settled next to her, in a cotton shirt and linen slacks, cobalt blue for fall. It's from my mother that I've inherited my love of linen—if such a preference can be handed down. On the opposite bench perched Gramma McKenzie, plump and small, wearing aqua sweat clothes, the top bearing a puffy-paint picture of a beach. She was toting a plastic purse adorned with Florida sea shells. Curled next to the old dear was my niece, in little jeans and a little U. of M. sweatshirt.

I said, "First of all, my name here at Sunnyside is Betty Jo Bialosky."

"Okay, Aunt Gayle," piped Rebecca.

"Aunt *Betty Jo,*" corrected Amanda.

"Betty Jo *Bialosky,*" mused my mother. "That name's so familiar."

"I use it a lot," I said. "Second, you all have to leave. Now."

"But Gramma McKenzie said I could see the lake," whined my niece.

"We drove all this way," murmured my grandmother. "I'd love to see it."

I *felt* like saying, "You wanna see a lake? Go back to Montrose and look at Lake Erie." However, I find it impossible to snub my granny, so I said, "All right. But remember, I'm Betty Jo, and you're the Bialosky family. Got that?"

They chorused, "Sure," "Yeah," "Of, course," and "I'm no fool"—this last from my sister. At that, we piled out of the trailer and hiked down to the beach, with Rebecca scampering ahead and me giving Gramma McKenzie an arm for support. Having had cataract surgery in July, she was enjoying the world with one clear eye, but she was a little frail at eighty, so she opted to view the lake from the bench on the bluff. I joined her.

With the fog gone, it was a luscious fall day, the waves gentle with barely a dab of foam. Gramma marveled at the azure of lake and sky. She speaks with a Southern-Ohio accent, which to my ears sounds less craggy than a Kentucky or West Virginia accent. "We went to see Lake Erie yesterday," she said. "It's more serious, you know."

I agreed. Lake Erie is greenish, grayish, rarely Lake Michigan's intoxicating blue, yet beautiful in its own way. "So how's the family?"

"Oh, your mom's been busy—helping out at the senior center three days a week. She sets out the lunch, rids up the dishes. Rebecca says fourth grade is too easy. And your sister—well, she's just fine."

Rebecca came flying up the steps. "Look at what I found!" She held out some smooth, indigo glass.

"Wow!" I said. "Milk of Magnesia."

"Milk of *amnesia?*" said Rebecca, a look of doubt on her face.

"*Magnesia.* It's medicine for a stomachache," said Gramma. "Comes in a dark blue bottle."

"That's the rarest kind of beach glass there is," I informed my niece. "Better hang on to it."

Rebecca deposited the find in her jeans pocket and flopped down beside me. By and by, my mother and sister returned. Mom said, "Long as we're here, we might as well go to town, take in the sights."

"Sure," I said, consulting Gramma's watch. "I have to get back to work in a few—"

"Oh, wait a minute." Mom sorted through her purse and handed me a set of keys.

"What do I owe you?" I asked.

"How would she know that?" demanded Amanda. "You're not done with the car yet."

"I put it on my credit card," explained Mom. "I'll let you know when the bill comes."

"Right," I said. "Well, it was real sweet of you all to bring the car. I appreciate it. Sorry you had to cancel work today," I told my sister, then forked over a check for thirty dollars.

She wrinkled her nose. "It's damp." That it was.

"And you," I said to Rebecca. "I'm real sorry you had to miss school."

"Oh, Aunt Betty Jo." She rolled her eyes.

We hugged all around and they left. I pocketed the article on Alzheimer's safety and walked back to work. No point in flaunting the shiny new rental. *White.* I wondered what had possessed my mother to choose that color. I like gray or silver best, for they fade into the background during surveillance. White sticks out, second only to bright red. Cop cars, for chrissake, are white. But for me to complain seemed vastly ungrateful, so I bit my tongue. I only hoped I wouldn't drown the damn car.

FOURTEEN

BACK AT THE MONTAGUE HOUSE, Fiona was up, looking somewhat less frazzled. She suggested we clean upstairs. I readily agreed, even offered to do the chores alone, but she insisted on charring alongside me. We stripped her bed, then found the linen closet empty. "I washed some sheets on Friday," I said. "I guess they're still in the basement."

"That's right," she replied and trotted downstairs to get them. My blood coursed faster at this unexpected boon: enough time to check for a secret passage. I threw open her squeaky wardrobe and pushed through a jumble of clothes to a space as dark and airless as death. My hands flew along the paneling, blindly seeking a door, yet feeling nothing but varnished wood—no hinges, no knob. Had Debby's gossip been a complete lie? When Fiona's quick steps echoed on the stairs, my heart flopped like a startled frog. I scuttled out of the wardrobe and was chasing dust balls under the bed as she bore the white sheets into the room.

Later, we took the old man out for a stroll, then Fiona asked me to preen the garden some more. As I knelt on the grass, yanking a stalk of ragweed, I philosophized that investigating a case from the inside was a lot like having a cold. In both instances you get to the point where you're bored and cranky and want to get on with your life, but you're in the middle of something that seems to move at the speed of concrete through an hourglass.

At five I came in to start dinner while Fiona drove to town to buy groceries, Dennis napped, and Sean busied himself upstairs. If only he'd been hammering the keys, I could have searched again for the secret door. After squishing together a meat loaf, I rewarded myself with a few calls on the kitchen phone. The first went to my hero, Sergeant Swinkey. As luck would have it, he was at the station, attending to the sizable paperwork portion of his job. "People have no idea what cops do," he griped. "Half the time we're filling in forms, writing reports, testifying in court—"

After four months with Leversee, I did have an idea. "I feel sorry for you, Swinkey," I said. "So, did Chief Glenn give his okay to call in the accident reconstructionist?"

"Oh, I see. My problems are nothing, while yours—"

"Swinkey, your problems are weighty as hell, but I'm really pressed for time."

"Yes, he okayed it."

"He's sort of a laissez-faire kind of chief, isn't he?"

"Not with everyone. But he likes you, Gayle. He thinks you've got grit."

"I've never met the man," I marveled.

"Gayle, you're like a rat terrier he's never seen but likes a lot."

"Swinkey—"

"As I was saying, the accident reconstructionist was supposed to show up today, but it's already after five—"

"Will you go with him?"

"Sure. If I can."

"Thanks a lot, Sarge. You're a big help."

We signed off, then I called the hospital. Keith remained unconscious, which made my spirits sink. Was he comatose or what? What had I done to the poor kid?

Sighing uneasily, I got out my long-distance calling card and dialed my answering machines at work and at home. Nothing there. I tried Iggy's number. No one answered, but I left a message: "Are you tracking A.N.? Please respond on my home answering machine." I refrained from leaving my name. Iggy prides himself on his paranoia, and I pride myself on being able to work within its parameters. Besides, he knows my voice.

Before I could return the phone to its cradle, red-haired Sean snuck into the room. I say *snuck,* because as usual he entered in floating silence. Whether or not he did it on purpose, it gave me the willies. I uttered, stupidly, into the receiver, "You must have the wrong number," and hung up.

"I didn't hear the phone ring," said Sean, rubbing his knuckles.

"It didn't," I said. "I was about to call the grocery and page Fiona to have her pick up salad olives, but a man was already on the line asking for someone named Greg." O agile liar that I am.

Sean waited a moment. "What about the olives?"

"Uh, right." I fumbled with the phone book, whereupon Sean sneered, Elvis-like, and left the room.

When Fiona returned, I gave her the article on Alzheimer's safety—I'd almost forgotten it. Then I headed for Sunnyside. Sure, I had enjoyed seeing my family, but with them gone I was free to crack into the little cedar chest. In a twinkling, I had dug it back out of storage.

It was a dainty chest, mellow with age yet in fine condition. I peered into the keyhole, then got out my picks and popped the lock in ten seconds flat. When I opened the lid, the sweet scent of cedar permeated the air. Inside lay a Petosky stone—hence the rattle—and a stack of notes. My back prickled with pleasant anticipation: I adore reading other people's mail.

Tied with blue ribbon and fragrant with cedar, the notes were slightly oily and rumpled, as if they had been handled many times. They lacked envelopes and were written on cheap white paper torn from a four by seven pad. Bits of adhesive that holds such pads together still clung to the tops of the pages.

The first note was written in what seemed a masculine hand.

Adorable,
Meet me at eight tonight. We're good together, aren't we?
Lover

Lover. That was vague enough. And who was Adorable? Probably not Dennis or Sean; the cedar chest and ribbon were too feminine. Old Mrs. Montague? Fiona? Or the most recent habitué of the trailer, Eleanor?

I read through the rest of the notes. All had been addressed to Adorable—a generic. Perhaps Lover was juggling too many women to remember their names. He had revealed little of himself, the contents of the notes ranging from "I need you" to "I want you" but always falling short of "I love you." The communiqués seemed hardly worth keeping but had meant enough to someone to hide them, beribboned, in a cedar box.

After tucking them back in storage, I stripped off my uniform, scrubbed its grimy knees and hung it in the shower to dry. I was relaxing in my skivvies when a series of knocks vibrated the Airstream like a witch doctor's rattle. "Just a minute!" I called. I threw on khakis and a shirt and opened the door.

It was *them*. My family. I ushered the quartet silently in, shut the door and asked, "What's up?"

They all started babbling about what a swell time they'd had wandering around Shore Haven, browsing knickknack shops, gawking at sailboats—and did I know that some drunken woman had plunged a car into the channel?

"That's something," I mumbled, managing to stifle a blush. "Excuse me, but why are you still here? Don't you need to get home?"

"Gayle Marie, don't be ungracious." My mother's comment was a corruption of one of Gramma McKenzie's sayings: *It doesn't hurt to be gracious.*

"We came to ask you out to dinner," said Amanda, in a petulant voice.

"I'm undercover right now," I impatiently reexplained.

"We're not planning to expose you," boomed Mom. "Aren't you hungry?"

"I guess," I said.

"Well then, let's go," said Mom.

As we trooped out of the trailer, Debby the dental assistant happened by. "God dammit," I muttered under my breath. I'd been wanting to have another tête-à-tête with blabbermouth Debby, and there I was stuck playing gracious daughter. Never again would I ask my mother to bring me a car, not even if I were stranded in the god-forsaken Gobi desert.

"Got company?" asked Debby.

"Yes, indeed," I said, forcing a smile. "This is my grandmother, my mother, my sister, and my niece."

"We're all Bialoskys," piped Rebecca.

Right on cue, the family curse set fire to each of our necks, cheeks, and ears—except those of the clever tyke. We stammered a few pleasantries, then hustled to the parking lot. Mom wanted to drive, but I figured we'd wrap up the family fun sooner if I got behind the wheel. I suggested eating at the Black River Inn and everyone agreed.

At the restaurant we were seated at a round table by a picture window that overlooked the river. My trip into its waters had given me a new appreciation of it—if cold sweat and nausea could be termed appreciation. As we awaited our meals, a tugboat towing a crane on a barge chugged past our window. The ungainly parade stopped mid-river, then two wet-suited scuba divers jumped from the barge into the water. Almost immediately, they bobbed back up and signaled the tug's captain, who towed the barge a few yards west. The crane operator lowered a huge hook into the river and the divers vanished once again.

"Whatever are they doing out there?" asked Grandma.

Rebecca said, "I bet they're pulling up the drunk lady's car."

"How do you know she was drunk?" I queried.

Rebecca went *tch*. "That's what the man at the ice-cream stand said."

"Sorbet shop," corrected Amanda.

Five minutes ticked by before the drivers resurfaced. The crane's cable began to inch up the boom and spool around a turning drum. Throughout the restaurant, necks twisted toward the picture window and eyes took in the scene. The front bumper of a car emerged from the river, gleaming like treasure from a sunken ship. As the crane pulled the car higher, black water and a brilliant orange carp poured from its open door. At last the car—my car—dangled dripping from the top of the boom.

A telltale blush sizzled my ears. My family had seen this LeMans just once before, on the Fourth of July when we'd all gathered in Montrose for a picnic and fireworks. This was before Gramma's eye surgery, but the rest of them had seen the car perfectly well. I waited for Mom or Amanda or Rebecca to say, *Isn't that your LeMans?* Yet no one did. My ears cooled. I had lucked out.

"It's like a big silver fish," cried Rebecca, "all wet and slimy!"

When a cheer went up in the restaurant, Amanda explained that the channel had been closed to deep-keeled vessels all day, so most sailboats could neither enter nor leave the harbor. The tug swung around and towed the barge, crane, and car back upriver to heaven knows where. I jotted a mental note to find out. Our food finally arrived, but the sight of my car suspended like a prize tuna had killed my appetite.

After dinner we headed down to the public beach, walking right past the scene of the accident. Two sets of skidmarks shown darkly on the street, one shooting straight downhill, the other curving sharply east. Remnants of the traffic sign lay scattered like kindling, and tire tracks rutted the lawn. Gramma said she was tired, so she and I relaxed on a riverside bench while the others trekked out to the beach. "How'd you happen to end up in the river?" she asked once the others were out of earshot. Old Granny doesn't miss much.

"I wasn't drunk," I said.

"I'm sure you weren't."

"It was work related."

"You're mighty hard on cars," she observed.

"I'd just as soon not tell Mom what happened. Not today anyway."

Gramma is a cool old lady. She nodded in agreement. "A letter or phone call down the road wouldn't go amiss."

The rest of the clan returned, and I was beginning to see the light at the end of the tunnel of this fun family visit. But as we drove back to Sunnyside, Mom complained of "queasiness," and Amanda suggested she lie down in the trailer awhile before they left for Montrose.

Back in the Airstream, Mom curled up on one of the padded benches. "Ooph! That chef's salad—I think the dressing was off."

I said, "How about some Vernor's?" Vernor's Ginger Ale is a family cure all—good for what ails you. Warm for stomach trouble, cold for fever.

"No…just a little rest."

Gramma extracted two packs of cards from her big plastic purse, then she, Rebecca, Amanda, and I played a cut-throat game of canasta. After an hour of shuffling, dealing, melding, and hoarding red threes, my patience was worn as thin as Mr. DeKat's lucky shirt. "It's getting late," I announced. "Hadn't you better go home?"

"Oh, my," called Mom. "It is late. Maybe we should stay over, leave first thing in the morning."

Amanda said, "Sure. Doesn't the trailer sleep five?"

I said, "Four." And no matter if it slept forty, I wasn't about to let them stay overnight.

"Pish tush," responded Mom. "Your dad and I stayed in a trailer exactly like this on our honeymoon in Grayling. It sleeps five. But as I recall, we didn't get much sleep, what with all the mortar fire."

"Mortar fire!" exclaimed Amanda.

"We stayed at the State Park," said Mom, "next to Camp Grayling. You know, the training site for the Army Reserves?"

"Why'd you need a trailer that slept five on your honey-moon?" I asked with a straight face.

"We didn't *need* it—we just happened to have it. Two could sleep up front—"

"And two in the back," I said. "That's four."

"No, *three* in the back." Mom reached between the padded bench and the wall and pulled up a big piece of plywood. "See? This fits up above, between those grooves. It makes a top bunk."

"Who on the earth would want to sleep on a plywood shelf?" I asked, rhetorically.

"Me!" cried my niece. "I would!"

"It's settled," declared Mom. "We're staying the night."

Rebecca said, "Oh, cool! I never slept in a trailer!"

"But what about school?" I countered.

"We can get her back in time for the afternoon," my sister said.

"Really?" I dryly replied. "Gosh, it's stuffy in here. Amanda, let's take a walk."

She gave me a blank look, so I kicked her shin under the table. Hard. She cried, "Ow! Okay." We grabbed our jackets and left that overcrowded tin can.

For privacy, I walked her down to the deserted shore where we commandeered a pair of abandoned beach chairs. We sat. A quarter moon had risen, shining pale light along the sand and faceted waves. "I don't want you guys staying over night," I said.

"That's pretty obvious."

"Look, I'm not here on vacation. I'm working. Undercover. Your being here compromises the case."

"I know. We were going to leave after dinner, but when Mom saw your car coming out of the water—"

"Oh, shit."

"She's worried. She wants to confront you about your drinking."

"Drinking?"

"Weren't you drunk?"

"No. I was rammed into the river by a criminal that damn near killed me and my passenger, who is still in the hospital, unconscious."

"Gayle—"

"That's right. So you tourists can just get the hell out of here. Before one of you gets hurt."

"But what about my report?"

"What report?"

"On the Montagues," she said in the withering tone she reserves especially for me.

"You got something?"

"Well, it seems that Dennis's finances are at low ebb, despite his having had a fine career on the concert stage. He could have held a tenured position at a university, but he was a free spirit, so he missed out on a salary, health insurance, and a pension."

"You would think of that."

With an impatient sniff, she continued. "He could've managed well enough on his concerts and recordings, but things started to go sour about fifteen years ago. His wife had a massive stroke. She was only forty-one."

"Unusual."

"Quite. She ended up in a nursing home. Dennis wanted to stay close to her and the children, so he cut back on touring and added some private students."

"He taught piano?"

"Of course. Dennis Montague drew students from Chicago, Detroit, Toronto—"

"Okay, I get it."

"And these students paid well. So he had income from concerts, students, and recordings. But the nursing home was draining his savings. Six years went by, then his wife had another stroke and died. Shortly after, he began to cancel performances. Eventually he couldn't get work. He lost his agent, his students." Amanda tossed a handful of sand at the lake. "Everyone thought he'd make a comeback. But he never did."

"Hm. What about Sean?"

"He's 'a promising young pianist.' He studied at Interlochen and Juilliard, where he worked with Nils Sörengaard."

"And?"

"He's been described as 'a young man with a lot of facility.'"

"Meaning?"

"He's got great technique."

"But?"

"The challenge is to connect technique to feeling," said my sister. "He's entered a number of major competitions, but he hasn't won yet. He's come in second twice."

"So the person who wins goes on to greatness—"

"A *chance* at greatness," corrected Amanda.

"And Sean goes home to beef up for the next bout. What about Eleanor?"

"Very talented—principal flute with the Manning Chamber Orchestra."

"Did she have a chance at a solo career?" I asked.

"Flautists don't really have solo careers."

"What about that guy—James Galway?"

"Sure. But he's a fluke."

"Okay."

"Have you heard him play?" she asked.

"Galway?"

"No. Sean."

"Yeah, lots," I said. "And the old man too."

"Dennis? You're kidding."

"He's…not well, but he still plays."

Even in the moonlight, I could see the awe on Amanda's face. "Sometimes I wish…."

"What?"

"That I'd stuck with piano. Not switched to organ. Maybe I could have…I don't know."

"I always admired your organ playing when we were kids."

"Really?"

"Yes! All those keyboards, pedals, and stops? And you could work the damn thing. Remember the first time you played at church? Just a little kid in a blue dress, hands skipping from keyboard to keyboard, feet playing those huge pedals. I was jealous," I confessed. "It was a kind of magic that you had and I didn't."

"It's not that big a deal," she said.

"It is."

We sat there a few moments, my sister speechless for once. I'd have to try compliments more often, if only to shut her up.

Back at the trailer, Amanda went to confer with Mom, who promptly rose from her sickbed. "We'd better be going," she said. "It's a long trip back."

"I wanna stay in the trailer," wailed the child, flinging herself across one of the padded benches.

"No," declared Mom. "You need go to school tomorrow."

"Awwww."

It took another ten minutes to gather their belongings, march down to the parking lot, and say goodbye. Mom hugged me. "Be careful," she whispered and they left.

Back at the trailer, I put on my nightgown and bathrobe, then lay on the padded bench contemplating what I needed to do the next day.... *Check on Keith, talk to Swinkey, locate my car, buy a new watch, go to the library, find the secret passage....*

THAT NIGHT I DREAMT of a bonfire. The smoke in my dream grew thicker and thicker, until my eyes popped open, only to be stung by real smoke. Coughing, I switched on the lamp. The trailer was hazed with smoke. I rushed to the door, but it refused to budge. I pushed and banged and yelled, "Help! Please! Someone help me!" but no one answered my cries. It was September and Sunnyside's summer people had packed up and gone home. My lungs were burning, my head was throbbing, my heart was pounding. I grabbed the phone to call 911.

The line was dead.

FIFTEEN

I DROPPED THE RECEIVER and fell to my knees, expecting to find less smoke, yet the haze was every bit as thick down by the cold, sandy floor.

The floor was cold—not hot!

If the trailer were on fire, I'd be cooking like a chicken in an aluminum roaster, but the Airstream was cold, the jalousies were open—the smoke was coming from outside! A surge of hope pulled me to my feet. I tore at the window above where I had been sleeping, but the glass louvers resisted all my efforts to dismantle them. I peered outside and all I could see was smoke. Most fire victims, I recalled with electrifying clarity, died not of charred flesh but of smoke inhalation. Quickly, I cranked the window closed.

Choking, I stumbled to the window opposite; its louvers were just as stubborn, but the smoke outside was thinner and I could see fairly well. A light shone in a trailer some eighty feet away. I pressed my mouth to a space between louvers and tested the air. Clear! I sucked in a cool lung full, then another. I yelled, "Help! Fire! Help!"—and kept yelling, praying that someone—anyone—would hear. As the smoke outside grew denser, the cloud within the trailer thickened, as well. I was coughing, screaming for help.

When I had controlled the trailer, it had felt cozy. Now that someone else had the power to lock me in and attack me with smoke, the Airsteam felt like a vile little prison. A long-buried memory flashed in my mind: when I was five years old I had accidentally trapped myself in an old refrigerator in my parents' basement. How frightened I had been! How hard I had fought to breathe!

Once more I screamed, "Help!"

And at last someone responded: "This way!" shouted Debby. "Hurry up!" hollered Patty.

The door shook and my heart surged with relief. I could hang on for a few more seconds as release was close at hand. Then Debby yelled, "It's too heavy!"

I screamed, "No!" and succumbed to a fit of coughing.

"Keep trying!" cried Patty.

As the shaking continued, my heart beat faster, and a siren screamed in the distance, closer and closer till it screamed in my brain. Abruptly, it stopped. Doors slammed, people ran toward the trailer. "Look at that!" called a man. A moment later, the door flew open, and a huge fire fighter in full regalia—vulcanized hat, jacket, pants, and boots—crouched into the Airstream and carried me out.

The fire fighter placed me on a stretcher and an E.M.T. thrust an oxygen mask at my face. I inhaled a lung full of dazzling O2, then pushed the mask away. "I'm okay," I said between hacking coughs.

A second, smaller fire fighter was hosing down a hissing black chunk of driftwood. A heavy pine picnic table lay toppled on the grass next to the trailer. "Arson," said the big fire fighter. "Someone dragged this picnic bench out of your neighbor's yard and upended it against your door so you couldn't get out. Then he hauled over that big piece of driftwood, placed it under your window, set it ablaze. And the phone line's been cut."

"My god," I murmured, grateful again that my family had left. If they had been hurt….

"You were lucky," he said.

"I'm not dead, if that's what you mean," I said with abundant sarcasm.

"I mean the fire wasn't close enough to your propane to blow it up."

"That's a comfort." I imagined a cartoon image of myself catapulted high over Sunnyside, then plummeting back toward a blazing trailer.

"You could've died from the smoke all the same," he mused. Great.

The handful of people still residing at Sunnyside were gathered around in their bathrobes, watching the little drama. They hugged their arms against the chill air and gaped at me. Standing closest by were my would-be rescuers, Debby in a blue baby-doll nightie and Patty in a fuzzy lilac robe. I scanned the small crowd. Was the firebug among them? I peered out into the darkness to where a pyromaniac might lurk. I began to shiver, my teeth rattling like dice. What the hell was I gambling with? My life? "May I go back in for a jacket?" I asked.

"Sure," said the big fire fighter. "Once the place is aired out. You can even sleep there if you want."

Sleep? Sure. Wondering if whoever pulled this "prank" would come back and finish me off?

The tall fire fighter set up a big fan to clear the smoke out of the trailer. The fan, which ran on gasoline, blew with such force, he had to brace it to keep it from flying backwards.

The far-off wail of a police car drew ever nearer. If the vehicle carried VanDee and Bigalow, my threadbare identity as Betty Jo Bialosky would be blown to shreds. I resolved to sneak off before they arrived, but my car keys were in the trailer. Hoping no one would notice, I dodged around the fan and started up the steps. Suddenly, a strong arm wrapped around my waist. "Wait a minute," said the big fire fighter. "Where do you think you're going?"

"You told me I could go in," I said, struggling to break free.

"I said *after* the trailer's aired out. Wait a couple of minutes—that smoke may be toxic."

"I'll hold my breath. I just need my purse." The police siren was growing closer.

"It can wait." And with that, the big fire fighter lifted me off the steps and set me down some five feet away from my goal.

Just then, the police car came skidding into Sunnyside, screeching to a halt behind the fire truck. The phrase "out of the frying pan into the fire" was taking on new meaning. VanDee would soon be grilling the witnesses, including his recent "date," Debby the dental assistant, who would refer to me as Betty Jo Bialosky, health-care aide.

However, to my great surprise, the officer stepping out of the cop car was neither VanDee nor Bigalow (nor Voight nor Swinkey), but some young baby cop I had never met. Truly, this was my lucky night, if you ignored the fact that I had inhaled enough fumes to blow a smoke ring around the lake. And that someone was trying to kill or at least scare the living snoop out of me. Babycop strolled my way. No taller than I and not much heavier, he had neatly trimmed blond hair, blue eyes, a button nose, and the pouty mouth of a Cupie Doll. I stepped forward and stuck out my hand. "Betty Jo Bialosky," I said.

He pumped my fingers and introduced himself as Officer Dill Cooper. "Is this your trailer?" he asked.

"I'm staying here a few weeks," I said, tightening my bathrobe around me.

"Please have a seat in my car, and I'll be back to talk to you in ten minutes."

I did as he asked. Meanwhile he pushed a dowel in each corner of the trailer's small yard, then carefully cordoned it off with crime tape. He spoke with the firemen, Debby, and Patty, writing notes all the while, then he returned to the police car and took my account of what had happened.

"Any idea who did this, Ms. Bialosky?"

"No…no…sorry. I figure it's a prank. You know—kids. Thought they'd have a little fun?"

"Fun?" he said, blinking his baby blues. "You could've been killed."

"But I wasn't."

"Well, thanks for the information. But to tell the truth, it'll be darn hard to find out who's behind this. Maybe the Montagues will have some idea."

"I doubt it."

"But it is their trailer."

"Yes, but I wouldn't bother them about it."

Officer Cooper narrowed his eyes.

"Not tonight," I quickly added. "Young Mr. Montague is fanatical about getting his eight hours. And if you woke *old* Mr. Montague, his daughter would have a devil of a time getting him back to sleep. You should wait till tomorrow. The later the better. They're extremely cranky in the a.m."

"But—"

"I'm not kidding. Call now and they'll take your head off."

"Well…all right." And he snapped his notebook shut.

"Thanks. I guess I better go put some clothes on."

"Okay, but try not to mess up the scene."

I regarded the taped-off area. It was slopped with water from the fire hose and trod into mud by Patty, Debby, two fire fighters, an E.M.T., Cooper, and me. I said, "Right," then hopped out of the car. Evading the tape, I climbed back into the smoke-stenched Airstream and shut the door. I'd be damned if I'd sleep in that deathtrap the rest of the night. I threw on some clothes, packed the rest of my stuff, and hustled on out of there.

Five minutes later I was in my rented luxury-mobile, driving south on the Blue Star Highway. The closer one gets to Shore Haven proper, the more often the farmland is punctuated by shabby Ma-&-Pa type motels with separate huts, each just big enough to shelter a bed. I stopped at the first one whose *Vacancy* sign glowed red in the night. Coincidentally, it was actually named *Ma & Pa's*. The office door was locked, but I banged it with a righteous fist until I had roused a scrawny bathrobed man I assumed was Pa and who muttered something about Ma forgetting to "turn off the goll-danged sign."

"I need a room," I said. "Got one?"

Old Pa wiped a few strands of hair across his pate. "Thirty dollars," he whined.

I excavated from my bag a Jackson and a Hamilton and placed them in his grip as if paying taxes to a king. He motioned for me to follow, and we hiked off to a shack in the farthest reach of his realm. After unlocking the door, he flicked on the lights and displayed the amenities: knotty-pine walls, saggy bed, electric space heater, and bathroom. I said, "This is great," and thanked him, whereupon he readily took the hint and wafted away on the breeze. I moved my car and unloaded my luggage, then fell onto the bed with a brain ache. Yes, my skull hurt like hell, and why not, what with the smoke, the stress, and the lack of sleep? I got up and sorted through my purse for my favorite pain killer. I swallowed two, chasing them with a glass of water that had the smell of a rotten egg dropped into a bucket of rust. I writhed with nausea.

I got out my gun, undid the safety and set it on the bedside table, where I could easily wrap fingers around it. If need be. Then I turned on the buzzing space heater, kicked off my shoes and slid under the meager covers, ready for sleep.

But sleep wasn't ready for me.

My mind got to grappling with a logic problem. I had nearly been drowned on Sunday, then almost suffocated on Monday. It was too much of a coincidence. Someone knew that the woman investigating the drug theft and the health-care aide working for the Montagues were one in the same. Someone knew that I had found the link between the Coulter robbery and the Montague murder. Seconal. Someone knew that I had to be gotten rid of— scared away or killed—before I exhumed the whole truth.

I WOKE EARLY the next morning to cold sunlight pouring through thin drapes. I had slept, but without conviction. My sinuses ached, my throat burned, and I coughed up a nasty chunk of phlegm. What a puny specimen I was. All it took was a dip into the Black River and a lung full of smoke, and I felt worse than road kill.

I rose and showered in rotten-egg water, then dressed in khakis, a madras shirt, and a blazer that stank of smoke. I had left my uniform drip-drying in the Airstream, but I wouldn't have worn it anyway: no place to stick a gun. With the outfit I had on, I could hide the gun in my pocket. I did. The lightweight Beretta barely sagged the jacket's seams, but an astute observer, such as a cop, would know exactly what it was, so I tucked the gun in the back of my pants where it would occasionally bite my spine yet remain well concealed.

I wanted to call the hospital to check up on Keith, but my accommodations had no phone, just a pathetic empty jack. If I had felt more energetic, I might have construed this anomaly as some kind of threat. Instead, I resolved to call later. Since I planned not to spend another night in knotty-pine smell-hell, I packed my duds and toted them out to the car. It was eight a.m.

Unsurprisingly, Ma and Pa hadn't offered croissants and fresh fruit (or even stale fried cakes and Tang) with the price of the room, so I drove a mile south to Dotty's Diner. Be it ever so humble, Dotty's had plenty of business. The tables were overflowing with working men, so I snagged a spot at the counter. As I peered bleary eyed at the menu, trying to find a special without eggs, a waitress stopped by to take my order. Her nametag read *Dotty*. I do that—read nametags. Anyway, it was Dotty herself, waiting on me. The middle-aged proprietress had the face of an amiable bull dog and hennaed hair secured with a net. "What'll ya have?" she queried.

"Oh, gosh, how about a bowl of oatmeal, hash browns, orange juice, tea, a side of sausage—and a pecan roll."

"You want that grilled?"

A police interrogation sprang to mind, then St. Lawrence martyred over hot coals. "Huh?"

"The pecan roll."

"Oh, sure. Why not?"

"Cost ya less if you get the number four," she advised.

I read the description of breakfast number four: eggs, hash browns, sausage. "I hate eggs."

"We'll hold the eggs," Dotty replied with a wink. She pivoted and shouted at the fry cook, "Grilled pecan, number four, hold the eggs!" Dotty dished up the oatmeal and brought water, juice, and tea. A few minutes later she slapped the pecan roll and a steamy, greasy plate of number four sans eggs before me. She was sweet. I said, "Dotty, you got a mighty nice place here." She spread her mouth in an undershot grin, then moved on to the next hungry patron.

I usually eat light in the morning, but that day I needed all the food groups, heavy on the grease, to smooth me out. Ordinarily, a breakfast like that would have left me snoring within the hour, but the cup of tea (and the residual adrenaline) would keep me alert until evening. Thus fortified, I took off for work, hoping that young Officer Cooper had taken my advice and held off calling the Montagues. I imagined the smoke-out would be just the excuse Sean needed to fire me.

A few minutes later I pulled into the Sunnyside lot, then walked to the Montague home. If only I had called in sick.

Fiona took awhile to answer the door. She seemed harried but made no mention of the trailer. I surmised that Cooper had not yet phoned. Good boy. Fiona motioned me in and said that she was readying the old man for a trip to the dentist. Sean was still in dreamland, so I would have to come along.

If Sean were to help Fiona take their dad to the dentist, I could search the house without Sean's sneaking around spying on me. The nerve of some people! I say this only half facetiously, for now I *knew* that Eleanor had been murdered. If Sean had killed her, he deserved my searching his house and exposing his turpitude; and if he hadn't, he still deserved the search, for he lacked the gumption to reject the M.E.'s too-quick determination of suicide.

"Which dentist?" I casually asked.

"Dr. Coulter. He's taken care of Daddy's teeth for years."

"I hear he's good." Once again, I can't say my fortune was all bad. My skin prickled pleasantly at the chance to scope out the dentist's office.

Dennis was sitting in the breakfast nook, already fed, and Fiona began to help with his grooming. "He seems to do better these days if I supervise," she remarked. "Daddy, are you ready to shave?"

The old man made no reply. "I can do it for him," I said, eager for us to leave before Cooper called.

"No, it's better if Daddy does it himself. Besides, we don't have to leave for the dentist's office for another half hour."

I nodded in resignation.

When Fiona passed her father the electric razor, he switched it on then ran it over his stubbled cheeks, chin, and neck for a good five minutes. At last he shut off the razor and set it on the table. He'd done a passable job and we praised him. Fiona gave him his comb and mirror, and he methodically combed, parted, and smoothed his hair.

"It's funny what he can and can't do," said Fiona. "He can

shave by himself, but he needs help eating. He can comb his hair, but he can't say *comb*." She paused to sniff the air. "What's that smell? Been to a bonfire?"

A perfect opportunity to tell Fiona about the smoke-out…but I didn't. "Sort of. Sorry about the uniform—I forgot to rinse it out last night."

"Oh, I don't care about that. You can wear regular clothes all you want."

"Thanks." I'd miss old greeny, the way it made me fade into the woodwork and washed so easily in the sink.

"I read that article," said Fiona. "The one on safety?"

"Yeah?"

"We ought to get something to cover up the l-o-c-k-s on the doors. If D-a-d-d-y can't see them, he might not g-e-t o-u-t."

"Great idea. Maybe little curtains?"

"Yes, that's what I was thinking."

"Curtains," repeated Dennis.

"I worry about your getting out," Fiona told him. "I want you to stay safe."

Dennis smirked and shrugged.

"He's pretty laid back today," I observed.

"It's the quiet."

"The Rachmaninoff agitates him."

"Especially the third movement," she agreed. "It's unfortunate. You see, Sean has to play."

"Has to?"

"He's preparing for the Rohrbach Competition. There's a fifty-thousand-dollar prize and a two-year concert tour. If he wins." Fiona gathered the shaver, mirror, and comb. "We really need the money. But it's hard for him, what with Daddy, and now Eleanor…." Her voice trailed off and tears spilled from her eyes.

"I'm sorry, Fiona." Perhaps I'd misjudged Sean. Perhaps the

pressure and grief were what made him so miserable to be around. "But it must be hard for you too."

"If Sean can just…." She paused as if his chore were too heavy even for Atlas. "Well, he's doing his best. We all are. Aren't we, Daddy?"

Dennis gave a Mona-Lisa smile in reply.

DR. COULTER'S OFFICE was located on Michigan Avenue, in an old stucco building with long windows whose glass dripped with age. The front door, however, gleamed with new glass. The enterprising burglar must have smashed the old pane, reached in, and turned the bolt from the inside. I detected no alarm system, old or new. The building was an easy mark.

The dentist was a short, dark-haired man, solidly built, about fifty-five years old. He wore one of those commercially-laundered white cotton tunics that crosses the chest and buttons down the side. He was exceptionally well groomed, except for a tad too much nose hair. Put a comb in his hand, he could have been a barber.

Coulter greeted Dennis warmly with a two-handed hand-shake, and the latter responded with closed eyes: he obviously could not place the dentist. Coulter seemed to take this in stride and ushered his patient into an operatory. "I'd better come too," called Fiona, hurrying after them. That left me with Debby the dental assistant. Debby wore a white synthetic pantsuit, her fair hair coiled into a hectic bun. She lacked her usual piece of tooth floss but surely could have laid hold of one at a moment's notice.

Debby immediately fell upon me, babbling about the fire. "I'm the one who called 911, then Patty and I tried to pull that bench off your door, but it was way heavy. Hey, I saw you with Dill. What d'ya think? Isn't he a cutie?"

"Dill?"

"Officer Cooper."

"Oh…to tell you the truth, I was too upset to notice."

"I was gonna invite you to stay at my trailer. But like that," she said with a clap of her hands, "you were gone."

"I went to a motel. I was fine, really. Thanks for helping. Maybe you saved my life."

"No—"

"Really, if you hadn't made that call, I don't know what would have happened."

She grinned for a moment, then a frown contracted her brows. "Who do you suppose did it?"

"Gosh, I guess it was kids. You know, a prank. No one was actually hurt."

"Well, I don't like it at all," she complained. "Anyone ever tried that with my trailer, I'd raise holy hell."

I nodded, then peered down the hall. "Would you mind if…could I see where the robbery took place?"

A conspiratorial smile crept over her pretty face, and we snuck to a large room near the end of the hall. "This is Surgery," she said in a low voice. I eyed the ghoulish accouterments of tooth pulling: the chair with straps, the tanks of oxygen and nitrous oxide, the autoclave steaming away fit to burst, the glass-fronted cabinets full of pliers and probes and enormous syringes I never wanted anywhere near my mouth. One of the cabinets was covered with white cardboard and adhesive tape. "That's where the drugs used to be."

I whispered, "Have any idea who did it?"

Just then, another dental assistant barged into the room. She was a no-nonsense type, with short dark hair and snapping black eyes. "Say, whatcha doing back here?" she bluntly inquired.

"I'm giving my friend a tour," said Debby, snootily inspecting her nails.

"It's quite a place," I said in my blandest tones.

"Debby, doctor wants you to watch the desk," the brunette said irritably.

"I better get going," I said. "I need to run an errand or two while Dr. Coulter's working on Dennis. How long before he's done?"

"Oh, forty-five minutes. Half hour if Mr. Montague gets antsy," said Debby.

I thanked her for the tour and bid her adieu. Then I hot footed it to the police station, where fate allowed me to bump into Swinkey as he sauntered out the door.

"Well, if it isn't Gayle Fisher, P.I.," he said.

"Dammit, Swinkey, tell the whole world, why don't ya?"

"Oo, touchy…."

"I'm *supposed* to be undercover."

He pressed his hand to the small of my back in one of his flirty gestures and steered me along the sidewalk. We strolled halfway down the block, his right hand groping my Beretta.

"Do you have to walk so close?" I demanded.

"Gayle's packin'," he murmured in my ear.

"It's legal."

He took his hand away. "I've seen you swing it around. Ya know how to use it?"

"Well enough. Where we headed?"

"The hospital," he said. "Keith's come around."

SIXTEEN

WE GOT INTO SWINKEY'S squad car and drove the short distance to the Shore Haven Community Hospital. I loved sitting up front where I could look at his gizmos—all similar to the ones in Leversee's car, except Leversee lacked radar. I examined the siren; *Hi-Lo, Wail,* and *Yelp* were the choices. "What's *Yelp?*" I asked, hopeful that Swinkey would demonstrate. Leversee never would.

"Leave that stuff alone," he said as we pulled into the hospital parking lot. Entering via Emergency, we encountered Nurse Ryanne, who was wheeling a whale-shaped patient to X-ray. Swinkey immediately switched on the charm.

I had to return to Dr. Coulter's office before long, so excused myself from their inane chatter. I boarded the elevator and just as the door was closing, Swinkey waved a hand before the electric eye. The door slid open and he stepped inside.

"Say, you're jealous, aren't ya?"

"Swinkey, I'd have to be pretty hard up before I was jealous over a married man."

"Ouch!"

"Yeah, Swinkey, keep on swinging. One of these days you'll hit a ball."

At that, he got a little testy. "Hell, I can hit a ball any god damned day of the week. I can hit a ball right out of the park. You know what that is? A *home run.*"

Fate smiled: the elevator lurched to a stop and the door glided open. We took off down the hall to ICU and asked if we could see Keith. The answer was yes, for within a certain parameter of requests, no one said no to Swinkey. Was it the blue uniform?

As before, Keith lay alone in the semi-private room. He looked even younger and thinner than before, dark hair bushing out on the pillow, face bandaged, and hand attached to an I.V. But he was no longer hooked up to monitors, and he was awake and grinning. "Hey, Gayle! Sergeant Swinkey!"

I bent down and gave the patient a hug. "How ya feeling, big guy?"

"I got a killer headache, whiplash, and a wompin' bruise on my thigh. Other than that, I'm all right. They're moving me to a regular room after lunch, and I can go home tomorrow."

"Imagine that. Just in time for school."

The kid cast me a mock-bitter glance.

Swinkey said, "Keith, I was wondering if you could tell me about the accident, what you remember."

"Sorry, but I can't remember a thing. *Nada*. I don't even remember going to work Friday."

"That sometimes happens with head injuries," commented Swinkey.

"Oh, Dr. Swinkey," I cooed, "will he regain his memory?"

"Maybe."

"What happened?" asked Keith.

"We were in a car crash and ended up in the channel," I said.

"And I can't remember that? Doood." A look of fright darkened his eyes. "Who was driving?"

I raised my hand. "Someone rammed us from behind, forced us into the water."

"Doooood."

I have to say that the kid got a lot of mileage and music out of that worn, surfer-esque monosyllable. I said, "You take care and don't worry. Sergeant Swinkey's on the case. He'll catch the filthy perp."

The big cop gave Keith his card. "Let me know if you remember anything, okay?"

Back down in the car, I said, "Shouldn't someone be guarding him? The creep that hit us is *probably* the same person who told Keith he had the skinny on the Coulter job."

"Yeah," said Swinkey, swinging left out of the parking lot. "Or it could've been random."

"Random? You don't believe—"

"Stranger things—"

"Swinkey, do you think Keith is in danger?"

"I don't know."

"Can an officer be assigned to watch him?"

"Look, Gayle, we don't have a bunch of spare officers we can assign to guard this person and that. Especially without any firm evidence that Keith's in danger."

So I told him about my little wienie roast of the night before.

"Hmm. That's why you smell of wood smoke."

"Keith and I are both in danger," I said.

"And that's why you're carrying that popgun."

"Brilliant deduction, Swinkey. You chose the right field of endeavor."

He pulled up to the curb next to the police station. "Look, I know Chief Glenn. He's not gonna put officers on overtime just to babysit you and Keith. He doesn't have the money in his budget, and you—you're not even a resident."

I chewed my lower lip. "Okay. See you around," and I started to get out of the car.

"Hey, wait a minute. Don't you want to hear about the accident reconstructionist?"

I got back in. "Sure. What happened?"

"He rescheduled for this morning. He might be over there right now."

I checked my wrist, where my watch should have been. "What time is it?" I sighed.

"Ten-fifty."

"All right, but I have to be at Dr. Coulter's by eleven." I crossed my fingers that the dentist would dawdle over the old man.

Swinkey drove to the Black River Inn, then we walked over to Hill Street, where the reconstructionist had blocked off traffic with four sawhorses and yellow *Sheriff-Do-Not-Cross-This-Line* tape. I'd say he was a shade under 5' 10", dumpy, dressed in a brown suit. If he were a lot smaller and had whiskers, he might have passed for someone's beloved pet rat. He scampered over to greet us, a lighthearted smile on his face. We shook hands. "Lieutenant Thurm Hollis," he said. "VanBurgen Sheriff's Department."

Swinkey thanked him for coming, then asked if he had found anything. Hollis said that the scene was "badly contaminated" by all the cars that had passed through since the accident, but "maybe" we could find some evidence. We hiked up Hill Street to the point where Keith and I had awaited our snitch. Close to the curb lay shards of red and white glass. "This is where he hit us the first time," I said. Hollis squatted to examine the glass. He opened his crime kit, put on rubber gloves, then whisked the shards into a plastic bag and labeled them.

A short black skid mark lay some ten feet downhill, and more broken glass lay a few feet further. Once again Hollis bagged and labeled the debris. Then came another skid, a blank spot, and a third skid that ran all the way down to the demolished road sign. The fourth and last skid paralleled the third for several feet, curved sharply right, ran another ten feet, and ended with a smear. Hollis scrutinized chunks of the broken barrier as well as ruts in the grass by the channel.

"Sorry I couldn't make it yesterday," he said at last. "It's best to examine the scene as soon as possible. But there's still plenty here. I need to take some measurements. Then if I could see the cars?"

Swinkey said, "Car number one's a Pontiac LeMans. It's at Wessel's, drying out. Number two? Who knows?"

"Hit and run?" Hollis rubbed his paws together as if he'd gotten a tasty piece of cheese. "Maybe we'll get him on the glass." He asked Swinkey to help with measurements, then the two cops pulled yellow surveyor's instruments out of Hollis's van.

I asked Swinkey the time.

"Eleven sharp," came his reply.

"Gotta go," I said, then took off running. As I rounded the corner to Michigan Avenue, I spotted Fiona and Dennis, the old man as chaotic as I'd ever seen him. "He tried to kill me!" cried Dennis.

"No, he didn't," said Fiona. "He was just checking your teeth."

"He was killing me!" the old man insisted, ripping at the green dental bib still clipped around his neck.

"Daddy, *please,* get in the car."

My first impulse was to rush to her aid, but I knew from my brief research that running would only excite him further. So I walked quickly toward him, then slowed. I tried to catch his gaze, connect with him, but he looked everywhere but at me. "Open the car door and get hold of his right arm," said Fiona. "Maybe we can ease him in."

I did as told. We tried to pull Dennis closer to the car, but he refused to budge. For such a sick old guy, he was as strong as a doorman at a Metallica concert and just as immovable. He flailed his arms. "Where are you taking me!" he shouted. "Help! You're killing me!"

"Daddy, please!" begged Fiona.

I stepped in front of him, making eye contact at last. "Dennis," I said slowly.

"Huh?"

"Dennis, it's time for lunch."

He took awhile to answer. "I just ate."

"It's time to eat again."

He said, "I don't *want* to eat," his wild agitation suddenly reduced to mere crankiness.

"Let's go home," I urged. I waited for this idea to sink in. And then, all on his own, he stepped into the car. Fiona fastened his seat belt, shut and locked the door. She and I got into the car and we made for the Blue Star Highway.

After a time she said, accusingly, "Where *were* you?"

"I'm so sorry. My watch got ruined and I lost track of the time. Debby said your father would be done around eleven, so I ran a couple of errands. I'm sorry—I should have asked first."

"Yes, you should have!"

She was right and I admitted it, so she had nowhere to go with her tirade. "I thought he was going to get away from me," she said, "right in the middle of town."

"I'm sorry," I repeated. "It must have been scary."

She gave a sarcastic laugh. "That's putting it mildly."

At home Sean was pounding out the feverish third movement of the Rachmaninoff; music churned through the house. Fiona parked Dennis in the breakfast nook and ordered me to watch him. The music clearly upset him—he was rocking with it, violently—then abruptly it stopped and Dennis sat stock still, staring at his hands. Feeling I could safely take my eyes off him, I searched the cupboard for lunch fixings.

A pot of vegetable soup was bubbling on the stove when Fiona and Sean marched into the room, both of them glowering. I backed against the counter, the Beretta biting my spine. Oh, jeeze. The trailer. The call from Officer Cooper. With all the hubbub at the dentist's office, I'd forgotten about it.

"Who are you?" demanded Sean.

Not exactly the question I had been expecting. "Betty Jo—"

"Who are you *really?*" asked Fiona.

"I—"

"We just called West Care," she said. "They never heard of a Betty Jo Bialosky. Are you a chippy?"

"A *what?*"

Sean said, "You were seen last weekend at Sunnyside entertaining two men in succession, and standing naked in the doorway of our trailer."

What could I say to that? I'd only had sex with one of them, but the other had stripped me bare? "It wasn't like that, and no, I'm not a, uh, chippy."

"Sean said Officer Cooper called today about a fire last night at the trailer. What about that?" inquired Fiona.

"Why don't you ask your brother," I said, grasping at straws.

"Are you accusing me of setting fire to our own trailer!" he shouted, his incredulity seeming real enough.

"Just tell us who you are," said Fiona.

The jig, as they say, was up. "I'm a private investigator." At that moment I was gladder than usual that I wasn't a man, for if I had been, Sean would surely have punched me out. Instead, Fiona slapped me across the face then hopped back with a little shriek.

My face stung in the shape of her hand and suffused with heat: there I stood, the blushing sinner. I seized the pot of boiling soup to defend myself. Yes, I did have Ms. Beretta…but she's shy.

"Why are you here?" said Sean, backing away from the pot.

"I'm not at liberty to reveal that information."

"It's Bill, isn't it?" gasped Fiona.

"I'm going to leave now," I said. "I gave two honest days' work and you can keep my pay. We'll call it even." I maneuvered out of the kitchen, jiggling my hot weapon before me. I grabbed my purse, leapt outside, slammed the door behind me, then dropped the soup and ran.

I wouldn't have put it past them to phone the police to register a complaint against me, whoever I was. Some snoop causing trouble? The Shore Haven P.D. would know who: Gayle Fisher, P.I.

Doubtless, Fiona and Sean would ring up Bill Feinstein to ream him out. In its own way, this day was turning into one of the lousiest of my life. I hated to be found out, my false identity stripped from me. I thought of a cloth being yanked from a table full of food, everything crashing to the floor in a god-awful mess.

But what did I expect? I had breezed into Shore Haven not even believing that Eleanor had been murdered, then I had assumed a false identity on the spur of the moment five miles north of a dinky town where five people already knew my real name and more were learning it every day.

When I reached Sunnyside, I spun around to see if I'd been followed. I hadn't. I was about to make my escape, when I realized that I had neglected to take the cedar box. Though I hated to go back in the trailer, I craved that box.

I had to duck under crime tape again to get into the Airstream, whose insides stank of smoke and vividly recalled my near suffocation of the night before. I practically tore the box from its hiding place and probably should have run out of there right then, but some secret part of my mind prompted me to open the lid and untie the pale blue ribbon. As I reread the notes, I was jolted by a detail I had missed the first time through. Two of the notes bore the vague imprint of words that had been inscribed on earlier sheets of the pad.

I snatched up a pencil and scribbled a light layer of graphite near the bottom of one of the notes. My pulse danced as pale words showed ghost-like through the gray: *forget the Tulip Fest*. The Tulip Fest was one of Shore Haven's myriad annual events, taking place in May. Not much of a clue. I scribbled the pencil lightly over the bottom of the other note and once again, words showed through: *5:00 p.m. Mark*.

There had to be a couple dozen Marks in Shore Haven, and these notes might have come from a non-Shore-Haven Mark, yet it pleased me to speculate that they'd been sent by the tomcatting Mark VanDee. Had he and Eleanor been lovers? If only I could get a specimen of his handwriting.

Ah, but I did have one—the reckless-driving ticket he'd written two nights before.

I repacked the letters, then wrapped the box in my smoky uniform. I drove straight to Dotty's, where I got the despised ticket out of my overnight bag to compare with the note. The black *Mark* on the ticket matched the white *Mark* at the end of the second note, right down to the little hook at the end of the *k*. So the mysterious lover *was* the lascivious VanDee. But who was the woman? Eleanor? She had spent a good bit of time at the trailer in the month before she died. Hm.

I stowed the ticket with the notes, then called Swinkey from a pay phone in the restaurant's foyer. He was out on the road, but I left a message for him to meet me for lunch at Dotty's—if he had a chance. The place was crowded, but I requested a booth, saying that I expected company. Time snailed. I read and reread the menu, the plastic kind with typed specials inserted daily. The waitress refilled my water glass three times, asking at length if I'd like to go ahead and order. I said, "The salmon patties look good."

"They come with creamed peas and a baked potato."

Just then, Swinkey swung into the restaurant.

"Sergeant Swinkey," she muttered. Most of the diners glanced his way, their faces assuming guilty expressions. They hunched over their chicken pot pies and fried gizzards as though praying to the poultry god to be spared. I smiled and he joined me, insisting that we change places so he could face the door.

Men. Cops.

He studied the menu a moment, then summoned the waitress with a wave of his hand. She hastened to our table and took his order: the meat-loaf special. "Dotty makes a great meat loaf," he amiably said. "With olives. So, why the invitation?"

"It's been a crummy day," I whispered. "Sean and Fiona busted me."

Swinkey gave his little chuckle and nodded his head.

"It isn't funny." My cheek still stung from Fiona's slap. I patted it gingerly with my right hand.

"Bad girl, bad girl, what ya gonna do?"

"That's right, kick me when I'm down."

"Well, what are you gonna do?" he asked.

"I don't know. Get my car. Get out of town. Maybe take Keith with me."

"Cut your losses and run?"

I shrugged.

"Aren't you the least bit curious about who rammed you into the channel?"

"Could've been a prank," I muttered.

"And the fire? Another prank? That's Shore Haven: Prank City, U.S.A."

"Swinkey, are you encouraging me to stick with this case?"

"Maybe."

"That's very uncop-like of you."

He stood, wrapped his fingers around my left biceps, and towed me toward the door. Many a head swiveled our way and one man muttered, "Hauling her off to the clink."

Out in the parking lot I shook Swinkey's hand loose. "That was subtle," I said.

"I need privacy for what I have to say."

"Okay, go ahead." I waved toward the diner's windows: we had an audience.

Swinkey said in a low voice, "I think Feinstein is right about foul play."

"And why do *I* have to solve the case? You're the cop, for chrissake. You solve it."

"The Montague case is closed, and Chief Glenn's not about to reopen it without strong evidence. That means more than Feinstein's crazy ravings and what *could* be a pair of pranks. You got anything three dimensional?"

I thought about the Seconal as well as the hidden door that might exist between Sean's and Fiona's rooms. "No."

"Is it at all possible you *could* get something?"

"Maybe." But I couldn't tell him about it. Swinkey was a great guy and all, but he was law enforcement, and to move forward on the case I'd have to break the law. That appealed to me not at all, so I said, "My schedule's too bloated to pursue it."

Swinkey stared down at me.

"Tell you what," I said. "I'll call Feinstein and talk to him before I decide. He's the one paying for my time."

"Fair enough," said Swinkey and we strode back into Dotty's to eat, occasioning more covert glances and mumbled speculation. Blushing fiercely, I attended to the salmon patties, creamed peas, and baked potato the waitress had delivered in our absence. They were divine. They put me in such a buoyant mood, I told Swinkey, "You should've let me eat first before asking favors."

"Well, then—how about going out tonight?"

I shook my head as at a naughty toddler. "Swinkey, we're both attached—to other people." In truth, I was feeling rather loosely attached to Leversee at the time, and Swinkey had begun to grow on me, rather like a friendly fungus, and he was a good looking, strapping guy, but how could I get past the smokes and the wife?

"Look," said Swinkey. "I'm not as attached as you think."

SEVENTEEN

"ALL RIGHT," I SAID, crossing my arms. "What are you? Partially married?"

Swinkey muttered into his mustache, "Getting a divorce."

"Hmm. As in *someday* you're getting a divorce, or you're in the *middle* of a divorce."

"Exactly in the middle. It's final in December."

"So why the ring?"

He stared at the gold band encircling his finger. When it declined to open a mouth and answer for him, he spoke: "It's hard to take off."

"Try soap," I said, dryly. "Or Crisco."

"Gayle—"

"Your wife wear hers?"

"My wife? No. Trish has been seeing another guy. You met him."

"Who?"

"Gono."

"Gono?" I repeated.

"Syph. V.D."

"Oh, Van*Dee*." A gong produced its sonorous tone within my head. VanDee was sparking Mrs. John Swinkey, AKA "Oh-baby" Trish. Not only was "Gono" promiscuous, but he was also disloyal to his brother in blue. As for Swinkey, he'd been trying, in his inept way, to get back into the swing of dating and mating, unwittingly aping a man he'd come to hate.

"What's he call you?" I asked.

"Swanky, Skanky, Stanky, Stinky, Slinky—"

"Uh-huh."

"So, what about tonight?" said Swinkey in a hollow attempt at bravado.

I said, as kindly as I could, "John, you're a nice guy, but I don't think so."

My erstwhile heavenly meal lay in my stomach like a lump of clay. As we awaited our bills, my mind scrambled for some less painful topic. "Have you heard back from the accident reconstructionist?" I asked.

"Preliminary findings suggest that your account of the accident is correct," Swinkey woodenly replied.

"Wahoo."

"Hollis dug the glass, all right. Some of it belonged to your car, some to another. He wasn't sure he could identify what kind—the pieces were small."

"And my car? Can you tell me where it is?"

While Swinkey gave directions to Wessel's, the waitress slapped our bills on the table. Swinkey grabbed both and I let him. Why be a complete jerk?

FIFTEEN MINUTES LATER I was eyeballing my LeMans at Wessel's Auto Repair. The silver car basked in the sun, windows down, a fall breeze flowing through, drying the interior. Or so I hoped. An old man in greasy overalls ambled over from the office, introduced himself as Herman Wessel, then smiled his face into a mass of yellow wrinkles and chaw-stained teeth.

I owned that the LeMans was mine. "Will it ever run again?" I inquired.

"It *could*," he said. "Gotta drain the fluids, replace 'em. Electronics might be shot. Right front fender needs fixin', an alignment wouldn't hurt. You hafta have new tail lights, of course. I got an old Rainbow machine's good at sucking up water. We'd run that on the interior. Got insurance?"

"Yes, but I'm not sure this type of damage is covered."

"And don't forget the cost of dredging your vehicle out of the channel."

"I'll take it up with my insurance agent, give you a call soon as I find out." I declined to shake the man's hand—it was black with grease—but I bid him as cordial a goodbye as possible, given that I didn't know when I'd get my car back or how deeply in debt the repairs would put me. Maybe they'd cost the usual: more than the damn car was worth. I rubbed my sore jaw and headed for the hospital.

By the time I arrived, Keith had been gurneyed to Floor I where he shared a room with a graybeard whose plastered leg hung in traction. I pulled the canvas "privacy" curtain—there's a misnomer—and squatted next to Keith. I whispered, "Remember anything yet?"

He mouthed a no.

"Let me refresh your memory. I asked if you'd heard anything about the Coulter job, and you said you'd check around. You called me later, said some guy with information would meet us on Hill Street at nine p.m. When we got there, a car rammed us into the channel."

A frown of concentration creased the kid's brow, then he slowly shook his head. "I'm sorry, I can't…."

"Nothing? Nothing at all?"

"Uh uh."

He looked so ashamed, I quickly said, "It's okay. But tell me, if you wanted to know who pulled the robbery, who would you ask?"

"I donno…folks who come into the shop?"

"Makes sense. Would you ask everyone?"

"No. Not people from out of town."

"Good," I said. "You'd talk to townies who stopped in."

"Yeah."

"And would you ask all the townies?"

"No, just the ones I know."

"And who are they?"

"Mostly clerks on their breaks, shoppers, guys from the hospital, kids from the beach."

"And how many guys would this be?"

"Let's see…twenty, thirty. Forty, if it's a good day."

"Keith, could you jot me a list? Male townies who typically come into the shop on Sundays—the ones whose names you know."

He grimaced. "My vision's kinda low-res right now—doctor says it oughta be back to normal in a day or two. Could I write the list then?"

"Sure, Keith. Whenever you're ready." I patted his hand, then said, "I'm worried about your safety. You can't remember who rammed us, but he knows who you are. You're a threat to this person. Understand?"

He nodded.

"Maybe he's long gone. Maybe he's hanging around, waiting for a chance. I want you some place safe."

"My house is safe."

"With your parents out of town? You'd be all alone."

His dark eyes lit up. "You could stay with me. There's plenty of room."

"I don't think so. I seem to be a magnet for disaster these days—flood, fire, plague of frogs, you name it. Could you hole up with someone up at Grand Valley? A friend? Preferably someone from another town."

"Well, sure, but I'd be more help if I was here."

"You know how you can really help? By writing that list and staying alive."

His dark eyes went wide. "Arty, my cousin, he's got a place in Alvindale. I could crash on his couch."

"Great."

Keith agreed to check himself out of the hospital right then. The supervising nurse labeled me a "negative influence" and urged him to stay. No dice. I drove Keith home to pack books and clothes, then I took him up to Alvindale and got him settled in Arty's apartment. Keith promised to write the list and call Swinkey if his memory returned.

I rolled back into Shore Haven about four p.m.—or so I judged by the westerly position of the sun. My first order of business was to buy a watch for $9.99 plus tax at the drugstore. Then I returned to the Shore Haven Public Library where the ginger-haired librarian shot me a bright smile of recognition. I located the latest version of the *PDR* and read up on Seconal: it's habit forming, a barbiturate, a sedative, and a hypnotic. It acts in as little as fifteen minutes, impairing mental and physical abilities. Caution is urged in prescribing it to persons with suicidal tendencies, as toxic effects and fatalities may occur following overdose, the symptoms of which include "sluggish reflexes, respiratory depression, circulatory collapse, pulmonary edema, and coma." If an overdose of Seconal hadn't made Eleanor malleable, nothing would. I flipped to page 414 for a color plate of the drug: a slim red capsule bearing the imprint, *Lilly F40*.

Then I looked up Tylenol 3, Nembutal, and Percodan, all heavy-duty painkillers that in a large enough dose could kill the patient along with the pain. Seconal, Tylenol 3, Nembutal, and Percodan—these were the drugs I'd found in Fiona's drawer. I was about to reshelve the *PDR,* when the librarian bustled by and said she'd do it for me. I was going to explain that having been a librarian myself, I could easily handle the operation, when she let fly with an explanation of her own. "People want to help out,

I know, but when books are misshelved it's such a mess. Why, it took me a week to find *The Encyclopedia of Music* last May." She adjusted the cuffs on her teal suit and grinned.

"Sounds frustrating," I commiserated. I'd had a similar experience myself, with *The Rubaiyat of Omar Khayyam,* in a library ten times as big.

When I handed her the PDR, she exclaimed, "Are you in the medical profession?" She wore a gold charm bracelet that jingled as she grew excited.

"Sort of. I'm a home health-care aide. I mean, I was."

"Really? Who for?"

"The Montagues, out on—"

"Oh, the Montagues! Mr. Montague was such a wonderful pianist! It's a shame…."

I nodded in agreement.

"And such an intriguing house."

"Beautiful—"

"Oh, more than beautiful. It was built by a bootlegger, you know, during prohibition. It's a perfect location—the lake on one side, the creek on the other. You'd be surprised at all the houses around here with secret doors and hidden passages."

"Really?"

"Yes. And hidey holes to stash money, Canadian Club, and the occasional member of the Purple Gang."

"Is that so…"

"Oh, yes," she said, jangling the bracelet with a flip of her wrist. "Shore Haven has had a 'purple' past."

Secrets doors, indeed! Had Debby been telling the truth?

I STOPPED AT DOTTY'S to call my answering machines. Iggy had left a message: "I'm on the case." Heh! Good old Iggy. There was also a message from Leversee, inquiring in his cop voice where I was.

Let him stew, I thought. Then I called Bill Feinstein in Detroit.

"What the hell did you do to them?" he demanded, in lieu of greeting.

Them, I presumed, was Sean and Fiona. "I cleaned their house, weeded their garden, and kept an eye on Dennis for two and a half days. For free. Think that's a jailable offense?"

"No." He sounded glum. Maybe he wanted me jailed.

"Besides, they don't know my name."

"Correction: they don't know your last name. I referred to you as Gayle."

I grunted in annoyance. "Do me a favor. Don't tell them the rest." Not that they couldn't figure it out easily enough.

"Did you *find* anything?"

"I'm no further along than I was the last time we spoke—except someone's tried to kill me again—or scare me off." I told him about the fire.

"And you say Sean might have set the fire?"

"I said it's *possible,* but I kind of doubt—"

"That murderous, anti-Semitic son of a bitch."

Bill was anything but logical when it came to Sean Montague. "Look," I said, "if he's anti-Semitic, why did he marry your sister?"

"I don't know."

"Well, why do you call him anti-Semitic?"

"What am I supposed to call a guy who refers to me as 'a crazy Jew'?"

"I see." I cringed a little before asking my next question. "I'm kind of curious about something, Bill. Could your sister have been having an affair?"

"What?" His voice had jumped an octave.

"I'm checking all the angles. If she were having an affair, that could give someone a motive." Someone, meaning Sean, VanDee, or any insanely jealous girlfriends *he* might have.

"I—I don't know, Gayle."

"Okay, here's where we stand. I'd been hoping to get into the room where your sister…was discovered. I thought I might dig up evidence to give the police cause to reopen the investigation. Now that I've been found out and kicked out, it'll be harder to get into that room. I don't know how long it'll take. Maybe I'll never get in."

I heard a sigh over the line. "Stay with it. Please."

I DROVE TO MA & PA'S and asked Pa if he had any cabins with a telephone. His wizened face crumpled in puzzlement, so I told him, "The cabin I rented last night had no phone."

"Dang it all, musta someone went and stole that thang." He squinted at me with suspicion. "That's the third 'un I lost so far this year."

"I didn't do it. So. You got a cabin with a phone?"

"Yeah," he said at last. I relinquished another thirty dollars, leaving my wallet practically flat. My host led me to a shack close by, this one appointed much as the last.

As soon as Pa had beat an arthritic retreat, I lay down on the sway-back bed to think.

This is what I came up with. The house next to the Montague's—the one owned by Dr. Krevitz from Chicago—was closed for the season. The yard was surrounded by a hedge. A great place to set up surveillance.

The temperature was supposed to drop to forty that night, so I dressed in two shirts, a sweater, a jacket, and slacks. I stopped at DeMuntt's to pick up supper—a small bottle of o.j. and a chocolate-chunk cookie, great for surveillance because they're filling, keep one awake, and require few trips to the sandbox.

By five-thirty I had parked at Sunnyside, trekked up Beach Street, peeked in the Montague garage to make sure Fiona's car was inside, and ensconced myself in the good doctor's yard. I waited there on the off chance that Fiona, Dennis, and Sean would all traipse off, maybe for ice cream, so I could break in.

I had brought along a few extra sleuthing tools, including a five-inch Mag-Lite and a set of lock picks. I hated to resort to these latter, because if I were caught using them, I could be jailed for home invasion. *Home invasion.* I love that term. Sounds like what an alien does before beaming you up to the saucer for some vile physical exam.

Little by little, the sun dipped toward the pink horizon. The breeze picked up and the air chilled. Waves smacked the beach. I wrapped a silk scarf around my head and waited. Sean was tormenting the piano. It was the Rachmaninoff, the passionate first movement. Presently, someone stepped lively along the road and up the Montagues' front walk. I peered through the hedge at Patty the practical nurse. She rang the bell and Fiona answered the door. They greeted one another with friendly hugs, and Patty entered the house. An hour later, she left.

By then it was dark. I stared at the luminous dial on my cheap new watch as the minutes ticked by. Suddenly, the Montagues' door swung open. The old man, in gray sweats and boat shoes, scurried down the walk; a moment later Fiona flew out behind him. "Daddy, please, come back. Daddy!" She seized hold of him, but Dennis shook her off, as he might an importunate stranger, then he strode out into the street, heading south. Fiona had little choice but to stay with him. I peeked between the leafy branches of the front hedge just as Fiona caught up with her father. She grabbed his arm to pull him back toward home, but he shoved her so hard she fell down. She cried out with pain and glanced back at the house, as though struggling over what to do, then scrambled to her feet and chased the old man down Sand Creek Road. I could have gotten up right then, run after Fiona, helped her. But I thought of the slap she had dealt me, the hatred in her eyes. So I chose to let *her* work it out—a decision I would profoundly regret.

From where I was hiding, I could see only so far down the road, and Fiona's calls grew ever fainter. I kept thinking she'd get him turned around. Meanwhile, Sean kept at the keys, playing intricate passages slowly, then faster and faster, like mounting hysteria. This was insane—I had to go help. I rose and ran to Sand Creek Road, yet by the time I arrived, both father and daughter had vanished.

Sand Creek Road bridges Sand Creek, beyond whose eastern bank lies a wooded area. Had Dennis entered the woods and Fiona followed? In the dark, they were liable to get lost or hurt. Maybe both. I called, "Fiona!"

From deep in the woods came a cry: "Help me! Please!"

I reached in my purse for the Mag-Lite, clicked it on, and picked my way between maples and oaks. I swept the flashlight back and forth before me, its thin beam lighting trunks and leaves—not much use. I yelled, "Fiona! I'm coming!"

"Gayle? What are you doing out here?"

"I thought you needed some help!"

She made no reply.

"Do you want help?" I asked.

"I twisted my ankle. And Daddy's got away, I'm not sure where. Please, go to the house, tell Sean to call the police!"

"All right, I'm going." I stumbled back out of the woods and sprinted to the house. I rang the bell and banged on the door, but Sean was thundering on his instrument and seemed not to hear me. I ran around to the north porch—a room littered with piano scores, CD's, magazines, and books. Sean was hunched over the huge piano, face shiny with sweat, fingers racing with fantastic speed and power. Then he bounced slightly from the plush piano bench and pounced on the keys, putting some shoulder into it, like a boxer. Despite the emergency, I couldn't help thinking, *What a marvelous pianist.*

I banged my fists on the closed windows and yelled, "Sean!"

Abruptly, he stopped playing. He turned to me, surprise, anger, suspicion, and worry all struggling to claim his face. He pointed a vehement finger toward the front door and I hurried to meet him.

"What do you want?" he coldly inquired.

"Your father's got out again. Fiona followed, now they're in the woods. She's hurt her ankle and your father's wandered off. She wants you to call the police."

Sean slammed the door in my face.

I began pounding the door with both fists and Sean opened it again. "I'm trying to call the police," he spat, then heaved the door closed with finality.

I trotted back to the woods. "Fiona?" I called.

"Yes?"

"Sean's phoning the police."

"Thank you."

Before long, Sean came loping down the road. "You can *leave* now," he told me, then started into the woods with no flashlight.

I caught hold of his arm. "Sean, don't go in like that—you could get hurt, too. Wait for the police."

He shoved me away, yelled, "Fiona! Dad!"

"Sean! Daddy's lost!"

A gust of wind shook the leaves in the trees. At that, the young pianist stumbled into the woods.

Two sirens sounded in the distance, one a howl, the other a *blaaaaaat*. The sirens grew louder, then I saw headlights, like excited eyes, racing toward me. I stepped into the road and waved my arms. A police car and a fire-department rescue truck skidded to a halt, five men leaping from the vehicles. The police were Bigalow and VanDee. "A woman's in the woods," I blurted. "She's hurt her ankle. And an old man with Alzheimer's, he's wandering around back there. And a young man too." I yelled into the woods: "Fiona!"

"Please hurry!" she wailed.

The three-man rescue squad took up big flashlights with strong beams and pushed into the woods. Bigalow detached the flashlight from his utility belt and followed. VanDee eyed me appraisingly, though I'm not sure as what. Prisoner? Sex partner? Torture victim? "You sure stay in the thick of things," he said.

"Sometimes it's unavoidable."

We stood there a minute, me thinking about him hustling Swinkey's wife and Debby the dental assistant—and Eleanor or Fiona. Maybe both. My gullet clenched with revulsion. What was it that they found so irresistible? Yes, he had the face and form of an Aryan god, but Nazi-boy would need a complete personality transplant before he'd appeal to me.

Just then the rescue squad carried Fiona out of the woods, Sean in tow. Under the flashlights' beams the siblings looked wild—clothes muddy, faces scratched, red hair tangled with twigs and leaves. "You've got to go back for my father," wept Fiona. "What if he falls into the creek? He could drown—"

EIGHTEEN

"TAKE IT EASY, MA'AM," said one of the rescue men to Fiona, as he and his partners lifted her into their truck.

VanDee approached Sean. "Now the old man, your father—he's senile?"

"He has Alzheimer's disease," answered Sean, eyes glinting with ice.

"People like that can be hard to find," said the cop, in a voice devoid of feeling. He might have been talking about a bolt in a basement workshop.

"What do mean?" demanded the young pianist.

"Sometimes they get lost in the woods or a corn field. Next person to see 'em's a hunter come deer season."

"But you're going to search," insisted Sean.

I cast VanDee a scowl of exasperation, willing him to shut up. "Sure they are," I said. "But it's tough at night—you understand."

"But he's out there alone," said Sean. "He must be terrified."

"Do you have a picture of your dad? A recent one? Maybe the police can have it put on TV," I suggested. "Then if he comes out on a road, someone might recognize him."

While VanDee and Sean strode off to the house for a photo, one of the rescue men waved me over for a powwow. "Looks like Ms. Montague's right ankle is sprained," he said. "We're taking her to the hospital to have it checked out. She wondered if you'd follow us, give her a ride home after the doctor's seen her, so her brother can stay here. In the event that their father shows up."

I said, "Sure," amazed that Fiona had gotten over her grudge so fast that she preferred me to a taxi. On the other hand, I was free and a cab might cost fifteen dollars or more.

I arrived at Community Hospital some twenty minutes later. Nurse Ryanne was at intake. At my request to see Fiona, she led me to a large room divided into two "Areas" by a huge canvas curtain. In Area 1 a baby screamed, then wept, while soft voices attempted without success to console it. Fiona lay on a gurney in Area 2. The damaged ankle—purple, swollen, and stripped of its sandal—reposed on a blue bag of ice. I ventured a grin. Fiona's lips quivered into a one-side smile, then subsided into a grim line.

A nurse came to clean the scratches on the patient's face; as she winced, I made myself useful by pulling twigs out of her red hair. When the nurse left, Fiona asked, "Were you spying on us tonight?"

I shrugged. "It's what I do."

"And your name's not Betty—it's Gayle?"

I shrugged again.

"Look, I don't know what Bill told you, but Eleanor was not murdered—and certainly not by Sean. It's ludicrous to think so."

"Why?"

"Well, Eleanor was crazy about Sean."

"That's great. But how'd he feel about her?"

Fiona leaned forward to adjust the bag of ice. "My brother's not what you'd call demonstrative. But they were practically newlyweds. That ought to tell you something."

"Newlyweds? I was married for four months and hated every minute of it." An exaggeration. For about an hour each day, I did experience marital bliss—my ex had certain desirable skills. But fifteen waking hours and eight dreaming hours of abrasion each day, day after day, will grind at the one good hour till it's worn to grit. Lest you think I exaggerate, let me remind you: we both worked at the Collingwood Public Library. He was inescapable.

I was ready to make a mountain out of Fiona's inability to meet my gaze. She was hiding something about Eleanor's relationship with Sean. Maybe, heaven help her, about her own.

The doctor chose that moment to abandon the whimpering baby for Fiona. Everything about him was tastefully subtle: nicely tall, quietly good looking, professionally warm. His costume included well tailored brown slacks, crisp white shirt, blue silk tie, and flapping lab coat. He introduced himself as Dr. Boyer, then gently rotated Fiona's ankle. When she bit back a cry of pain, his amber eyes turned sad in silent apology. I assessed him as young, nice, rich, and ringless—a perfect match for Fiona.

Dr. Boyer ordered an x-ray of the damaged joint, extending our visit by an another hour. Finally, he was able to affirm that the ankle was badly sprained but unbroken. He injected the patient with Prednisolone, then strapped the ankle, doled out ten Tylenol 3's, and loaned her a pair of crutches so she could get around. But not at the hospital. We had to go through the rigmarole of the wheelchair. You know, they wheel you out to your car so you can't fall down while leaving the hospital and sue them.

Fiona and I got back to the house by midnight. Sean met her at the door and helped her into the living room. "You can go now," he informed me in his typically arrogant way.

"No," said Fiona. "I want her to stay. We have nothing to hide—and maybe she can help."

"Help? She's trying to prove I killed my wife!"

"But you didn't, so what's the harm of having her around?"

"Why not Patty instead?" said Sean.

"Oh, for heaven's sake, she's already been here once today," replied Fiona. "Let the poor girl sleep!"

Sean opened his mouth, but Fiona glared at him and he said nothing.

I gave what I hoped was an angelic smile.

"Any word about Daddy?" asked Fiona.

Sean replied, "No. They're not even looking tonight. Officer VanDee said they'd have fifty people out first thing in the morning."

Fiona's face flamed as red as her hair. "That—that son of a bitch! Tomorrow's too late! It's much too cold for Daddy outdoors."

"I know. I was just waiting for you to get back," Sean said, grabbing his jacket from the closet.

"No, Sean, please don't!" she implored. "What if you get hurt?"

He was rifling through a kitchen drawer. "Christ, Fiona, that's our father out there!"

"Please, Sean—don't go!"

Sean snatched a flashlight from the drawer and bolted from the house, leaving Fiona in tears. I did my best to calm her, then persuaded her to lie down on the couch and prop her ankle on a bag of ice. I fetched a glass of water so she could take a pain pill, my altruistic behavior counterbalanced by my desire to get into the locked room. If Sean stayed away and Fiona dozed off, I might get my wish.

At least, that was the plan. Fiona wanted tea, so I said, "All that caffeine's liable to upset you." *And keep you awake,* I mentally added.

"It's not coffee," she said. "Tea's relaxing. Just a little cup."

I couldn't very well say no, so I made her a cup, letting the bag steep for a ten count and no longer. After a sip, she said the tea was too weak, I should go get the bag and let it steep some more. I said, "Sorry, I threw it away."

She said, "Never mind," and clicked on the TV with the

remote control. There she lay watching an old Hitchcock film
that starred Teresa Wright as a sweet young girl and Joseph
Cotton as her sly, murderous uncle. I watched too. Betty Jo
might have volunteered to wash the windows or wax the floor,
but I was Gayle and Gayle said to hell with it.

During a newsbreak a picture of Dennis flashed on the screen,
and a beefy newsman announced that the famous pianist was
missing in Shore Haven. I glanced at Fiona to catch her reaction,
but she lay with eyes closed, oblivious.

Time to move.

I looped my purse over my neck and made for the stairs. I
climbed them in silence, avoiding the creaker with a giant step.
I closed myself into Fiona's room and turned on the bedside
lamp. The wardrobe stood open. I parted the clothes and swam
into the dark, the roots of my hair tingling with elation and revulsion at what I might find. As Fiona's clothes pushed at my
ribs, I groped the wardrobe's back panel for signs of a door.
Nothing: no hinges, no hasp. A flush of annoyance suffused my
body, and I chided myself for believing the secondhand blather
of Debby the ditz.

But then my fingers touched a seam. I traced it from the top
of the wardrobe down to the floor, then across to the right a
couple of feet, then up again to the top. A door. When I shoved
it hard with my hip, it popped open with a *suck* and stopped with
a *clunk*.

I pushed through the opening to the other side, expecting to come
out in Sean's wardrobe, but instead I stood in a narrow passage. It
was airless, black. Something skittered across my feet, light as
animated bones. I stifled an "Eek!" then shuddered with claustro-
phobia. Once again, I recalled being locked in that old refrigerator.
I had pounded and screamed but no one had heard, and finally I
had passed out. Luckily, my father had rescued me from the white
prison before I suffocated, but ever since, I've hated to be confined.

I had to force myself to shut the secret door behind me.

I got out my little Mag-Lite and flicked it on. I was in a two-foot-wide strip between Fiona's and Sean's rooms, a bootlegger's hidden closet that stank of mouse scat and dust. The closet was cobwebbed and stacked with boxes at either end. Before me stood another door, its hasp closed by an old wooden clothes pin. I removed the pin and placed it on the floor, then pulled at the door until it gave.

I stepped forward into another sea of clothes, wriggled through them, and at long last pushed at Sean's wardrobe door. It refused to budge. With rising anxiety, I heaved a shoulder against the door—once, twice, three times—until it popped open, and I stumbled into a frigid room.

Evil vibrated the air, like a bloated corpse somehow alive.

The beam of my flashlight played along the Matisse prints, the disheveled bed, and the plaster littering the oriental carpet. I aimed the light at the ceiling, into a big black hole and along an exposed beam. I envisioned the sheet and the swaying corpse.

Suddenly a shape dived at my head. I crouched, heart racing, as it sailed past my ear. It was black and had wings. A bat? No, a blackbird! Curtains floated in the wind, beckoning the bird. It seemed to hang in mid air, then plunged into the night. I giggled—half in horror, half in relief.

I swept my light cross the mahogany dresser, which no longer blocked the door. The drinking glass was still on the beside table, but the pillbox was gone. A gust of wind played at the curtains, and they fluttered and flapped as if alive.

Just then someone seized me from behind and spun me around. "What do you want?" he demanded. It was Sean, a man whose ability to sneak dwarfed even my own. He had entered the room as I had, but silently. The Mag-Lite dropped from my hand, leaving the room nearly black. Sean began to shake me, whipping my head back and forth, clacking my teeth like castanets. "Why are you here?" he shouted. "You voyeur, you ghoul!"

I couldn't let him rattle my head off my shoulders, so I jammed my knee into his groin, contacting soft organs and hard pubis. As he crouched groaning in what I hoped was agony, I snatched the Beretta from the back of my pants, clicked on the bedside lamp, and took aim. Sean writhed into the fetal position, rendered temporarily harmless.

"What are you looking for?" came his anguished cry.

"The truth. Eleanor's death was no locked-room suicide and you know it. Why didn't you tell the police?"

Sean pressed his eyes to his forearm. "I—I wanted it cleared up as quickly as possible. The passage only complicates matters. I knew Fiona and Dad and I hadn't—"

"You had no reason to want her dead?"

"No, she was my wife, I loved her—"

"Loved her?" I said incredulously. "What do you know about love, you icy son of a bitch?"

"I hope you lose someone you love to suicide—see how you feel."

"She must've adored that vengeful streak."

He pierced me with a knife-sharp gaze. "Fuck you."

"Let's see now. We've established that you're a liar, a sneak, a person who hides evidence from the police, cold, vengeful—"

"Shut up!"

Of course, that didn't necessarily mean he was a murderer. I shared the same traits—except for being cold and vengeful—and I was no murderer. Not that I wouldn't protect myself if someone tried to kill me.

Sean lay huddled on the floor. But as what? Killer? Grief-crazed widower? Selfish prick? "You should have told the police. Suppose your wife *was* murdered—by someone other than you, let's say. Would you want that person to go free?"

"No, but—"

"But maybe she did hang herself. Maybe she learned some grotesque truth and it drove her to suicide."

"Like what?" Sean looked up, anger and puzzlement corrugating his face.

"That you and Fiona were lovers."

"What? *What?* That's insane!"

"Are you telling me that you and Fiona aren't lovers?"

"She's my sister, for God's sake. What you're saying—it's monstrous."

"Yes." I studied his face, and no, he didn't *seem* to be lying. "Someone told me that Eleanor had found you and Fiona in bed together. Naturally, this disturbed her. So much so, she ended her life. But you or Fiona—or both of you—might have killed her to silence her."

"That's deranged. Who would spread such lies?"

"I'm not at liberty to say."

"Anyone who'd say that is hateful, crazy—"

"Whatever." I gestured with the gun for him to stand, then I slid back the bolt on the bedroom door. I turned the knob, but the door would not open.

"You need a key to open that door," he said.

"Then open it," I said.

"I lost the key." The smug look on his face made him look quite jolly.

I kicked the door, expecting it to fly open. It didn't. The bolt might have been a flimsy gimcrack but oddly enough the lock wasn't. I kicked the door again with enough force to hurt my ankle, knee, and hip; the door shuddered but remained closed. I wasn't about to turn my back on him to pick the lock open, so Sean and I would have to exit the room as we had entered, a chilling prospect.

Fiona called from downstairs, "What's going on up there?"

"She's pulled a gun on me!" shouted Sean.

"Get through that wardrobe," I ordered, "and don't try anything slick or I'll shoot."

He slid through the wardrobe and when I waded in behind, he banged the door in my face. If he could slip the clothespin back into the hasp, I'd be trapped. But I had foreseen this trick; I jammed the Mag-Lite into my back pocket and slammed into the door with my tender shoulder. Sean fell back and I surged into the secret closet. He pounced on me and I was so scared, I forgot to be claustrophobic. Meanwhile, from out on the stairs came a series of thuds, growing ever closer.

Fiona.

As Sean tried to rip the gun from my hand, I flicked open the safety, then struggled to pull our hands down to where I, a head shorter, would have greater control. But Sean pulled inexorably up, his massive fingers squeezing mine against the gun until bone met metal in crushing pain. My only chance was to turn his power against him. I shrieked, "Get away!" and jerking our hands straight up, I shot off a thunderous round. Fiona screamed. Sean let go of my hands, pried open the door to Fiona's room, and dashed through. I followed, both of us tumbling onto her bed.

I leveled the gun on him. "That shot was just a warning," I gasped, scrambling to my feet. "The next time I'm aiming at your heart." Fiona stood on crutches in the doorway, jaw dropped. She gaped first at Sean backing off, hands raised; second, at the wardrobe; and third, at the gun. I used it to motion her into a room that was now as horrific as the one next door. Opening the passage seemed to have released Eleanor's righteous anger into the rest of the house. "Have a seat," I commanded. "Both of you."

Fiona obeyed, settling awkwardly on the bed. Sean sat next to her, then seemed to think better of it, sliding cross-legged to the floor. "Someone told 'Betty-Gayle' we're incestuous," he blurted. "Eleanor supposedly found out, so we supposedly killed her."

Fiona's face blanched with outrage. "But you can't believe—"

"Oh, I can believe all kinds of things. Your brother just attacked me—twice."

Fiona cried, "Sean!" and burst into tears. Sean rubbed his musical knuckles as though yearning to punch me.

"Who was it?" she demanded. "Who spread such filth?"

"That's my secret," I replied. I told Fiona to drop her crutches off the bed, and she obliged, letting them clatter to the floor. "Where do you keep your stockings?" I asked, as if I didn't know. Sobbing full-bore, like a devastated baby, she pointed at the top drawer of her dresser.

I turned the gun on Sean. "Kneel and hold your arms straight out behind you," I said.

"What is this? An execution-style killing?"

"Do it."

He threw me a hate look, which I patiently returned. Then he complied. I knotted a pair of beige pantyhose around his wrists, told him to lie flat on his stomach, and wrapped another pair around his ankles. Amazingly useful items, pantyhose.

At last I took my leave of the Montagues, Sean trussed neater than a Christmas turkey and Fiona weeping on the bed, crutchless. I ran downstairs to the kitchen to call Swinkey. When his answering machine kicked in, I said, "I have new information on Eleanor's death, maybe good enough to reopen the case."

Then I phoned the station and Bigalow answered. After identifying myself, I told him I had new evidence regarding Eleanor's death and suggested he pick up Fiona and Sean for questioning. I said, "Do it as soon as possible." I banged the receiver back into its cradle, hastened out to Dr. Krevitz's yard to pick up the debris of my abandoned surveillance, then raced to the parking lot at Sunnyside. Wheezing, I searched my purse for car keys. Fiona might have untied Sean by then, and he could be out hunting me—with a gun, for all I knew, though his bare hands were lethal enough.

What I saw next stopped me cold.

Parked on the far end of the lot was a dark old beater. Naturally, I pulled out my Mag-Lite to investigate. The vehicle was a Chevy Malibu, navy blue, its front bumper creased and right headlight broken. I wrote the license number in my note pad: 574PRC. Was this the vehicle that had chased Keith and me down Hill Street? Were Sean or Fiona keeping a second car in this lot? The Malibu's locks were the old kind that could be flipped up with a hanger, so I retrieved one from my trunk and speedily fashioned a straight wire with a hook at one end. I wiggled this impromptu tool through the rubber stripping by the driver's window and raised the lock.

To keep my prints off, I wound my head scarf around my hand. Then I opened the car, beelining for the glove box, often a treasure trove. In this case, the trove held nothing but audio-tapes of piano concertos.

I copied the Vehicle Number from the dashboard onto my note pad, just in case. Once upon a time, when I was a junior detective, I sought information on a BMW that turned out to be wearing a stolen plate. Had I taken the Vehicle Number, I could have used it to learn who owned the car and if it had been reported stolen.

A search under the front seat turned up a quarter, two dimes, and a nickel. The back seat yielded six empty Faygo cans, nothing more. Beater car plus broken headlight plus piano concertos might just add up to Sean Montague ramming my car into the channel. I jotted one last reminder on my note pad: *Have Swinkey run 574PRC ASAP.*

NINETEEN

BACK AT MA & PA'S, I parked behind my cabin, in case—well, just in case. I phoned Swinkey at home, again raising the answering machine. After my refusal, perhaps he had gone out and hustled someone else. Some nurse or waitress or beach bunny. As the sailors say, any port in a storm. I didn't really begrudge him the shore leave, but I wanted that plate run. I left him a message to call me at Ma & Pa's, no matter when he came in.

True, I could have asked Carry Veen at the Collingwood County Sheriff's Department to run the plate. But she would have lectured me first, then dribbled out the information in her own sweet day or two or three. As for Leversee, he would have lectured, then given me zip.

Exhausted, but still nerved up from the evening's events, I jammed a chair under the door knob (the poor-man's dead bolt), set my gun on the bedside table, then lay down on the covers fully dressed, except for my shoes. Sometime in the night I drifted off.

I woke before the sun at 5:05 a.m., according to my new watch. As the cabin was frigid, I switched on the space heater and showered, the soothing warmth on my aching body offsetting the water's sulfur stench. I stuck my limbs into the same clothes I'd worn for the past twenty-four hours; why gussy up for a stalk through the woods? I phoned Swinkey a third time. Still no answer. I cursed him for his night of lust, then packed my belongings into the rental's trunk. Again.

The lake breeze had grown cold, making me to shiver beneath my jacket. I thought of poor Dennis in the woods: how could an old man's flesh endure a night so cold?

I took off for Dotty's. Unable to stomach breakfast, I ordered a large cup of hot tea to go, then drove to Sand Creek Road to join the search for Dennis Montague. The shoulder was lined with police vehicles—a Shore Haven Police car, an idling State Police cruiser, and three Chevy Tahoes marked *K-9*. I parked and walked to the cruiser where a trooper was studying a topographical map. When I tapped on his window, he jerked in surprise, patted his holstered gun as though touching a rabbit's foot for luck, then slowly emerged from the car. He was the quintessential trooper: a good six-six, in his early thirties, dark eyed, dark haired, and extremely well groomed, even at 5:45 a.m. That's a trooper for you, part he-man, part pretty boy. Instead of the state-police uniform, he wore midnight-blue fatigues. Search garb. We introduced ourselves to one another; his name was Henson. I asked how the search was going.

"There's three dog teams working the area," he said, "but we haven't found the old gentleman yet."

"How long they been at it?"

He examined his watch. "A little over two hours. It's not a bad night for the dogs—cool, moist, a little breeze—but they've got their limits. It's a big area. Woods, swamp, creek, fields."

"And Mr. Montague's a fast walker."

"So they say."

"I'd like to join the foot search, if you have one planned."

"We ought to know in an hour," he said. "The dogs track off the freshest human scent, so we need the area to be free of civilians. If the dogs fail to find the old man, we'll call in the helicopter. The area has to be clear for that as well."

"I could help," I said. "If people drive up, I could tell them to stay out."

Henson smiled, revealing perfectly straight teeth, except for a twisted lower cuspid. "That's my job," he said. "But thanks anyway." He returned to the map and I trudged back to my car to sip tea. I had nearly finished it when branches began to shake at the edge of the woods. In the light of pale dawn, a German shepherd in harness led a wiry young man out from among the trees. The dog was stocky and blunt-faced, a European shepherd, as most Michigan search dogs are. The young man wore boots, dark fatigues, and infrared headgear for night vision. A few minutes later two more teams burst from the woods, dogs and trainers all slick with mud. My stomach knotted with fear for the old man.

More vehicles began to arrive, mostly small trucks, giving Trouper Henson some work to do. Meanwhile, the handlers watered their exhausted dogs, loaded them into the Tahoes, and left. A helicopter arrived, all pocka-pocka noise and artificial wind, making multiple passes overhead, until at last it, too, wheeled away.

A queasy feeling climbed my esophagus.

At full dawn the road was crammed with the cars and trucks of volunteers who had come to hunt for Dennis Montague. I recognized several of the searchers: Mrs. Hogoboom of the Black River B & B, some good old boys from Dotty's, Patty the practical nurse, scrawny old Pa, and Sean Montague. I wondered how long it had taken Fiona to untie him and if Bigalow had deigned to drop by.

Swinkey had arrived, as had a lieutenant from the VanBurgen Sheriff's Department and a dozen members of the Sheriff's Reserves. The rest of the crowd were members of the County Disaster Team, volunteer fire fighters, fruit pickers on loan from the Defresnes Winery, hunters in hip boots, and assorted townies—some fifty searchers in all. The Montagues may have been artsy and aloof, and Dennis Montague a demented old pianist; but the Montagues were *their* artsy and aloof fellow citizens, and Dennis *their* demented old pianist.

Swinkey explained to the crowd how to avoid getting lost or hurt, as well as how to approach a man with Alzheimer's so as not to "spook him"…should he still be conscious. Small compasses were distributed, as were metal whistles. Searchers were to blow one long blast every two minutes if they got hurt or found Mr. Montague. Two blasts of a car horn would signal the searchers to return to the road. Then Swinkey assigned them to the marsh, woods, or corn field, according to their tracking abilities or lack there of. People asking questions besieged him, but at last I had a chance to speak with him in semi-privacy. "Did you get my messages?" I asked.

"What messages?"

"I left them on your home answering machine. If you spent the night in your own bed, you'd know."

"I was out here all night with the State boys," he griped. "Didn't get home till four-thirty. I slept two hours, washed up, came back."

"Poor Swinkey," I said, ashamed of thinking he had been carousing. Up close, I could see circles under his bloodshot eyes.

"So what's the message?" he asked with impatience.

"I found a car last night, parked at Sunnyside. An old Chevy Malibu, navy, front bumper dented, headlight broken out, license plate number 574PRC."

"You gotta have more than that."

"I looked around inside—the door wasn't locked," I lied. "I found a bunch of piano concertos on cassette in the glove compartment. So I'm thinking maybe it's Sean's car, but there's no room in the garage for his car, so he parks it at Sunnyside."

A spark shone in Swinkey's tired eyes. "Follow me," he said. We strolled back to his police Caprice, where he typed the plate number into his lap top. While awaiting an answer from the Law

Enforcement Information Network, he asked the Shore Haven dispatcher to forward his messages from the station. These came up in an e-mail box within the larger screen. I was eyeing the first message, a tip about a stolen dirt bike, when Swinkey said, "Do you mind?"

"Sorry."

While he reviewed the rest of his messages, I played with my little compass. A GPS would have been tonier, but a compass costs a hell of a lot less and would do in a pinch. I wondered if people with dementia could be rigged up with a signal sender, so if they wandered, they'd be easier to find. "You about done?" I inquired.

"About."

When I looked back at the lap top, the e-mail box was closed. On the main screen blinked the answer to our license-plate query. The car belonged to one Velma Bancroft, 20 Beach Street, Shore Haven, Michigan.

"Not Sean?" For a moment I was as disappointed as Bill Feinstein might have been. "Well then, who's this Velma Bancroft?"

"Never heard of her. Let's see…seventy-seven year old white female, 107 pounds, eyes brown, no outstanding warrants. Not likely to be a rammer."

"Twenty Beach Street. I could at least go see her, ask if anyone's taken her car."

"You got your work cut out," said Swinkey. "Twenty Beach is Sunnyside. All of it. And you're just guessing about the car."

"Gee whiz…." I envisioned myself traipsing around, trailer to trailer, eventually finding Velma Bancroft, and her telling me, *No, no one's taken my car.* But I had to try.

"And I got a message from Keith. He says his memory's coming back. It was an anonymous, whispered phone call that set up your meet with the snitch."

"Anonymous? Great. Just great. So how did Anonymous know to phone him? And if Anonymous was whispering how did Keith know it was a guy?"

"Those are good questions, Gayle. Maybe you oughta give Keith a call."

"Me? Well, I'd be glad to give Keith a call, but isn't this a police matter?"

Swinkey groaned. "I'm pretty busy here, Gayle. Can I get on it tomorrow?"

"John—oh, god—I'm sorry. But there's one more thing I need to tell you. This girl, Debby Fenton, gave me some second-hand story about Fiona and Sean—Eleanor caught them together in bed and that's what drove her to suicide. Debby claimed there was a secret door between Fiona's and Sean's bedrooms. Well, I found it last night. It was not a locked-room suicide."

"Debby knew about this door?"

"Yeah. It might be worth your while to ask her a few questions. And your pal VanDee—"

"He's no pal of mine."

"Okay. VanDee, your archenemy, maybe was having an affair with Eleanor."

"What?"

"I hate to tell you this, but VanDee's a real loose goose."

"Piece of shit," growled Swinkey.

"Maybe it *wasn't* Eleanor. Maybe it was Fiona. I'm not sure which and I'm not sure when. Anyway, it's a possible motive for someone to do something."

Swinkey rubbed his eyes. "I have to get back to the search."

"You think they'll find the old man? Alive?"

He shrugged. "Dogs couldn't find him. Copter couldn't—"

"But how could it, flying over corn stalks and trees?"

"It's got a FLIR."

"A what?" The only Fleer I knew made Double Bubble Gum.

"A forward-looking infrared camera. F-L-I-R. It shows heat. Pilot spotted a few deer, but no humans—far as he could tell. But old people lose heat real fast. They lose too much, they die. I gotta go."

I returned to the Sunnyside lot, only to find that the Malibu had vanished, Velma probably with it. Muttering a few curses, I stoically shuffled into the trailer park, determined to at least find out where she lived. I knocked on every single trailer door to inquire, but no one was home. No one. As I left in disgust, I reasoned that most residents were gone for the season, and those who remained were either at work or searching for Dennis. I could probably get Velma's trailer number down at city hall, but that would have to wait. Though I was no expert on tracking in the woods, I liked the old man and I wanted to lend a hand.

By the time I got back to the search area, Swinkey had put Officer Voight in charge and joined the hunt. "He put on some waders," said Voight. "Took off due north."

"Say, would it be possible for me to borrow a pair of waders?"

"Sorry," said Voight. "This operation's strictly BYOB."

"Huh?"

"Bring your own boots."

I thanked him for the information, then thinking I might as well hunt with Swinkey, I headed north.

So many searchers had been tripping around in the woods, the foliage was beaten flat. Therefore, all I had to contend with were blackberry runners, toppled trees, tricky vines, and animal holes big enough to swallow a leg. After half an hour, I came to a marsh where the footprints of earlier searchers turned east. Who wanted to be sucked down into loathsome, murderous muck? Not me. I, too, turned east.

I walked alongside the marsh until the boot prints had all but vanished. "John Swinkey!" I called. Receiving no reply, I took out my Cracker-Jack compass and followed the bobbing needle north. By and by I saw two people up ahead, creeping quietly along. The woman had golden brown hair, railroad-striped overalls, a blue sweater, and hiking boots. The man had red hair, a fisherman knit sweater, brown corduroys, and muddy loafers. They turned to look at me, noisy behind them. Patty and Sean. Patty cringed, eyes wide, mouth ajar, and why not? Sean had doubtless told her that I'd shot off a gun in his house and hog-tied him. To avoid this duo I turned abruptly east.

I felt stupid slogging around on the off chance that I might run into Swinkey or Dennis Montague. I went on another ten minutes, then paused to look around me. There on a blackberry runner fluttered something that made my pulse leap: a shred of cotton fleece, like a tiny gray flag.

Had Dennis passed this way? And if so, where had he gone from here? He was an old man, probably terrified, stumbling in the dark, no compass, no short-term memory to aid him. He might have walked in circles. He might have tumbled into the creek. If the dogs hadn't found him, if the helicopter hadn't, how could Swinkey or Sean or I?

At last I came to the field. The corn had grown high, with stalks still green and plump ears ready for harvest. I stepped between two rows of stalks and headed toward Sand Creek Road. The warming sun was high overhead, and I was deep in thought about my clammy feet, tired legs, and empty stomach, when I saw a crow float down two rows to my right. I walked on, slowly, then another crow swooped down with a caw.

TWENTY

I cut through tall stalks to where the crows had boldly perched on the huddled body of Dennis Montague. One hopped forward to peck an eye already black with gore. I screamed, "Get off, you son of a bitch!" and flailed my arms, causing the crows to flap skyward on broad black wings. I fetched out my whistle, blew a sharp blast, and—this is awful—cheers went up throughout the field.

I knelt by the old man. His face and hands were scratched, pecked, and bloodied. His gray sweat clothes were torn and dirty, his boat shoes caked with mud. Hoping against hope, I pressed my fingertips to his neck, searching for the carotid artery, but it was as cold and inert as clay. The spark was extinguished, the great pianist gone. People were running toward us from all around, and suddenly a reserve deputy, Pa, and two fruit pickers burst upon us. Their collective gaze fell upon the body, then veered away from the handiwork of the crows. The deputy called in on his cell phone that Dennis Montague had been found, whereupon two blasts of a horn rose up from the south.

More cheers.

The deputy checked the old man for signs of life, then shook his head. When he reported in the bad news, he was told to stand guard until the EMT's arrived to examine the body. Pa, the fruit pickers, and I all headed for Sand Creek Road. After awhile, we met up with the EMT's, who carried an aluminum stretcher and an equipment box. We pointed them back towards the body, and continued out to the road.

One by one and two by two, volunteers emerged from the woods, learned the sad news, then walked silently to their vehicles and drove off. Sean was one of the last to come out from among the trees. An eager look on his face, he ran to Officer Voight. They exchanged a few words, then Sean stood as if in shock—not moving, not speaking—until at last he shambled off toward home, cold fate having blighted his family once more.

A bit later, Swinkey straggled out of the woods, ungainly in waders. After he had conferred heatedly with Voight, I went over to update him on Velma Bancroft. Four hours of fruitless search in the swamp had done nothing to improve his mood, for before I could get a word out, he fended me off with his hands. "Gayle, you better cool it with the Montagues."

"But you believe Eleanor was murdered, don't you?"

"Look here, Voight just gave me some more bad news. Fiona's applied for a personal protection order. She claims you stalked her family, shot off a gun in their home—"

"I shot off a gun because Sean physically attacked me. What's more, Fiona *invited* me into their home."

"Yeah, she admits she invited you in, but she wants you to stay away from now on. She says you made a lot of wild accusations, tied up Sean in her *pantyhose*—is that right?—and basically scared them silly. What with Eleanor's death and now the old man's, she can't deal with you. So the judge gave her the P.P.O."

"God dammit."

"And when the chief got wind of what you did, he slammed his office door so hard the glass broke."

"Oh, really," I said. "But he couldn't care less that whoever killed Eleanor is running around free as the breeze, tra la?"

"I'm sorry, Gayle, but I can't help you anymore."

As he started to leave, I latched onto his arm. "What about Keith?"

The big cop gave a sigh of exasperation. "He doesn't know anything—he'll be all right."

"What about Velma Bancroft? Maybe *she* knows something."

"Gayle—"

"What about VanDee?"

"I am not gonna to ask if he was screwing Eleanor," he hissed.

"Maybe Officer Voight—"

"Gayle, if you don't leave now, you're gonna lose your P.I. license."

"What? Are you gonna take it?"

"Chief Glenn said he'd have it yanked." Swinkey held his thumb and index finger half an inch apart. "He's this far from having it reeled in. He can do it, Gayle. Is that what you want?"

"But I have to come back for my car," I whined, "and that stupid reckless-driving beef."

He grasped my shoulders. *"Don't come back."*

The people still on the roadside gaped at us. Swinkey swung around to return their stares, swore a "God damn son of a bitch" under his breath, let go of me, and stomped off to his car. Meanwhile, I had colored as I hadn't in days—a ten pointer, full McKenzie, sunrise over Lake Erie—from sternum to crown and every place in between—neck, face, ears, scalp—a red-hot Technicolor drama for gawkers like Mrs. Hogoboom, who stood not ten feet away, a satisfied smirk on her lips.

A SCANT HOUR LATER, I was home. What choice did I have? I was furious with Swinkey, Chief Glenn, Fiona, the judge—and especially myself, for blowing it. I had never made such chaos of a case. I, who had claimed discretion as my specialty, had blown up discretion like a Silver Salute on the fourth of July. Not only had I blown my cover, but I'd been run out of town, and I thanked my lucky stars that the town I'd been run out of had been Shore Haven and not Collingwood, for despite its many flaws, I love it.

Finding myself in a particularly self-punishing mood, I phoned Bill Feinstein to update him on the case. I simply said that I believed without a grain of doubt that Eleanor had been murdered, and that Sergeant John Swinkey knew it too, but his chief was preventing him from pursuing the case.

"What about you?" demanded Bill. "Can't you pursue it?"

"Not at this time."

"Why not?"

"Look, it's been a rough few days. I'll send you a report and keep in touch with Sergeant Swinkey. I'll prod him along." Swinkey would love that.

"You could go back—"

"No, I can't. Fiona's got a protection order out against me, and Chief Glenn's thrown me out of town."

My client hung up with a bang. Whoopee!

AS I TOOK A LONG soaking bath, my mind retraced the maze of this case. I ended up feeling like a cowardly little creep who'd quit because the cops had said boo. I knew in every cell of my body that Eleanor had been murdered. How could I turn my back and walk away? It was insane.

After bathing, I dropped into bed, too tired even to fill my growling stomach. I fell into a dream…. *A woman with long dark hair sat facing a window. She wore white lace, like someone from the Victorian era. I touched her shoulder…she turned…it was Eleanor, face black and bloated with death, head tilted on a broken neck, tongue black and protruding*—and I was jarred awake by horror, sweating in my own hot bed.

I knew how she was killed, but not why or by whom. Was it Fiona? Sean? VanDee? Someone else? I'd been over it in my mind a hundred times—Sean and Fiona had the most to gain, if what Debby had said was true. They'd be rid of Eleanor, free of fear that she'd tell their secret. But was it a secret? Debby the dental assistant knew. Someone had told her, and she'd told me and maybe a few dozen other people. I bet she handed out gossip, along with the free toothbrush, at the end of each patient's visit.

I had to stop thinking about it, get my mind on something else. I was starving, for instance. I'd eat. I phone-ordered a mushroom-and-pepperoni pizza from Luigi's, then waited on the stoop for the delivery guy. Within a half hour, I toted the pizza upstairs, the odor of garlic, basil, and tomato working on me like medicine. I chomped on the greasy treat and felt a lot better—good enough to play back the message on my answering machine. It was from Iggy: "Find me." I made a soundless laugh. Sorely in need of diversion, I took up the challenge.

The time was just after four, perfect for what I had in mind. I called Oxford Investments, Alex Naylor's business. A woman answered the phone, and I immediately recognized the purring tones of Miss Felicia Pearl, whom I suspected of being Naylor's secret squeeze.

"Is Mr. Naylor in?" I asked.

"I'm sorry," she replied. "He's in a meeting right now. May I take a message?"

I hummed as if contemplating the options, then said, "I'll call tomorrow."

I threw on chinos, a tee-shirt, and a jacket. I considered retrieving my gun from the pants pocket of my dirty khakis, which along with the rest of my search attire, lay heaped on the bedroom floor. But why would I need a gun?

Why indeed?

I drove down to the Collingwood Bank & Trust Building whose entire sixth floor was occupied by Oxford Investments. I found a parking space half a block away but facing the building. At 5:20 p.m. the tall, trim Naylor strode out the front door, elegantly dressed in a tailored gray business suit that set off his fair hair, graying temples, and tennis tan. He was a walking advertisement for himself, for being rich and marrying rich. They say that clothes make the man, but I knew he was a son of a bitch. He entered the parking structure, soon exiting in a silver Cadillac Seville that I recognized from when I had spied on his wife.

I tailed him out to the Business Loop, west on 94, north on 131, and out Maple Street to Raptor's Run, Collingwood's newest "planned community" for "young professionals." I followed him along a tree-lined drive that curved through ten condo complexes. Up ahead lay the clubhouse, tennis courts, and Olympic-sized swimming pool, beyond which loomed big houses, like gigantic sugar cubes, along a swamp.

The Seville snaked into the last condo grouping—the Alexandria. Unlike its sister complexes, it nestled among natural rises, ravines, and older trees, its units either freestanding or duplexes, each a unique design but built of the same cedar and sandstone. The effect was pleasing, to say the least. The Seville pulled up the driveway of 1456 Alexandria, the garage door magically arose, and the car slipped inside. I parked my conspicuous white rental as far away as possible, then hopped out for a stroll around the complex. I hid behind a tree when a nondescript green Dodge drove past and parked three houses away from Naylor's tasty new digs. The driver seemed to be checking a map. I stole up beside him. It was Iggy, fiddling with his Remote GPS. When I tapped on his window, he started like a dog jolted from a dream of chasing a fox.

I made a winding gesture for him to roll down his window. He motioned me to go around to the passenger side. I obliged. He reached over to unlock the door and I slid in. "How's it going?" I asked.

"Ducky."

"Got anything on him yet?"

"Who wants to know?"

"Dammit, Iggy, *I* want to know."

"You're not my employer."

At that I opened the car door and started to leave. Iggy caught my sleeve and yanked me back into the car.

"So touchy," he declared. "As suspected, Naylor's been making it with Felicia Pearl." He said her name as if it were holy. "God, what body—"

"You *would* notice that."

"I'm not the only one."

I had to admit that Miss Pearl was an eyeful. She had thick dark hair, creamy skin, violet eyes, full lips, and the body of a lingerie model straight out of an old Frederick's-of-Hollywood catalogue. As far as I could tell. "And where do these assignations take place?" I inquired.

"Sometimes at her apartment, conveniently located at 1625 North Dillworth."

"That's not far," I amiably put in. "Anywhere else?"

"Sixth Floor, the Collingwood Bank & Trust Building."

"Combining pleasure with work. Hmm. Got any pics?"

"Yeah—and you'll appreciate how I got 'em."

"Do tell."

"I put on my yellow overalls and was admitted to the big shot's office to perform 'biennial supra-maintenance on the air-conditioning system.' While there, I installed a tiny cordless mike and a tiny video camera, just this big," and he shoved his broad thumb nail under my nose.

I leaned my head back, said, "If the camera's only that big, where do you put the film?"

"It's not film—it's video tape. The tape's in another part of the camera that's hidden inside the air-conditioning vent. Ha!"

"How do you get the sound and the visuals to match up?"

Iggy waved his hand in disdain. "Trust me. Anyway, I stopped back a couple days later to install a new temperature regulator—"

"Really?"

"No, not really. I was there to pick up my equipment."

"Good for you."

Then he pulled a file folder from beneath his seat. He licked his thumb, pressed it to the folder and made a sizzling noise, before passing it to me. I flipped it open to pictures of Naylor sneaking into and out of 1625 North Dilworth. Next came large color photos of Naylor and Felicia Pearl, hard at work at the office. All I can say is she's one hell of a receptionist.

"How'd you do these?"

"I used a video-capture program to take snapshots off the video tape, imported them into Photo Shop, then outputted them on hi-res glossy paper."

"Wow."

"Yeah," he said modestly.

"Well, Iggy, with all this, er, evidence, how come you're still watching Naylor?"

"Gayle, there's no such thing as too much dirt."

"Come on—you're milking this gig."

"What if I am?" he said. "Therese *Defresnes* Naylor can afford it."

"You don't even like surveillance. In fact, you hate it."

"What makes you think that?"

"You told me so when you were watching her last May."

"Well, see that was *way* different. First of all, you were paying me dirt-cheap wages. And second, she was crying all the time. I hate tears. My current situation is far superior. Mrs. Naylor is paying me fifty an hour. Plus I get to see—and hear—Naylor and Felicia Pearl doin' it." He chortled.

"Okay, whatever yanks your weewee." On that note, I took my leave.

I hadn't been to the office since Sunday, so I motored over to the DeKats Arms to catch up on mail and proofread my ignominious report to Bill Feinstein. Maybe if I had all the words spelled right he wouldn't notice that I had failed him completely. As usual, the lobby sofas were loaded with hotel denizens, the after-dinner smokers and nappers—some especially adept gents doing both at once. Mr. DeKats waved a cigar at me in lazy greeting. He was used to my coming and going at odd hours or disappearing for days.

I nodded and pointed at my office door: *Work to do.*

He cocked an approving eyebrow. This meant, *Good, I'll get my rent on time.*

We're semi-telepathic, Mr. DeKats and I, when it comes to money.

I opened the door wide and hoisted the window to evict stale air. I whipped through the postman's offerings, winging eighteen out of twenty-one pieces into my special receptacle for unsolicited bulk mail: it's called a trash can. Then I got on the phone. I called Keith at his cousin's apartment in Alvindale. Fortunately, Arty recognized my voice. "Otherwise," he said, "I'd've never told you he was here."

"Good. You keep that up and maybe he'll be okay." Was that reassuring or what? Keith got on the phone, and I queried him about Anonymous. "What was the voice like?" I asked.

"Whispered."

"Man? Woman?"

"Gee, I donno. I *thought* it was a guy…but I guess it could've been a woman. It was just this hissing I could hardly hear."

"You been working on that list?" I asked.

"Male townies who eat sorbet on Sundays?"

"Yeah."

"Some," he mumbled.

"Better start adding female townies."

"Okay."

Then I told him not to go to class on Thursday.

"Hey," he complained, "I gotta go to class sometime."

"It's not safe yet," I said.

"When *will* it be safe?" He sounded exasperated—and rightfully so.

"I'm not sure. Soon, I hope."

"Dude—"

"Call your profs, tell them you've got a concussion. It's the truth. Teachers like that."

"You want me to tell 'em somebody tried to kill me?"

"Hmm. That might be too much truth. Just tell them about the concussion and get your assignments."

"What about next week?" he griped.

I thought about this a moment. "Wouldn't you rather stay alive?"

"Sure, I would. But I won't have to worry about any maniac murderer if I flunk out of school. My parents'll kill me."

"I know. I'm really sorry I got you involved."

"Wait a minute," he said. "I *asked* to be involved."

"Yeah. But I didn't have to be so damn eager to grant your request."

"Gayle?"

"What?"

"You got anyone watchin' out for you?"

"Sure," I said, flexing my fingers. "Any maniac murders come after me, they'll get tackled by ten of my biggest, burliest friends."

I told him I'd call as soon as I had news—good or bad. And he promised to lie low—until Tuesday, at least.

We signed off, then I leaned back in my chair. That's when it occurred to me that whoever had killed Eleanor might come to Collingwood to finish me off because I knew too much. And there I was, lazing around the office, door wide open, no gun in my paw. So I got up and shut the door. Too bad Leversee had been such a brat. He would have let me lie low at his house, but as things stood, I'd feel funny about it. So if someone was coming, I'd have to be ready. *If* someone was coming.

My last call was to Therese Naylor. When I asked her to join me for a drink at Georgie's, she agreed to meet me at eight. After hanging up, I wondered if baby brother would be tagging along again.

While waiting for eight p.m. to roll around, I put the finishing touches on my report for Bill Feinstein. For all the time I'd applied to the case, I'd found nothing but the pills, the love notes from Mark VanDee, and the secret door—which might or might not spark an investigation into Eleanor's death. I felt frustrated enough to knock down a brick wall with my fists.

At 7:55 I crossed the street to Georgie's. It was a good time to visit—in that melancholy lull between happy hour and the lively evening crowd. The majestic Georgie was leaning against the bar among four young men, engrossed in a Charlie Parker disk. She wore a dark red pants suit with bead trim, natty as hell, and her friends resembled an ad for Armani. I'd been absent awhile, so Georgie disengaged herself from her companions and made over me the way she does: "Gayle? Where you been? I never see you anymore. Been taking your business elsewhere?"

"Georgie, I've had a rough time of it. I was picked up for drunk driving over in Shore Haven."

"Girl, you don't even drink."

I crumpled an imaginary traffic citation, tossed it to the floor. "Maybe they'll drop the charges."

"And they *ought* to with that big cop boyfriend of yours. When're you two getting married?"

"I don't know," I said. "Marriage is kind of a big step…into a big black hole."

TWENTY-ONE

GEORGIE SHOWED ME to my favorite spot, a rounded, red-leather booth, where I ordered an orange juice over crushed ice with a dash of bitters and a cherry. She gave a shiver. "Gayle, where do you come up with ideas like that?"

I shrugged my shoulders. "I thought it'd make my juice seem more like a drink. I only did it to please you."

She shivered again—was it disgust?—and floated regally back to the bar. It occurred to me that she wouldn't be satisfied until I ordered a triple vodka straight up.

A little after eight, the front door swung open and there stood Bobby and Therese. They hesitated a moment, then Bobby led the way, casual yet self-assured and masterful, as befitted the Count of VanBurgen County. Therese hung behind, in dark glasses, a black silk shirt, black cropped pants, and black sandals. She looked like Lynne Jeffers the last time I saw her. All in black. The day she was killed.

They joined me, and I swiftly sensed a shift in their relationship. I'd seen Bobby the Protector and Bobby the Bully, but this was Bobby the Estranged. Therese removed her dark glasses and offered me a tentative smile. I returned her smile, less tentative than tense.

Georgie put some vinyl on the record player, and Ella Fitzgerald's voice filled the place with whooshing blue waves. Georgie sailed over with my drink and set it firmly on our table. I hoped to heaven that Bobby wouldn't treat her like one of his waitresses in Pauling, for although he was the count of his county, Georgie was the queen of this bar. She said, with great dignity, "May I take your order?" The regal power in her eyes squelched his emperiousness at once. He quietly requested a shot of bourbon.

Therese asked for a glass of Chardonnay. She lit herself a B & H and inhaled deeply.

"How's it going?" I inquired.

"Waiting," said Therese, within a cloud of exhaled smoke. "I hate it. I'm so wound up I could scream."

"Have you talked to Iggy?" I asked.

"Yes. He had good news."

"What's that?" Bobby demanded.

"Alex and his receptionist," said Therese. "Caught on videotape. And it's graphic. Wes Peevy thinks we might avoid going to court, but—"

Just then, Georgie returned with their drinks, placing them ceremoniously on cocktail napkins. She cast me a questioning look. I merely smiled, and she sailed away on the wave of Ella's voice.

"But what?" I said.

"Imagine a set of scales," said Therese, holding out her slim hands, palms up. "On one side place Alex in a dalliance with his receptionist. On the other, put Lynne and me, planning to divorce our husbands and run off to Oregon. Which side do you suppose weighs more?"

"Oh, for chrissake," muttered Bobby.

"I know Alex," continued Therese. "He loves to win—*has* to win. He'll say I drove him to Felicia Pearl. And maybe I did."

"Like he drove you to Lynne?" I countered.

Therese took another drag on her cigarette, blew a cloud skyward.

"What about the audit?" I asked. "Any word on that?"

Bobby said, "Not yet. Alex is stalling."

"Maybe he's got something to hide," I said.

Bobby rolled his eyes. "Of course, he does. But we probably won't have it by September thirtieth."

A smile curled at my lips. "The court date'll be postponed."

"What are you, psychic?" Bobby's tone was suspicious. No, accusing.

"The thirtieth is Yom Kippur. The Day of Atonement. Marty Klein and Judge Baumann will both be at Temple all day, praying."

Therese crushed the end of her cigarette. "Bobby, I should just come out—"

"You don't care who you embarrass," complained her brother. "It's yourself you're worried about. What people will think. So I have to hide and pretend. Well, I'm not hiding anymore."

"Please—think of yourself," he begged.

"Dishonesty makes people vulnerable, and that's exactly what I'll be till I stop living a lie."

"You'll be vulnerable," said Bobby, "till people stop fearing anyone who's different."

"Are you afraid?" she asked. In answer, Bobby downed his drink and walked out, the heavy door swinging closed behind him.

"Your brother's pretty sore," I observed.

"He'll be all right," Therese said. "Believe it or not, he's adjusting to the 'new' me."

"The 'new' you. So, when I'm called up to the stand, you want me to tell it like it is?"

"Sure. Why not?"

"You may not care, but what about Lynne?"

"Lynne's too dead to care." She had been murdered by a gay-hating psychopath.

"What about her family?" I asked. Lynne's husband, rare man that he was, had graciously accepted the relationship between Lynne and Therese. But Therese's outing herself at the trial might damage his fledgling career as a TV newsman. What's more, the last time I'd spoken with Lynne's sister, she had begged me between sobs to hide the affair because her homophobic father couldn't handle the truth.

"I'm tired of being responsible for other people's prejudices," said Therese.

What could I say to that?

"Look, I better go or Bobby's liable to call a cab." She jangled a set of car keys and said, "I drove."

"And the truth shall set them free."

She left and Georgie made for the table. "Mind telling me what Bobby Defresnes was doing in my establishment the night before the Pauling Wine Fest?"

"Wine Fest starts tomorrow?"

"Yes, indeed. He should be preparing for the onslaught."

"Well, he was tidying up a bit of business." Our business, unfortunately, felt as tidy as a shattered vase. Before Georgie could accuse me of dodging her question, a couple of young jazzophiles bebopped in and carried her off on a stream of *copacetics* and *sublimes*.

I was sucking the dregs of my o.j. when the bar door swung open on Lieutenant Steven Leversee. Ella had just sung her last blue note on Side A, and Georgie sashayed to the bar to flip her over.

Leversee peered all around, the way he does, in case he might chance to spot a criminal or, better yet, a crime in progress. That little ritual complete, he approached my table. Once again Ella was swinging in the background.

"What brings you to Georgie's?" I wondered.

"You."

Leversee arranged his long body in the booth, rolled his neck, and popped a vertebra.

"You need to see a chiropractor about that neck."

"I need something, but it's not a chiropractor."

I almost laughed. "I need something too. But it's not a jealous son of a bitch."

He glanced down, then up, an apology in his eyes.

"You think I'm the type who'd go roll around with any guy—"

He shook his head.

"If I did, it'd be because you drove me away. Is that what you want?"

"No."

"That cop over in Shore Haven's a nice guy, very cooperative, good looking, but what am I gonna do with a married man who smokes?"

Leversee smiled. "Gayle, I know I acted stupid. But the thought of you two together…."

"What?"

"Bad memories."

"Of *me?*"

"Kathy. My ex-wife. It was hell losing her to another cop."

I suppose Swinkey felt the same about his wife. Most men would. I said, "Sure it was. But I'm not Kathy."

FURTHER NEGOTIATIONS led us to a treaty, then to the parking lot outside. I craved him as though I'd gone celibate for months. He fell on my mouth with warm kisses and we twined ourselves around one another. "We ought to go somewhere," he whispered.

"Mmmm."

"Your place is closer."

I pictured the clothes and towels scattered on the bedroom floor. "It's a sty. Let's go to your place. The extra five minutes'll do you good."

He stared at his stainless steel wristwatch in horror.

"Come on…" I wheedled.

He groaned. "Let's go."

That's how we ended up at his little house in Compton. We were wrapped in one another's arms, lying on cool white sheets. He was nibbling the freckles on my neck, following the spotted path to my breasts. He told me for the hundredth time, "I love your freckles," and I murmured for the hundredth time, "Don't stop."

I AWOKE IN THE DARK. Leversee lay next to me, snoring gently. I like sleeping with Leversee. He smells nice, he's warm, and he gives me sweet dreams. Compared to the rest of my life, sleeping with Leversee is simple and good. That night, it had even removed some of the sting of the Shore-Haven debacle and the horror of Dennis's death. I glanced at the clock that glowed on his bedside table. Six-forty a.m. He was still working afternoons, so there was no big rush to get up and get going. I curled around him and drifted back to sleep.

I woke again at eight to the sound of the shower. Leversee was beautifying himself for me—or so I assumed. However, when I joined him under the steamy spray, he informed me that he had to be at the office by nine. He had to prep himself for a court case that convened at 10:30 a.m. He was to give testimony regarding what he jokingly referred to as "a heinous east side murder." Apparently, the east side has more than its share of killings, and they tend to be nasty and drug related. The sad thing is, joke or no joke, the murders are all heinous. Drive-by, head-and-heart, gut-shot. Forget the hangings and stabbings: the east side favors guns.

He quickly dressed while I luxuriated in bed, but as soon as he left, locking his three deadbolts behind him, my Shore-Haven obsession returned. I wanted the poop on Velma Bancroft, and who better to ask than Debby the dental assistant?

I phoned her at home and she answered on the first ring.

"Hi, Debby," I said. "This is Betty Jo Bialosky."

"I can only talk a minute," she replied. "I'm late for work, and Dr. Coulter's very—"

"I won't keep you long. Listen, Debby, I have to get hold of Velma Bancroft. You know where she lives?"

"Mrs. Bancroft? Why, she's out on the Red Arrow in Pauling."

"I thought she lived at Sunnyside."

"She did. But she died, and now she's in the graveyard on the Red Arrow Highway."

"But I saw her Malibu at Sunnyside."

"That's Patty's car. Patty is Mrs. Bancroft's granddaughter."

"Is she?"

"Mrs. Bancroft raised her after her mother died. In the trailer next door? Mrs. B. turned up her toes, couple years back."

"What happened to Patty's mom and dad?"

Debby whispered: "Her mom died of an overdose when Patty was little. Her dad—he was a biker or something."

"A biker?"

"I don't know—nobody knows, ya know?"

"Well, thanks. I suppose Patty's gone to work already."

"Nope. She went on vacation. Up to Manitowoc."

"You mean Wisconsin?"

"Yeah, the state park. She loves to go camping." Debby yawned, then said, "Oh shit, look at the time! I gotta go, or Dr. Coulter—you know? See ya 'round, Betty Jo." And she hung up.

Patty? On the surface she was bland enough, but scratch a little and all sorts of odd details began to show. She knew all the Montagues and doubtless knew, care of Debby, about the drugs in Dr. Coulter's office. Patty could have been one of the townies who frequent *I Know Your Vice;* her father was unknown, maybe a biker. She had told me, "It's not a nice place over there," referring to the Montague house. She could certainly have been the one to tell Debby about the "incest." She drove a car registered to a dead woman (a minor crime), kept cassette tapes of piano concertos in her glove box, and maybe rammed Keith and me into the channel. But why?

She visited the Montagues often enough and was searching for Dennis with Sean. Was that it? Patty and Sean were in love and Eleanor was in the way? Then why not get a divorce?

No. Patty *wanted* Sean and Eleanor was in the way. Patty knew of the ritual ice cream after dinner; and she knew that Eleanor would let her into the house. A lifelong resident of Sunnyside, Patty probably knew all the bootlegger eccentricities of the Montague home, including the secret passage between bedrooms. It clicked for me then. Even with all the *coulds* and *maybes,* I knew it was true: Patty was the one.

I picked up the phone and dialed Swinkey at work, but he was out. I tried him at home, the phone rang, and the answering machine turned on. I said, "This is Gayle. Please call," and I rattled off my apartment and office numbers. Then I headed home to pack. Sure, I was *persona non grata* in Shore Haven, but I had not yet begun to rub people the wrong way in Manitowoc. I'd drive up to Luddington, catch the car ferry, and land in Wisconsin by sunset.

Back at home, the message light was flashing on my answering machine. Was it Swinkey? Plopping down at my desk, I pressed the playback button and was assailed by my mother's voice demanding that I call her. She, Gramma McKenzie, and Amanda were "worried sick." I reflected that my mother was positively psychic about sex. Every time I had slept over at Leversee's, she'd left a message about being worried sick.

Next came a call from my insurance agent, asking me to contact her regarding my drowned LeMans. At last! I sure hoped my policy covered the car's resuscitation—dredging, drying, deep frying—whatever it needed.

The third message was as follows: "Gayle, this is John. Chief Glenn's started proceedings to have your P.I. license revoked.

Sorry it turned out this way." The machine emitted a final beep that, along with Swinkey's message, sent a chill up my spine. I heard a rustling, the sound of drapes shifting in the breeze before an open window—except my windows weren't open. The chill raced up my neck and grabbed my head in an icy claw.

Slowly I turned to face the doorway. There stood Patty the poisonous practical nurse, hands sanitary in latex gloves, aiming a Glock nine-millimeter at my chest. Why did everyone but me have such a rip-roaring big-assed gun? If I was lucky, she wouldn't know how to use it; the recoil would knock her on her can, and she'd end up blasting a hole in the wall. If I was lucky.

"Hi, Patty."

She was wearing blue jeans and a pink sweatshirt inscribed with the motto, *Hug a Nurse.* Great big fat chance of that, with her holding a gun on me. She waved me out of my office into the living room, pointed at the couch and said, "Sit."

I obeyed. Why get the golden-haired sociopath all nervous and upset? "To what do I owe the pleasure of your company?" I asked.

She chewed on this awhile. "Owe it to the process server who went door to door at Sunnyside last weekend looking for Gayle Fisher. He—what is it they say?—blew your cover?"

"Iggy?"

"Yes. I asked for a description and he showed me your picture. I said, 'That looks a lot like Betty Jo, over in that little Airstream.' Next thing I know, you're answering the door in a blue sheet and he's stripping you naked."

"You've got keen eyes," I said, scrawling on my mental notepad: *If Patty doesn't kill me, wring Iggy's neck.* But she did plan to kill me, didn't she? "How'd you get in here?"

"Back door. It wasn't locked," she explained, the shadow of a smirk playing over her mouth.

"Shit." I must have forgotten to lock the back door after I'd brought in my damn cell phone.

She pulled an aluminum flask from her back pocket. "Drink this," she said, holding it out to me.

"What for?"

"It's not poison," she said. "It'll relax you."

"You need to relax me to shoot me?"

Her laugh was calm and throaty. "I'm not planning to shoot you—unless you make me."

Unless *I* made her. But wasn't that always the way with her ilk? Any time a psychopath performs some rotten act, it's someone else's fault. "Then why're you here?"

Still pointing the gun at my chest, she leaned back in my recliner. "Drink that and I'll tell you."

"I'd rather not."

"I see," she said. "You *want* me to shoot you," and she pushed back the safety on the Glock.

"No need to do that," I said, unscrewing the cap of the flask. I took a sniff, whiffed nothing but tea. "What's in here?"

"Oolong tea."

I lifted the flask and tested the liquid with my tongue. The tea was bitter, adulterated with what? Seconal? Tylenol 3? Nembutol? Percodan? Rat poison?

"Drink," she ordered.

I pressed my tongue to the mouth of the flask, tipped it back, and faked swallowing motions with my throat. Pulling the flask from my mouth, I wiped my lips on the back of my hand.

Patty hopped to her feet, seized the flask, and sloshed the liquid around inside. She grimaced, then jammed the cold muzzle of the Glock against my temple. "Drink it all," she growled.

So I did. Every bitter drop. Except what I let stream down my chin and through the opening of my shirt to where it pooled between my breasts and soaked into my bra.

"That's better," she said. "Now you'll be relaxed."

"If you want me relaxed," I countered, "take that gun off my head."

And she did. She returned to the recliner and checked her wristwatch. "You've just taken five Seconal. In fifteen minutes, we'll be ready to continue."

Five Seconal? An overdose. "Continue with what?"

Patty leaned forward in the chair. "I've something special planned for you, Gayle."

"Such as?"

"Like what I did with Eleanor."

"You mean you plan to kill me," I said.

"We'll see."

"The Shore Haven Police are already suspicious of you, you know."

"Look, Gayle, the only one they're suspicious of is you."

"Look, yourself. You'll never get away with doing me in."

"Gayle, I drove up to Luddington yesterday and took the car ferry to Manitowoc. I'm vacationing right now at the Manitowoc State Park. And I'm not coming back until day after tomorrow."

"So how d'you happen to be here?"

"I drove around the lake. And when I'm done with you, I'll drive back, then take the car ferry home to Michigan."

"That's a lot of driving," I commented. "How old's your car?"

"Not to worry," she said, reassuringly. "My car may be old, but it's reliable."

But her car—her grandmother's car, I should say—was a loose end. If Patty succeeded in terminating my life, Thurm Hollis might still be able to prove the broken glass on Hill Street had come from her car. It wasn't much, but it was a dab of consolation.

Consolation! Adrenaline jolted through my body. Consolation be damned. I refused to let her kill me. I'd get out of this. I would. Somehow. She had a gun but I had brains.

"Too bad you had to hang Eleanor," I murmured.

"It was her own fault. She shouldn't have married Sean."

"But it's not just Sean. It's that four-hundred-thousand-dollar house. With Dennis gone, it goes to Sean and Fiona, right?"

"Yes. And me, when I marry Sean. But with real estate so strong right now, I figure we can get seven-hundred thou—maybe more. Those Chicago big shots, what can I say? They'll pay anything for a house on the lake. Plus Dennis still has money in a trust—two hundred, three hundred thou. And Fiona? She'll meet with a hideous end—she'll drown, poor rat—and the money will be all ours, Sean's and mine."

A million dollars. People have murdered for less. Far less. "What makes you think Sean would marry someone like you?"

At that, she jumped out of the recliner and slapped me with the Glock. My face exploded with pain, my mind spun, and my ears rang like a huge bell: Bong. "Sean'll marry me," Patty was saying. "I know he will. It's only a matter of time."

"Yeah," I muttered, licking blood off my lips. "Sure, he will."

"I'm the one he loves—the one he's always loved. But she got him all confused, the little flute-playing bitch."

"And you pretended to be her friend?"

"She was stupid—the kind who believes anything. *You* know what I mean."

"And you told her Sean and Fiona were—"

"Yes, I did. I said, 'Fiona's been forcing herself on Sean since he was a little kid.'"

"And she never said anything to anybody?" I asked, hoping to find a crack in Patty's scheme.

"Eleanor—she was so easy to handle. Shy, lonely, sweet—in a sickly wimp sort of a way."

"So you, you killed her."

"Oh, no. Not right away. First, I gave her pills to weaken her: 'Eleanor, take these, they'll help you sleep.' Old Dennis was always stumbling around at night, making a racket. Fiona was supposed to watch him nights, but he kept waking Eleanor and she couldn't get back to sleep. So she took the pills—"

"Tha' you stole from, from Dr. Coulter."

"At first I stole pills from the hospital. But that stupid R.N. in Ward Two got suspicious."

"Taking 'em from the hospital 'ould be too obvious," I said, working my jaws over the words.

"Right. Then Debby told me about all the drugs at Dr. Coulter's office, so I broke in and took them."

"Di'n Debby suspect you?" I asked, rubbing my head. It was starting to feel like a giant bottle of pills, stuffed with a great big wad of cotton to keep them from moving around.

"Why would she? She told everyone about those drugs."

"Kin' of a blubbermouth."

"And I kept giving Eleanor pills, hoping she'd O.D. But she didn't. Then I realized she was going to need more help—to die, I mean."

"More help," I echoed.

"Yeah. I watched and I waited. Sean and Fiona and Dennis liked to go out for ice cream and a walk in the early evening. Usually took forty minutes and that was long enough."

"Eleanor di'n go?"

"She used to, before I turned her against Fiona. Then she couldn't stand to be around her. So I got in the house. They never locked the door, and see how it turned out for Dennis?"

"Uh huh."

"Then I made Eleanor take three Seconal. She got real pliable. I took her upstairs and dropped her on the bed."

"Youcarriedher," I mumbled to the three gun-slinging Patties sitting before me.

"What?"

"You—carried—her," I enunciated.

"Yes, I'm strong, *strong, strong,*" said the three Patties, one after the other. "I'm a nurse, I lift people every day." The Patties were starting to spin now—clockwise. "Then I went into Fiona's room and came through that secret door. Punched a hole in the ceiling, strung her up, *up, up*...."

"Hid...pills...Fiona's drawer."

"Sure, I thought I'd incriminate her in case of an investigation. But I didn't think there would be, and there wasn't. The VanBurgen M.E.'s notorious—a lazy, incompetent slob."

I drifted off...until a slap stung my cheek.

"Sign here, please," said the Patties from far, far away.

"Huh?"

The Patties pushed up my eyelid, and each held a piece of paper before me.

"I need your signature, Gayle." They wrapped the fingers of my three right hands around three pens.

"Wha' for?" I didn't know which of the three papers to sign. The Patties pulled my three right hands to the three papers.

The pinwheeling Patties were picking up speed. They drew closer and closer. "Write your name," they intoned.

I did.

Then blackness.

TWENTY-TWO

THE GLASS ON the bedside table, a red pill box below, the dresser looming against the bedroom door, the sheet hanging from the hole in the ceiling, Patty slipping into the wardrobe, grinning cat-like at what she'd done. Eleanor Montague, hanging, head swollen and dark, body limp as a rag doll's, a child body draped in lace, tiny feet sticking out below. Eleanor, spinning ever so slowly...clockwise.

I take a slow breath, fight to open my eyes.... Something important is happening.... If only I could remember. Something vital. My left cheek is pressed hard to the wooden floor, drool puddling at my lips. Oh, god—have I been drinking? We promised ourselves never again. Mandy and I, fifteen and thirteen. We shared a pint of gin. An experiment. What it's like. What a pair of heads the next day! Hated it. Swore off. Told Mom and Dad we had the flu.

Something important.... I open my right eye. What's that? A quilt? I'm in the bedroom. A crash! I draw a sharp breath. Out of the corner of my eye, I see Patty. She stands on the bed, a heavy glove on her hand. She punches the ceiling and plaster falls like snow. Cold. A hole now. A big black hole to nowhere. I'm icy all over. She looks up into the hole and smiles.

I take a breath. Where's Eleanor? Patty looks down at me, at my slit of an open right eye. "It won't be long," she says, baring her teeth. The cat assuring the mouse that their game is nearly at an end. She hops down from the bed, pulls the sheet loose, wraps a corner around my neck. Her face brushes mine as she ties the knot. She exhales a sour smell. She takes my right hand, shapes it into a fist, punches it into the pile of fallen plaster. It hurts. Then she props me next to the bed.

Now I remember. She gave me Seconal. A central-nervous-system depressant. Brings relaxation, sleep. Too much brings suffocation, death. I've got to stop this. I'm on the floor in my own messy bedroom, yesterday's clothes scattered around me. Patty is pulling the sheet taut. "You shouldn't have mixed in," she says. "This is your fault," she says. Her Glock is lying on the bedside table, next to the phone. I take a breath.

There's a piece of paper on the floor, near my head. The angle's bad, but I can just read the typed words: Sorry I made such a mess of things. Then my signature, but it looks all wrong. What mess of things?

Ah, an all-purpose suicide note.

I'm cold.... all the way down to the marrow of my bones. No!

I take a breath, try to move my hands. I try to make fists. My hands feel weak.

"I'm scared," she mocks. "Oo-oo-oo!"

My Beretta Jaguar is in the pocket of yesterday's pants, somewhere nearby. If I can make fists, I can move my arms.

Patty is standing on the bed, pushing the end of the white sheet up into the hole. The knot around my neck pulls me up, so I'm sitting straight.

"Here's one piece of information you couldn't have gotten— no one knew but me and my mom and my gran, and they're both dead. Dennis Montague was my father. That's right. Back when Fiona was a baby, my mother worked for the la-di-da Montagues. Cooked and cleaned and tended their baby. Dennis was in his fifties, but still young enough to make Fiona and Sean. Still young enough to screw my mother and make me. Sean's my brother. We're exactly the same age.

"I've always loved him. Always, always. When we were kids, we played in the sand together, swam together, rode the school bus together. Then he went up to Interlochen for high school, and I hardly ever got to see him. And somehow, Eleanor got her hooks in."

The gun, the gun, the gun, the gun. My right hand reaches for the khakis, inches them toward my lap while Patty is busy securing the sheet across a beam—for surely that is what she is doing.

"Yes," says Patty. "With Eleanor gone, Sean's coming back to me. He and I are meant to be together. Let Fiona try and cause trouble. She'll get hers, just like Eleanor, the old man, and you."

I breathe. Most people are right-handed—90% of men, 96% of women. But I'm not. My left hand fumbles its way into the pocket, pushes at the safety. My index finger hooks into the trigger. I could shoot her now. She tugs again at the sheet. I will myself not to be lifted.

"You're heavier than you look," Patty complains, hopping down from the bed once more. She's coming at me.

"Stop or I'll shoo'," I mumble.

"You'll what?" She keeps coming.

"I'll shoo'." My elbow braces against my hip. My finger pulls the trigger.

A red-black hole has formed in her cheek. Her hand flies up to the spot and blood pours between her fingers like water from a cracked pipe. Red is draining down her arm to the floor. Her eyes are furious. She tears off the big glove and reaches behind her for the Glock. I'm glad she's so close—otherwise I'd never hit her. As she jerks her trigger, I squeeze mine. A huge weight slams into my right shoulder—I've been hit—and she stumbles back, also hit—chest?

I can hear Leversee riding me about my .22. *"Wouldn't stop a cat,"* he says.

Oh, it'll stop a cat, all right.

"Big bad Jag," laughs Iggy.

Beretta Jaguar. You bet it's bad.

Patty is back on her feet. She's coming at me again, the lunatic. I squeeze the trigger, keep squeezing, until I fill her full of lead. She falls—

My head is muzzy. My brain is pickled in formaldehyde. I'm sitting up against my bed and Patty is lying face down across my lap, a pool of blood widening around us. Horror—or is it cold?—raises the hair all over my body, a prickly sensation. My right shoulder hurts like hell, like a railroad spike's been jammed through it. With my left arm I shove the slack weight of Patty off my lap, roll her to the floor. I'm drenched in blood. Teeth rattling, I kneel, press my fingers to her bloody neck, searching for a pulse. I can't tell if she's dead or alive. My hand is wet with blood—hers or mine? It's all red. I half crawl, half fumble to the phone next to the bed, hit the speed dial for Leversee's line at Public Safety. If he's already at the courthouse—

The phone rings, rings, rings, is starting the fourth ring that will shunt me to his voice mail, when he picks up. "Lieutenant Leversee speaking."

I open my mouth to speak, but nothing comes out.

"Who's there?" he asks.

I try again. "Gayle," I whisper. "Come quick."

I drop the phone, fall back, stuff my khakis against my bleeding shoulder. The stench of blood and cordite… It's hard to breathe.

I hear sirens—a hoot and a screech—it's taken four minutes—I'm watching the clock—anything rather than view Patty or my own bloody self. Oh, how I long to wash away the blood.

There's a thundering of feet up the back stairs, pounding, a cry of "Gayle!" a crash in the kitchen.

I stumble up to meet him, but the sheet's still tied around my neck at one end and the beam at the other. I rip at the blood-soaked noose….

MONDAY AFTERNOON, I was back in my office printing out my report for Bill Feinstein. I had called him Saturday, told him about Patty killing his sister, and he'd said, "And Sean was in it too?"

"No. Patty acted alone. She was obsessed with Sean, but he had nothing to do with her killing your sister."

Bill was quiet awhile, then said he'd like to pick up my report and pay the rest of my fee.

"I can mail you the report and my bill."

"I'd rather see you in person."

I didn't know whether he planned to pin a medal on me for finding his sister's killer or punch me out because it wasn't Sean. But I'm open to all sorts of experiences. "Sure," I said. "How about Monday, seven p.m.?"

So I had three hours left to proofread the report. I'm obsessive about stuff like that. As far as I'm concerned, a sloppy investigator writes sloppy reports. I got out my special purple proofreading pen, uncapped it, and sure enough, the phone rang.

It was my insurance agent, Mavis Quimby of Quimby & Pugh, calling to find out if I'd gotten her message. I said I'd been tied up. Then she told me that the fearful expense of dredging my car out of the Black River was fully covered by my auto insurance, at was cost of repairing the water damage to the engine and interior. So I phoned Mr. Wessel in Shore Haven and gave him the go ahead to fix my car. He said he'd have it ready in a week, providing the car's computer wasn't "brain damaged." I told him I had complete faith in his neurosurgical abilities—rah rah—and hung up.

All of that reminded me to reimburse my mom for the rental car she had brought to Shore Haven. Leversee had returned the pricy car to the airport, and I had taken a cab to Rent-a-Wreck where I'd picked out an old Pinto for twenty dollars a day. I wrote my mom a check, stuck it in an envelope, stamped it, and dropped it in the out tray.

I had called her on Saturday and told her I was fine—a lie that would save me a lot of grief—but I was a lot better than I'd been on Friday. I'd been taken to the hospital and my stomach had been pumped, a painful, revolting experience I was too drugged to remember with much clarity. I do recall doctors mumbling about dialysis, then deciding against it. The tunnel through my shoulder turned out to be a flesh wound, through the meat: a smaller hole in, a larger hole out. As they started the second pint of blood, I had had the presence of mind to demand that a plastic surgeon look at the wound. I told her I already had a knife scar on my right calf, thanks to some crazy murderous creep, and I had no desire to sport two more melted-wax blobs of scar tissue when I swam at the Y.

Dr. Kaloff worked her magic, then told me as I lay in postop, "You'll still have a couple of scars."

"How big?" I groggily inquired, working my bruised jaw.

"Oh, bigger than a vaccination, smaller than a bread box."

Iggy visited me in the hospital. He brought a bouquet of purple chrysanthemums that looked hacked out of someone's garden—and certainly not his own. Despite this larcenously sweet gesture, I laid into him about his blabbing my true identity to Patty the poisonous practical nurse.

"How was I to know?" he asked, jamming the mums into my plastic water jug.

I sighed, too tired to wrangle with him.

"How long ya in for?" he asked, as though I were lollygagging in the pen.

"I get out tomorrow, first thing. It's not a bad wound."

"Huh?"

"It's a flesh wound."

"Ole Patty's not much of a shot, eh?"

"Nope. Honestly, when I think about it, it's amazing. What

the hell was she aiming at, anyway? Five feet away, a nine-millimeter Glock, and she can't do any better than a flesh wound?"

"Afraid of blood?" he suggested.

"She's a nurse, for chrissake."

"Saving you for the noose?"

"What's the point once she's shot me? How's she gonna make that look like suicide?"

Then he said, "Hey, you know what'd be cool? If you and her were roomies."

"I don't think so, Iggy."

"Why not? There's another bed in here, no one in it. Just the spot for Patty. You and her could talk over why she's such a lousy shot. You could give her some pointers."

I changed the subject. "How's the Felicia Pearl Show going these days?"

"I'm off that," he said, waving his hand in the manner of one shooing away a plate of greasy corn dogs. "All I gotta do is type up the report and the bill."

He faked a punch to my injured shoulder and I cringed. "Damn it all, Iggy, you're driving me nuts."

"Just trying to take your mind off your troubles."

"Look, Iggy, I'm not so laid up that I can't get you in another head lock."

"That so? Then why're you lying around in the hospital?"

He was right. But I had nowhere to go. My apartment was a crime scene, and although Leversee had offered to put me up for the duration, he thought I'd be arriving the next day.

Then Iggy did something with his face.

"What the hell was that?" I asked.

"Huh?" He was playing dumb.

"You *know* what you did."

"I didn't do anything," he said.

"You didn't do anything? You winked!"

"So?"

"I hate that crap—that eye-scrinching business. You know, I read in *Psychology Today*"—this was a lie—" that winking is an effort on the part of the winker to control the winkee."

"The winkie?" he repeated. "You mean one of those nauseating chocolate muffins with the white gop inside and the black icing?"

"Not the winkie—the wink*ee*. You're the winker and I'm the wink*ee*."

"Me control *you*," he scoffed, then aimed another punch at my throbbing shoulder.

"Don't you dare!" I wailed, rolling away from him. "Get out!"

As Iggy slunk away, I called Leversee to spring me, and he did.

MY FRIEND KEITH tells me that Sean and Fiona have already had the old man cremated. In Michigan, if cremation is done within forty-eight hours of death, there's no need to embalm, thus saving the family money. That's why Eleanor was cremated right away: no embalming, no casket, no marker. Cheap, cheap, cheap. There will be a memorial service at St. John's Catholic Church in Shore Haven on Friday, with lots of melancholy music performed by Dennis's famous former colleagues. But I'm not going. I figure I'm the second to the last person Sean and Fiona want to see right now.

I expect the siblings will keep on as they have, till their father's estate is liquidated. Plus Amanda says that they plan to reissue *Dennis Montague's Piano Favorites;* it ought to sell like hiphop now that he's dead. Then they'll have plenty of samoleons to invest and follow their dreams. Maybe Sean will win the Rohrbach competition; maybe Fiona will show her photographs.

I'VE THOUGHT A LOT these last couple of days, and I've decided that it's bad for young people to lose their parents. It wasn't good for Bobby and Therese to lose theirs. Not good for Bill and Eleanor. Not good for Sean and Fiona. It certainly wasn't good for me to lose my dad. I had rushed into a disastrous marriage as if I might raise him from the grave by saying, "I do."

Mandy and I are lucky to still have our mom, for even if she is a pain in the glute, it's good to know that someone cares if we've got a car to tool around in, or if we drink too much, or if we're dead or alive.

LEVERSEE HAS BEEN an upstander, letting me stay at his place. Not only was my apartment sealed as a crime scene, but it was also a god-awful mishmash of fallen plaster and blood. Oh, yes, and the back door was demolished. All the times I've scoffed at someone else's cheapola door or lock, and here I'd been living, as if invincible, with both. My landlord's insurance ought to cover the cost of repairs and clean up, but I have no idea when I'll be able to return. To tell the truth, I'm not sure I *want* to return. Who can sleep in a place of violence? I'd be drifting off and catch a whiff of cordite. Or blood.

Regarding the "suicide" note Patty made me sign, Leversee said he would never have accepted a "scribbled right-handed signature." Amanda said that she would never have bought that I was sorry for making a mess. "You live to make messes," she said. Iggy remarked that he would never have fallen for that "sissy note, looked like it was signed by Timothy Leary on acid." He didn't care how long it took, he'd find whoever did it and gut him. Or her.

Right….

AS FOR PATTY the practical nurse, my "puny" Beretta did its bit of damage. Shoot ten .22-calibre bullets into anyone, he or she will at least stop and think about it for a minute. In Patty's case, she lost her right kidney and a whole lot of blood, but she did not die. She has been charged with the first-degree murder of Eleanor Montague in VanBurgen County. I am to be the prime witness, and I'm eager to tell *all* in this particular case. Fortunately, I'm not all the prosecutor has got. Eleanor's body and its drugged blood may be gone, but a toss of Patty's trailer turned up three ziptop bags containing what's left of the drugs she stole from Dr. Coulter, Eleanor's favorite flute, and several obsessive scrapbooks of photos and articles about Sean. None of it proves that Patty killed Eleanor, but it helps. Bottom line, Patty may walk on the murder rap. Yet, if she does, Collingwood County will charge her with attempted murder of yours truly, and there's no way she'll weasel out of that. Hi ho, hi ho, it's off to Riverside—the state prison for the criminally insane—she'll go.

THE COLLINGWOOD *Evening News* ran front-page coverage of Patty's crimes—oh, excuse me, *alleged* crimes. I was mentioned as "Collingwood investigator, Gail Fischer." Where'd they get that? Never mind the misspelling. An old lady who read the article has already engaged me to locate her lost Maltese. Not a falcon—it's a cat.

In an article in the *Shore Haven Gazette,* VanDee was quoted as saying, "Fisher's an amateur. In both murders she so-called solved, she only succeeded in turning herself into a sitting duck."

Chief Glenn, in what can only be called a fit of remorse, dropped all charges of reckless driving against me, mailed me my driver's license, and halted the proceedings to have my P.I. license revoked. Moreover, the VanBurgen M.E. has changed his "opinion" on Eleanor Montague's death. In compliance with the county prosecutor, he's now calling it a murder.

Swinkey and I are back on speaking terms. In fact, he's the

one who gave me the inside scoop on Patty as putative daughter
of Dennis Montague. Fortunately the Medical Examiner kept a
bit of Dennis on ice; with such a high profile citizen and death,
it was impossible to skip the post mortem. Dennis's and Patty's
DNA are now being run through the gene grinder to see if the
pianist and the nurse are truly father and daughter. She doesn't
look like him, but stranger things have happened. No father is
named on her birth certificate. Her lawyer had the luminous
idea that if she were an heir to Dennis Montague, she could pay
for her defense with her share of his estate.

Meanwhile, Swinkey asked Voight to ask Bigalow to ask
VanDee if he'd been sexing Eleanor. The answer was no; it was
Fiona who had "enjoyed" his attentions.

Keith is doing okay, glad to be out of his cousin's apartment
and back home. Apparently home is the ideal place to recover
from a concussion. His parents are still tumbling around out
west but have promised to return in time to rake leaves. They'd
better hurry. I sent Keith another five hundred for his assistance
in solving this case. Swinkey says I shouldn't encourage the
kid—next time he's liable to get killed. All I can say is *what next
time?*

At a quarter to seven, I strolled across the street to Georgie's
and found my favorite booth. Georgie was no where in sight yet
had put my favorite disc on the CD player. Coincidence? Who
knows. I leaned my aching shoulder against the padded booth
and nodded my head as Coltrane riffed a solo in "All Blues."

The door swung open and there stood Bill Feinstein, the righteous brother. His dark eyes locked on mine. Oh, yes, I could see
it—he still thought he'd screwed up, left his sister to die, but there
was a certain satisfaction…and humility as well. He had avenged
her death, and I had been the sharp sword that, despite his aim,
cut true.